LEARNING
MONKEY AND
CROCODILE

NICK WOOD

Text Copyright © 2019 Nick Wood
Cover Design © 2019 John Cockshaw
Harvester Logo © 2019 Francesca T Barbini

First published by Luna Press Publishing, Edinburgh, 2019

Of Hearts and Monkeys. *First Published in PostScripts 22/23, 2010.*
The Girl Who Called the World. *First Published in Fierce Family, 2014.*
Thandiwe's Tokoloshe. *First Published in African Monsters, 2015.*
Five Hundred Photons. *First Published in 365 Tomorrows, 2017.*
God in The Box. *First Published in Interzone 187, 2003.*
Bridges. *First Published in Albedo One 40, 2011.*
Azania. *First Published in AfroSF, 2012.*
Lunar Voices (On the Solar Wind). *First Published in Redstone Science Fiction, 4, 2010.*
African Shadows. *First Published in Infinity Plus, 2003.*
Mindreader. *First Published in Escape Velocity 2, 2008.*
The Paragon of Knowledge. *First Published in The Future Fire 33, 2015.*
Case Notes of a Witchdoctor. *First Published in The World Science Fiction Blog, 2013.*
Dream-Hunter. *First Published in Omenana 6, 2016.*
Thirstlands. *First Published in Subterfuge, 2008.*
The Guardian of the Grain (original to this collection)
A Million Reasons Why (original to this collection)
Beautiful Meat (original to this collection)

www.lunapresspublishing.com
ISBN-13: 978-1-911143-95-6

To our 'disappearing' wild animal cousins,
and the bugs that bite and pollinate.

Contents

Bonus Material

Of Hearts and Monkeys

We are amongst the last of the last, the 'do not dies' as the living dead now call us. They follow us, the dead do, whispering and pulling at our ears and hair. The other two don't notice, although they do see and comment on the occasional cock of my head, as I listen without comprehension to dry and meaningless whispers from shadowy lips, the occasional repetition of that one phrase all I can make out: 'Do not dies...' We make our way down the mountain slope to the dense bush and protea trees below, the draw-string bag bumping on my back. I laugh at their comments about me—my niece and her partner; for I'm old enough to have earned the right to be called mad.

But why do the dead follow me? I am not an *amagqirha* or traditional healer, nor have I drunk *ubalawu* to make contact with them either here, or in my dreams. I carry very little knowledge of the old ways within me anymore. Perhaps this is why they harry me so? None do I recognise; none seem tied to my birth. Their shapes change like the shifting smoke on the horizon, their features blunted and blurred.

The path branches through thick grass both left and right at the bottom of the slope; the fork to the right is more heavily trampled and leads between two large boulders. The bushes, laced with yellow flowered sour fig creepers and the blackened cone protea trees, crowd the paths more than *Bontebok* high, scratching and pulling at our skins with a greater intensity than the dead can muster. The foliage releases a wet, stinky, oily heat that leeches our bodies of sweat too, and Bongani turns with a relieved hunch to his shoulders, onto the well-flattened path to the right.

He stops at my whistle.

Four of the dead are dancing and waving in warning on top of the large boulders ahead.

I point left and immediately regret it.

Bongani stiffens and shouts: "I'm in charge, you silly old woman. You'd both be dead if it weren't for me."

I am still (just) the good side of sixty. His words hurt a little, even though there may be some truth there; he is quick on his feet and good at herding dam and river fish into the shallows, me, my bones are slow and stiff, but I have caught a few. Penny, she always just likes to sit and watch.

(Still the dead dance.)

I place my hands together in supplication and bow to him, showing *ukuthoba*. His face softens a bit, but he shakes his head. "I've had enough of fighting this bush, MamBhele," he says, "We've earned ourselves an easier path for now."

The dead obviously don't think so, but can you really trust them—especially when you can't hear what they have to say? I have asked them about Janet, but they just gape at me and whisper to each other.

I have nothing to give them in sacrifice, whoever they might be, apart from dragging a thorny branch across my right wrist to gouge a weal of blood. One of the dead prods at it with suspicion, but I feel nothing. The other four have left the boulders.

Perhaps it is enough. Perhaps we are indeed safe now.

Bongani and Penny are almost through the boulders as I follow them down the path.

Penny's scream freezes me. Bongani is lying on the path, his body crumpled. An *umlungu*, a white man, stands over him with a broken branch in his hand. Penny's scream rips shut as strong brown arms grab her mouth and body from behind one of the rocks and pull her behind, out of view. Hairy, muscular arms…at least two men, two young and strong-looking men.

The man with the branch looks up at me and smiles, his hair wild and bushy. The blood on my wrist curdles and stings. I turn and run, back up the path, crashing through the thickened grass that slices my ankles beneath my shorts, before realising I'm still in sight to anyone chasing. I stop and duck under the branches of an acacia tree, cowering behind the rough and wide base of the trunk; seeking shelter behind thorns.

It is long moments before I can hear anything other than pounding blood. Then there is just stillness and the distant bark of a baboon.

My ears stay good and I would hear a chase. Of course, I am old and they have caught enough now for a good few days of sex, whatever their fancy.

But why did the dead stay behind with them?

I cry.

I had promised my brother I would take care of his pale daughter for him, even as he lay and haemorrhaged his life quickly away on his bed. I was the only one there to speak to him, his white wife already two days dead. All over town, all over the land, all over the world, people lay dying to the final deadly twist of *Umbulalasizwe*, this Nation-Killer virus, which takes to the winds like an Invisible Angel of Death. At the end of a week of global carnage, very few were still there to watch and share the dying. There is just a sprinkling of us left now, spared by God for an unknown reason. Bongani had said it was as if we were born of the tough survivors, those who'd developed a resistance to HIV during the days the government refused to roll out anti-retroviral treatment to its people, when it had been an older and kinder virus. He always was a clever one, that Bongani, but now he may be a dead man too—with his words, like his body, dust.

Why spare me, God, I am just an old woman?

So many have died and yet I still live. Why me?

Yes, I am a 'do not die', but I fall asleep with my wet face crusted against a hard tree-bark, endlessly saying sorry to my brother.

*

The cold wakes me, cramping my bones in my hips. I see the sun is down, the night and an early autumnal mist stealing in. Light enough still to see, but I know I must move if I am to stay alive.

I stand with aching difficulty and stretch stiffly, raw hunger and thirst pulling me back into a hunch. I strip a few tough leathery brown figs from the succulent sour fig creepers, bite the barky stem and sip the sour, sticky moisture from within. The wound on my wrist itches but has scabbed. I haul the bag off my bag and unpack the last of the *dassie* meat, cooked and still smelling fine. It had been killed by my lucky stone as it had lain sun-bathing on a rock amongst its faster brothers and sisters.

But why should I eat? Why should I go on? Alone, I am nothing.

Even Janet's shade avoids me and she is now more than six lunar cycles dead. It must be rising seven months since I was last held in a loving rather than a dying embrace by her. The dead don't hug and even they have left me too, chased away by this damp and creeping fog… or perhaps something else? No, I will not think more on this and yes, *why* should I raise this food to my lips, even though my stomach begs me to?

Because… at least for now, I still can.

It tastes good, seasoned by my prayer for Janet's shade. I leave the scraps for morning…none can I spare for my ancestors, I only hope they understand.

So I follow the path less travelled, winding its way along the flank of a mountain peak, somewhere south of *Silvermine* I think, a ways from old habitations where a few of the do not dies, Cape leopards and caracals, vultures and baboons still look for easy pickings. The stench of death and rotting flesh used to be a good guide to when you were getting close enough, but it's all disappeared after the Big Burn tore through Cape Town and across the Flats, reducing so much

3

to blackness and charcoal. The *fynbos* is used to fire though, growing rapidly again to strangle everything on the slopes. There is even some dryer and thornier vegetation like the acacias, marching in from the Karoo, now that the people are almost all gone.

All I want is cover for the night—somewhere high, in a tree perhaps. I could strap myself against the trunk with the elastic exercise bands from Penny's aerobics classes I had kept for her in my bag. To tie myself onto a tree trunk on high would be the safest thing to do now that I am alone—above and beyond ground scavengers.

My wrist burns so I wipe it with the last of the sour, soothing juice from a plucked fig.

Cries hang on the air. A child's cries, I'd recognise them anywhere, despite never having had any of my own.

I follow the shrill sound of a young and miserable voice.

As for me, I've been a mother to quite a few, even though my preference for women's company had meant my family wanted little to do with me; but I'd been faithful to Janet for twenty years. Thankfully people's need for work usurped the stiffest of their principles and I was good with stories and playing with their children, spinning a good few *rands* from child-care. Janet, though, had been the *real* business woman behind it all, sharp as hell. (Paper money is just good to wipe your bum with now. At least coins are still good to open rusted food cans.)

But, for me, dead babies still hurt the most to look at.

This child is very much alive, deep in the underbrush and trees, in the flats away from the mountain slope. I creep in through the bush slowly and carefully—a live child is bound to have adult carers and I age this one by its cries as between five and ten.

The sobbing stops and there is a low murmur of adult voices so I slow my creep to a careful hands and feet crawl, testing the ground gingerly ahead of me before placing my weight, praying there are no sleeping snakes.

A small clearing ahead opens up and I hear and smell the crackling bite of a smoky fire—have they a golden stock of matches too? A middle-aged woman sits and cuddles a listless looking child awkwardly in her arms; a second older child of preteen years—a girl in a tattered green dress—stands and looks on helplessly. A small man circles the clearing suspiciously, thankfully on the opposite side of the clearing, so I pull back slowly into the deeper shadows of the trees. They have a small tent. It is an organised family; I can smell insect repellent.

I can also smell the younger child's sickness.

The man comes near and I play musical statues to the thump in my chest and head.

He returns to poke the fire.

The child retches and vomits, the woman holds her wrong, some of the vomit may stick in her throat.

I have had enough of death…

"*Molweni*, hello my friends," I enter the clearing, hands raised.

The man turns and points a gun at my head.

I struggle to hold my water in, despite there being so little left in my bladder.

The woman recoils. The child in her arm coughs and keeps coughing. It is a younger girl and she is choking, face up in the women's clutch of fright.

The man cocks the gun, a noise that cracks through my head and wets my legs.

But I cannot stand still if a child might die.

"Let me help you with her," I say, holding my arms out.

The man lowers his gun-hand down and I can breathe again. The woman stands up, but does not hold her child out.

"Turn her over," I say gently, "and pat her back."

She does so, watching me warily and her child coughs the last of her sick from her mouth onto the ground and begins breathing a little easier, though still panting a bit.

I breathe a bit easier too as the man sticks his gun into a belt around his waist after carefully un-cocking it. He has a sallow flat face, as if he has distant San or Khoi ancestry.

The woman is brown but not as dark as me—her girls are even paler still. The older one smiles at me, but says nothing.

Her mother speaks in Afrikaans: "Wat is jou naam?"

"Noluthando," I tell her, relieved and more relaxed, "Noluthando Ngobo Bhele." Only the worst of the *skollies* or *tsotsis* ever ask for names from those whom they intend to kill, as if it gives them further power over their quaking victims—and they certainly don't look after children. Still, the virus has been no discriminator of moral character; I have seen that.

The man holds his hand out to me: "Are you on your own, *gogo*—do you want to join us?"

I smile and nod gratefully, blinking tears away, even though I am no grandmother.

The older girl shows me a space by the fireside. They have some meat on a spit of wood over the fire and it looks (thankfully) like chicken.

I wipe my legs discreetly with a scented wild mint leaf from my bag before sitting down.

They give the little one some moistened, crushed *buchu* leaves for her stomach.

One by one they introduce themselves—Habib and Marlene, Shannon and Tracy; although Marlene talks for Shannon, the older girl herself still says nothing. They'd had to move and move fast when the

Big Burn swept through everything, lit by God or someone who was hoping to purge the world of Death's stink. The Mountain had been wet with late winter rains; so like us…. Like me, they'd found refuge in the woods alongside rivers and the larger dams.

Tired of just surviving, Habib has finally decided to head west and north, where he says some of his family may still live—way up the West coast, deep into dry Nama country. He says the names of his family with a spattering of clicks.

"Cousin," I nod, for us amaXhosa learned our linguistic clicks from much shared history deep in back-time with the Khoi-San people.

He looks at me with narrowed eyes. Is it that my comment was over-familiar? Or perhaps he is one of those who think we have taken everything from them since the white man finally gave power over to us; one of those who claim they are the sole indigenous people of this area and country? If so, a silly squabble to hold onto, with such a large and empty space now left for so few.

And it would indeed be a long, long walk, but I have nowhere else to go. Although I have not seen the shades of any of my family, deep down I know they are all dead. Yet my ancestors have not told me this—I have nothing to give them, apart from my own life, is this why they do not come and why they show me nothing?

I voice this belief of mine and our words dry up.

Behind me, I hear the whispers of voices and turn quickly. There is a cloud of children, hanging in the bushes, talking much, saying little. I do not know them. Why are they here? What do they want?

Habib stands next to me, peering into the bushes, holding his swaying gun in front of him. "What is it, *gogo*? What do you see?"

"Nothing," I sigh, turning back to the last flickering coals of our fire.

Shannon watches me. In her eyes, I can see she has seen them too.

We settle for the night, them in their tent, me on a rolled mat from my bag.

The dead children quieten their whispering when I wave an angry arm at them. I have not yet died and so I fall asleep with some little hope.

*

I wake to find something sniffing at my face.

In my vanishing mist of dream, I imagine it is Janet at first—until it grunts and flashes its teeth from its grey, hairy face, backing off with my bag in its deft dark hands.

I sit up, *knobkierie* straight and stiff with shock, biting back a scream.

It has found the last of the *dassie* and is cramming the meat into its mouth, grimacing at me. I look around, but it is alone—it must be a single male baboon, roaming the bush in search of a new mate, in the hope of starting a new troop.

I avoid eye contact, careful not to raise a challenge and slowly stand up, backing even further away. Despite myself, I let out the slightest of fearful whimpers.

The baboon throws my bag down and turns to lope off into the bush. Behind me, I hear a little chuckle. It is Marlene, stretching her arms wide from the flap of the tent-door, as if embracing the new day.

"You've already had a visitor," she says. "Did he take everything you had left to eat?"

I retrieve my bag and feel inside, nodding shamefully.

"Families share," she says simply, turning to pop her head back into the tent. "Get up you lazy lot, it's getting late."

She has a working watch I notice; to me the sun is only just creeping over the bushes. The child shades have gone, as if driven away by the sun.

We eat the last of the chicken, sip and splash sparsely from a water jug, pack our goods.

"Forty-three minutes," she says, "It's now seven twenty-five," she hitches up her Y-frame back-pack. Habib smiles mildly. The girls move easily and quickly, as if in a well-rehearsed routine. The oldest one, Shannon, takes my hand. Tracy looks a lot brighter herself in the day's gathering heat.

"How will you find your way," I ask Habib, "By the sun?"

He grins and holds out a scratched compass. "I also have a *Slingsby* map. Once we get to the Atlantic, we just keep it on our left."

And so it is that we set off west, heading for the sea. Habib leads the way, with Marlene taking up the rear with Tracy. Shannon walks behind me, occasionally skipping ahead as the mood takes her and if the vegetation allows, but still saying nothing. Marlene mentions she has said nothing since almost her entire class died around her, including her three best friends. Instead, Tracy behind me has all the words, eight years of age she is, chatting about how she finally realises she does actually miss her school—she'd been in her third year at Muizenberg Primary, although perhaps it was her own best friend she missed most, Shireen, who likes dappled ponies…

Habib takes up the theme before we drown in Tracy's words, "So what do you miss most about life before the Week of Invisible Death, *gogo?*"

"My partner," I say shortly, thinking too of my online sisters on Behind the Mask.

"Oh…" he is suitably quiet for a while, "As for me, I miss watching Manchester United and Ajax Cape Town play soccer, perhaps with the odd Castle Lager for company."

"Or Jack Daniels, you old hypocrite," shouts Marlene from behind: "I just want a supply of tampons at the right time of the month and some birth control pills."

Perhaps being an old woman is not all bad.

We stop for lunch in the heat after making our way up and along another slope that affords us a view of a glittering beach in the distance: "Noordhoek," says Habib, the Atlantic coast indeed.

The children groan when he hauls another chicken out of his rucksack, salted and sealed.

"I was a chicken farm manager," he says to me, "And I have a map of all my company's free-range farms as well as their security access codes in the Western Cape, all the way up the coast. The farms do get very few after Saldanha, so we will need to learn to catch fish and eat mussels and *perlemoen* on the way."

"Hooray for fish," shouts Tracy, suddenly turning to look at me: "Can you tell us a story, *gogo*?"

The flies are buzzing now and we are all well pasted with insect repellent, the birds quiet in the mid-day warmth as we shelter under a pincushion *protea*, still charred but having burst its seeds. I try to think of a story that fits our plight and remember our morning visitor. Ah, 'The Day Monkey Saved his Heart'—not an amaXhosa tale from my own culture, but a Bemba tale from Zambia that my Aunt Mams had told me when I was of an age with Shannon.

So I launch into the story of how God had created the world of man and animal as separate and they had never seen each other, until Monkey was elected by the animals to visit man, as he was both clever and quick. Once Monkey saw man from a distance, all fur-less and carrying shiny tools that were planting and harvesting strange foods in the field, he was not so sure it was wise to meet them, however. So he waited until it was night and then he stole into the field and ate the wonderful food until he was stuffed like a melon. As he was about to head home, a man leaped out with a net to catch him saying: 'In my culture, we take the heart of all who steal from us. I know not what manner of creature you are, but I want your heart…'"

"And?" asks Tracy, her eyes big.

"More tonight," I say, "At bedtime."

"That's not fair! I wanted a whole story."

"Endings don't come in one easy telling," I say, "It is good to learn to wait for them."

There is a grumble behind me. Turning, I spot a few vague and shifting child shapes in the bush. Some dead still follow—what will they have of us?

We head off again, Tracy moaning until her tired legs eventually still her mouth. It is sticky hot but cooler in the blustery South-Easter moments as the wind swirls through the reeds and bushes around us. Three children pace alongside in the nearby bush, as if herding us.

Marlene calls the evening camp within sound of the surf thumping through wild dune vegetation ahead of us. She was P.A. to a middle-manager of a local lumber company I hear and a well-good one at that it seems.

She looks at the plant ground-cover underneath us with some curiosity; a strange mix of thick succulent creeper leaves with thorny aloe edges, trailing from the bushes we'd just gingerly negotiated. "Better put plenty of soft reed bedding underneath, this *fynbos* is *deurmekaar*—weird man, true's God, I don't know this plant. It's like things have changed since it's re-grown from the Big Burn."

Habib snorts: "Evolution doesn't work that fast, 'Lene."

She looks at him severely: "I'm talking God and devil stuff here, 'Bib, not science."

He's another man of intelligence, with words like that. He shades his face from her and rolls his eyes at me, smiling. I'm not sure though—I'm not a plant person, but I've never seen anything like it before either. Habib sighs: "*Fynbos* is the most diverse range of plants per area in the world—do you women claim to know every one of the thousands of species here?"

He is right. I'd heard a tourist guide say the same thing about *fynbos* before, a good few years back now.

I make sure the bedding is very thick, spending the better part of an hour, according to Marlene, collecting both wood and *restio* reed bedding to put between our mats and the spiky creepers.

Night comes in fast and some baying noises hover momentarily on the dying breeze, curdling my blood, for I do not recognise the sound either. I scratch my itchy wrist as Habib gets the fire going. He is aiming to char the last of the chicken and says he is hopeful that we will reach another company farm by tomorrow evening, Hout Bay way, on the coastal path along the ridges of the Twelve Apostles that spine Table Mountain.

"Please finish my story, *gogo*," asks Tracy. Shannon comes to sit next to me. She gives a little discreet wave and I look up. The three dead children sit on a *protea* bush, as if settling down to listen too.

"So Monkey thought quickly and told the man that animals don't keep their hearts in their bodies but their Lion king keeps their hearts for them and could the man row him to the king so that he could give him his heart. The man agreed but as he rowed the Monkey to the forest shore, Monkey started singing, calling on the crocodiles to help him. The man could not understand the animal language and so the crocodiles surrounded them, forming a bridge from the boat to the

9

land. The Monkey ran across their backs and shouted back from the safety of the jungle: 'Foolish man, don't you know that animals keep their hearts in the same place that men do, and feel pain as strongly as you do?' Today, if you see a Monkey, watch what they do to their chests. They beat their fists in the place their heart lives, as a reminder to man they have hearts also…"

"Wow!" says Tracy, "So do chickens have hearts too?"

I laugh and nod, wondering if my answer will put her off chicken even more. Still, hunger always tells in the end.

Aunt Mams stands before me and a chill trickles through my body. I feel I have almost told her story well, but the words have perhaps slipped a little too easily off my tongue and sound both strange and detached from the twilight burnt bush around us. Mams puts a finger to her lip, pointing her left arm behind me. The hairs on my neck tingle as I turn.

The thick vegetation is quiet and still. I move towards Habib, who raises a questioning eye. He startles with alarm when I reach in and pull out his gun from under his nearby jersey.

With a rustle of leaves two men stand in the twilight, one wielding a tree-branch, the other a knife. They have big toggle-bags on their backs and wild hair and thick muscular arms. The one I have not yet fully seen from yesterday stands both darker and shorter than the other. Habib leaps up, small and fierce, with a large *panga* in his hand that I had not noticed before, big enough to gut an ox.

They laugh and step forward as if two to one, but I level the gun to stop them. It is heavier than I expect, waving a little as I try to steady it in their direction.

"Where is Penny? Where is my niece?" I ask the white man with the tree branch and the wildest hair. He hears me, his glance flickering to his companion. I see her death in the shorter man's eyes.

With horror that feels like cold vomit in my bowels, I pull the trigger.

But the gun is not cocked.

They laugh and both move now as if to flank us, for I am just an old woman, I can see it in their smiling faces.

I drag the hammer back with a loud and vicious click. I rest the gun on my upper left arm and spread my legs to brace for the recoil, aiming squarely at the taller and bolder one. (I have dealt with a few men before, who would correct my sexuality.)

He frantically waves the other man to stop, but it is too late.

I hear screams behind me.

And Janet hovers like a ghost over both the men, shaking her grey, pony-tailed head.

My finger freezes. The men turn and run clumsily, crashing through the woods, scratching themselves silly in the process, no doubt. I wish the creeper spines had been laced with Puff-Adder venom, to give them a slow and painful death.

With sudden stillness, they are gone.

As is Janet, not even a drifting mist on the breeze.

She didn't even stay one moment to say goodbye. The gun is a block of pain in my hand and Habib takes it quietly from me, un-cocking it, while I sink to my knees with a salty blurring in my eyes.

Shannon cradles my head in her wiry, bony arms.

I cry like a baby, ashamed, but unable to stop.

I feel her small hand in my trouser pocket. Child, my pockets are empty, I have nothing to give you.

It seems as if the dead have all gone too. Do they still have *their* hearts?

(A glimpse of Janet is not nearly enough. Why did you come for them, killers and monsters, but not for me, Janet le Grange?)

*

The others sleep, but not me.

I feel the pull of the sea and walk over the dunes and down towards the water, feet straining through sand in the bright moonlight. The surf churns out at me like froth from space and my ankles chill with the cold ache of its touch. There is no one riding the surf-foam that batters my body and steals my breath—not the dead, nor my ancestors, nor Janet herself. The night and the sea are numbingly empty ahead of me.

I carry on walking although I cannot swim. It will be all the more quick then, I hope.

The water burns the wound on my wrist and I stop, waist high. Wait. Perhaps my clothes might still be of use to them.

Marlene has *isandla esishushu*, a warm hand indeed underneath her brusque manner, and the oldest girl feels kind, hanging on my words as if she has none of her own. (Habib himself had refused to put down his gun and had given me a warning look before sealing their tent for the night.)

I turn back to shore, unzipping my track-top and folding it neatly on the wet sand. The tide is on the way out; my clothes should be safe here for a while. I feel in my shorts pockets to empty them first, in case there is anything of use to leave lying in sight there, like a coin or two.

There is indeed something, a little hard and feathery. I cup my palm and hold it up against the half-moon's light. It is a flower-head—dark and heart shaped, translucent papery petals wet and fraying from its edges. An *everlasting* it's called, I'd seen them sprouting from a few of the bushes along our march to the coast.

I remember Shannon's thin fingers in my pocket.

Gingerly, I put the flower-head back in my trouser pocket and shivering, zip on my damp top.

I look up at the sky.

Above me flies the half-moon, bounced along on scudding clouds.

The moon is an alien world, scarred, old and barren. There must be dead men and women there too, I think, the lunar base now filled with emaciated corpses rotting in diminishing air; supply rockets from China and America stranded like huge, empty steel candles on Earth.

But I can't see them in my mind's eye. The moon blinks down on me, white and cold.

The wind howls like *Machelanga*'s cries for the moon, long let loose from his pot by one of his children, who falls and dies trying to get the moon back. The moon is too far gone now and there's no going back, it's above and beyond his failing reach, drifting ever further away.

And I can't see *Machelanga* either, the stories in my head are harder to piece together, the meanings of the words dry and crack further on each telling and retelling.

A voice calls my name from the sea; parched and thin, but twenty years familiar. I step forward until the waves are round my ankles and knees, tugging me in. A cloud of shadow and vague shape spins before me but I can smell it's her, she always had a slightly musty—almost mint— smell on her skin.

"It's good to see you, 'Thando, but the dead ask me why you pursue them, sister."

"I don't, they pursue me!" I try to think of something else to say, but there is nothing in my throat, my heart is squeezing sore. I am no sister.

"They ask why then came you so deep in water when you cannot swim?"

Ah, I understand. I hold out my hand, but the shape spins away from me, her smell recedes, leaving a trace of sadness in the air: "I can't stay, 'Thando, for now, there can be no more."

"Why?" I plead.

"I may not find you if you walk to your death—even now, old lives and memories fade, new spaces and new lands call…so please stay… and you'd better learn to swim, Thandietjie."

I cannot say anything, but she is gone anyway. She leaves me the last of her tart comments, sweetened by that Afrikaner miniaturisation of my name, which had always been a sign she wished to repair things.

But what was there to repair? She has gone…but 'for *now*,' she'd said, and I can still smell her sadness hanging in the salty air. The dead do have hearts, it seems, but I am left alone in the here. How long is 'for now'—what is time to the dead? Where has she gone? And why did she die *before* me; after twenty years of love and strife and love again?

Questions fly through me but I know better than to ask them of this cold wind.

I breathe the last faint whiff of mint on the breeze and pull on my numbed ankles, my feet locked under wet sand from the retreating tide. There is only the sharp stinky smell of sea-weed. Janet is gone. I do not know if I will ever see her again.

I turn from the sea, but stop as I glimpse a huge dark woman with fiery eyes rearing out of the ocean, an army of living dead and massed cattle spattering out of the waves behind her. Her name ripples through me—*Nongqawuse*, the prophetess of old who claimed the living dead would sweep the British into the sea, provided the amaXhosa all had faith and slaughtered their cattle.

More than a hundred thousand died for their faith. (Perhaps now, a hundred and seventy years later, she has finally repaid their dead doubts?)

Her blazing red gaze sweeps the land, but she doesn't see me. Perhaps I am too small.

Small is good. I feel the tiny fragile cone and leaves of the damp *everlasting* in my pocket.

Me, I would live.

Yes, there is someone *I* would see still. I have looked into her brown eyes. Shannon they call her, but she deserves a new name in a new world. She is building a story inside her and I want to be there when her mouth opens to speak, for it will be a strange and terrible story indeed.

Shrieks, cries and howls erupt from further along the shore to the north. I don't know what they mean, but still I shiver… we must go that way tomorrow. We must learn the words of the monkeys and the crocodiles if we are to survive in this burnt but flowering world.

I walk over the dunes, looking back just once to see the empty and pounding shore.

I walk down the slope to my new family. As my amaZulu brothers and sisters say '*umuntu ungumuntu ngabanye abantu.*' We are only human through sharing our being with others.

Ow. I am indeed glad the creeper thorns do not have Puff-Adder venom.

A host of dead children stand on the edge of our camp, a few turning to glance as I pass, if only briefly. (They no doubt wait to share the young girl's story when she finally finds her new voice and learns her new name.)

As for me, my name is Noluthando Ngobo Bhele and I am still alive.

We shall see what stories the new day brings.

The Girl Who Called the World

So it is we skirt along the beach-line, heading into the waking sun, scavenging kelp and herding what little fish we can. Occasionally, we dart away to hide in coastal vegetation at the slightest sign of trouble, but all we see is one large band of noisy and rough looking men marching past on the dunes, several woman dragging behind them, bound with ropes.

That night, we sleep in the bushes, too afraid to venture out, even to find food. I sleep little, certain they can hear the thunder of my pained stomach and will return.

A new day breaks, just like any other.

We scramble down to shore and I head out to boulders, knee deep in water, showing the youngest where to look on the swirling brown seaweed for the rich pickings of fat Great-White shark egg sacs.

It is Tracy who sees them first, all eight years of vision and curiosity, looking up at the sky. She points above, towards the shards of late afternoon sunlight that flare along the blackened seaside cliffs. "Look, *gogo!*" she says.

How sweetly she calls me grandmother, even though I have no blood-link to her.

I glance up briefly to humour her—Tracy is only a curious young child after all, still bewitched by so much. I locate the man and his wife, unpacking the tent higher up the beach, their mute older daughter looking on, under the shadowed gloom of the cliff face.

"Look, *gogo!*" The young girl has arched her back as she stands on the rock alongside mine, pointing upwards urgently: "Birds! Big birds!"

I stare upwards, teetering on the edge of a boulder, fingers splayed before my eyes.

They jump us from above, descending like angels on broken sailed wings.

Big winged shadows wheel and spin around the warm sea breeze filtering off the cliffs, growing in size as they descend. Two large shapes—but they are human in both their shape and intent.

I stare back up the beach in fear.

The girl who says nothing, Shannon, stares upwards too, arms raised, as if welcoming the visitors from the air.

They glide in on short para-wings, AK-47 rifles cradled gently across their midriffs, like two big and deadly birds of prey. I cry out, but the late evening breeze bounces off the cliff and tosses my shout back over my shoulders and into the grey Southern Oceans roaring behind me.

Sweeping in low over our heads now; the young girl and I duck and I scrabble to keep my footing. The wing canopies flap with a 'crack' that shudders the air, as the two gliders rear and stall, falling to earth with a shooosshhh of sand. One figure stumbles slightly, but their guns remain level. Grey sails drop onto the skeletal frame of the gliders, concealing that part of the beach from Tracy and me.

She turns to me, "What do we do, *gogo?*"

What can I say? I am not truly her grandmother—just an aging woman, a woman without weapons, a woman who always stands on the edge of things; at best, just a teller of tales.

I have an urge to run, to move on, away from guns and dangerous men. This is not my real family, after all.

But Tracy has skipped over the last rock, landing in sand, heading up the beach in a bouncy run towards the pitched sails.

"Stupid girl; never stops to think," I snap. Now suddenly without choice, I scramble over the last two rocks to try and reach her first. But my limbs are too old and slow. I make the beach, but a man waits for us, unharnessed and rifle ready.

The girl is shrieking when I reach her, limbs locked in shock, but the man keeps his finger on the trigger. I come up behind her and place my hands on her shoulders. "What do you want of us?" I ask the man, "We have so little."

He shrugs, and then—with much relief—I see him snap the safety on. "As do we, Aunty. We just do what we must, to live."

He is short and dark, umXhosa like me, in blue council overalls. He speaks in slightly apologetic tones, with hints of loss in his words too. But there is nothing apologetic about his swinging gesture for us to step ahead of him, as he herds us towards the cliff face, where his big white colleague with bushy ginger hair has Marlene and Habib squarely in front of him, their arms raised in defensive posture, palms empty.

The mute older girl stands watching, hands by her side, mouth open, as if waiting for something else to happen. Shannon has still not uttered a word since I joined them, already two lunar cycles ago—her tongue has been stiff, since the invisible coming of *Umbulalasizwe*.

The *umlungu* is less relaxed than our umXhosa guard and is seemingly unnerved by the older child's posture. "Tell your girl to raise her hands."

Marlene glances across to Shannon and gestures with her hands.

Shannon smiles and raises her hands smoothly, as if in worship.

The white man is in combat safaris and relaxes slightly, flashing his colleague a curt nod, "That's all of them, 'Yiso?"

"*Ja, baas*," he says curtly and I sense the edge between them. The white man just shrugs and laughs, turning to Habib, who has kept his face blank throughout. "We're just here to do a little redistribution of wealth, *boetie*. Starting off with any weapons you have."

Marlene it is who speaks first though, moving around to hold Shannon protectively and giving me a grateful nod as I cradle Tracy protectively behind me. "Please," she says, "We won't survive without at least something to protect us."

The white man grunts. "Let's see what you've got first," he says, "Firearms are non-negotiable."

Negotiable? Men who 'negotiate,' despite being behind automatic rifles? They are perhaps not quite what they seem.

Habib bends down and slowly pulls a firearm out of his bag. His face tilts slightly as if alert to both rifles raised now, one aiming at him, the other at the loose huddle of us females.

He can be an impetuous man—please *don't, umfana*—I brace myself for disaster.

But, instead, he clips the safety on and cautiously tosses it across to the white man's feet, scowling.

"Ammo?" asks the *umlungu*.

Habib tosses two long clips of bullets to the same spot and stands up, square and bullish. "So what are you going to do with us?"

"We will pray for you," says 'Yiso, "for we are The Raptured."

I choke with surprised laughter. We have heard passing tales of a few bands of people who felt abandoned in the wake of what they considered the immanence of the Lord's Arrival—wandering and searching for ways to be lifted up with the multitude of others already gone, high into the clouds, to join their brothers and sisters and the Oncoming Christ.

Just wild stories, we'd thought… but all is wild now, so perhaps it should not surprise me so much.

As 'Yiso launches into the words of the Lord's Prayer, his words seem to drop like stones into the sand. I steel myself upright, restraining an old childish habit to fall to my knees.

A cooler Antarctic wind sweeps in from the darkening sea as 'Yiso finishes the prayer, his rifle propped against his thigh, arms lifted to the dulling pinkish glaze of the sky. His eyes stay open and watchful though—they have no doubt survived so long by not *fully* trusting in the Lord.

Indeed, the white man has kept his rifle level, although he has mouthed along silently too.

Shannon keeps her arms raised, swaying slightly to the words, face flushed—here, but not here.

And, as 'Amen' sinks into the sand, I see three dead young children crawling down the face of the cliff. Stick figured, gaunt and blurred as only the dead can be, they range from ten years of age at death, to three. I sense their ages, but their names elude me, floating past in the breeze. The smallest child, a girl, scrabbles at a fern frond, almost losing her grip.

Shannon turns in her mother's grasp to watch the dead children climb down, but seemingly no one else has seen them. They huddle at the base of the cliff, unable or unwilling to reach for their father.

'Yiso smiles, prayer finished, but seeing nothing. How can he be so blind to his own?

I catch the flash of an old memory of Noluyando, stillborn to me thirty years ago, her father vanished months before. Janet had helped me bury her shrivelled body under a tree in an Edgars' shoebox, size 8 men's, brown Italian leather.

There had been no men for me since.

I have kept doing what I can to help this family, long after the passing of *Umbulalasizwe* has almost emptied the Earth of both humans and apes...

...And Janet.

I have seen so much death that I stand and cover Tracy even more; with only the slightest of tremors in my limbs, as 'Yiso picks up his gun again.

Habib leaps, as if anticipating the two men's hearts and minds are lingering in their monologues to God.

With one quick motion, the white man swivels his gun and crashes the butt into Habib's face. The small man staggers back, falling onto hands and knees, blood bursting above his right eyebrow. The white man steps back and takes aim.

Nearby, someone screams.

Shannon has broken free and stands in front of the gun. The *umlungu* hesitates and for the first time in over sixty days, the young girl-woman speaks.

"No, Andries," she says, "Annelise does not approve."

The man's face crumples and his rifle sways in his grasp.

"Annelise?" His voice is strained, pleading and yet suspicious.

"Does not want more death," says Shannon, who is now more than a fourteen-year-old girl; although I cannot see the *idlozi* she carries.

The man lowers his rifle, but he still keeps it hovering alertly, at around forty-five degrees.

"What does she want me to do?" he asks.

'Yiso drops his gun too, staring at the base of the cliff, as if seeing something for the first time. His three shadowy children are reaching up for him.

As for the white man, Andries, he is bending down and grasping at sand, as if reminding himself of where he was, rifle on the ground beside him. I can make out the dull gleam of the ring finger of his left hand, sifting beach sand in trails of whiteness.

Shannon steps forward and pats his bent, wild ginger head with sadness and a strange sense of calm. "Just remember me," was all she says, in a voice hers, yet not hers.

Marlene moves forward to hug Shannon from behind.

"Hello, mother," says the girl, in her own voice again.

Andries turns to her in his crouch and snarls: "Satanic witch!"

Habib wipes blood from his face with his right hand, as he lurches back to his feet, pushing himself upward with his left arm.

And, with one fluid motion he steps forward to pick up 'Yiso's fallen gun, swinging the strap over his shoulder as he braces his legs and opens fire.

I turned and push Tracy into the sand, covering her small body with my own, as bullets spark and spray in the gathering evening gloom. A sharp, staccato burst of raw and rude noise and a flock of black oystercatchers wheeling in for the night scatter across the sky, screeching in panic.

My ears sting and my nose weeps at the smell of burnt chemicals.

Habib holds the gun steady, body rock solid, right eyebrow dripping red.

It takes me some moments to realise that no one is hurt and he has fired warning shots above all of our heads. Does he not know the flawed accuracy of this deadly gun?

I roll off Tracy and hold her; she is crying through sandy eyes and mouth.

Habib may be a small man, but he is powerfully built and he sweeps his left hand into the sand near the tent behind him, whipping up a long and wicked *panga*. With a few strides, rifle cocked in right hand, but *panga* waving in left, he has reached the men's para-gliders and—with a few deft slices of his long blade—he leaves the sails on both gliders in tatters.

Then he swings to face us. "Run," he says, "Both of you men, run like hell and never come near us again. Or I will kill you. Go. Now!"

His voice rings with a harsh and clear certainty.

'Yiso has turned away from the cliff; his spirit children cling to his back. He wipes his eyes with a forearm and looks at the *umlungu*.

Both men turn to look again at Habib.

One look is all.

They run.

They run with wild desperation, heading west from where we have come; towards the distant burnt husk of Cape Town. They run until we can see them no more, struggling around the cove headland, now blackened in the broad red beams of the sinking sun.

Three dead children spiral above us, swirling and breaking up like smoke.

Gone: Mandisa, Andiswa and Sibusiso junior, I think, although without any reason or certainty.

The cool breeze from over Cape Agulhas brings with it the sparkle of icebergs in the distance, remnants from the greening continent that straddles the South Pole.

Habib clips the safety and drops the rifle and *panga*. Stiff-legged, he walks stiffly over to his wife, hugging their eldest daughter too, but without tears. The blood is drying on his cheek, crusting his right eye closed.

I hesitate for a moment and then step over to them, with Tracy holding my hand. Marlene takes her from me with a bittersweet smile. "Thank you, 'Thando."

The short man, father of two, bows slightly towards me. "Yes, I thank you for protecting her, *Mambhele* Noluthando Ngobo... and I am so sorry for those words I spoke to you, sometime after we brought you along with us."

Marlene glances at both of us, but I say nothing, respecting the man's bravery for an apology in front of all, for private comments made to me a while hence. Just a few words he'd said really, but biting deep they were, warning me not to touch his children in strange ways.

I bow slightly and say nothing, turning to head back down towards the water, past the lacerated husks of the two dead gliding machines. The tide is coming in through a gap in the rocks and I hitch my trousers up to feel the numbness of the water as it rushes around my ankles.

Where should I go now? What should I do?

If I follow The Raptured men, would they take me in?

Was this family I stood with now, indeed truly mine?

And why still, did none of the spirits of the dead ever come for me?

"*Gogo?*"

I turn to face Shannon, who has followed me down to the water's edge. Habib and Marlene are fast packing the tent behind her, as if planning to move on and find a new and safer place before night has fully settled in. Tracy stands alongside, watching them, holding her teddy bear.

The teenage girl is looking at me with clear brown eyes, her pony-tailed brown hair bobbing behind her. She holds out her hands and I move up the beach towards her.

It is then that I see she has again become more than Shannon.

"*Molo, mamma,*" Shannon-Noluyando says to me and I step forward to hold her.

But, just as suddenly, I can feel she has gone—if she ever was there, her greeting lost, like the sound of the waves receding behind me. Although my eyes sting, I can see the girl is just Shannon again, any trace of my long dead baby daughter erased from her eyes.

Still, she touches my arm lightly, smiling as she stoops to pick up a stone.

"Can you skip a stone on the water with me, *gogo*?" she asks.

I laugh, welcoming a bit of play to dull the memories of threats, gunfire and a lost infant.

Shannon whirls a flat stone at the incoming wave, bouncing it twice off the green surface beyond the oncoming white crest.

I pick up a thin stone and sends it flashing in four spectacular bounds over the water in front of us.

Shannon turns to laugh at me: "Now you're just showing off, *gogo*!"

"Come, you two!" shouts Marlene; she and Habib are strapped up and ready to go, Tracy's right hand clutched tightly in Marlene's left. "Collect your bags, we need to find a new camp site before nightfall."

It is indeed darkening fast now, the sun gone, leaving a cold bite in the air. Shannon dashes up the beach.

Habib's right eye is plastered up, but it does not look as if he had been watching us especially closely.

Janet, where are you, beloved?

The bitter water swirls in again; my ankles and knees lock with the numbing surge of water that seemed to come from the ends of the Earth. I look up. The purple-black sky is empty; no one is coming in on the clouds.

"*MamBhele*?"

I turn. It is Shannon who has so correctly and formally addressed me. She has returned, straddling a small boulder with what looks like a sure and solid sense of her body.

"Come," she holds out her right hand, "Please come, grandma."

I laugh. My fears of being left behind vanish, just like those dead children of Sibusiso's. What else could I do, but take the young girl's hand and go?

Shannon she is—or else She-Who-Had-Called-The-World.

The eldest of my granddaughters...

Who cares about the dead?

I have a live family now.

Thandiwe's Tokoloshe

Thandiwe knew it was *her* Rainbow the minute she saw it, through the window of their sleeping room—just the other side of their neighbours' shiny corrugated roof, where kind Mrs Motlala lived.

But it was the rainbow Thandiwe was watching.

The rainbow was huge, bright and fresh in the early morning sun, hovering against dark clouds and dropping with a splash of colour into the nearby field. Not far, just the other side of the wire fences. Mamma had told her it was homework time, especially as she was due to start a new school next year—a bigger, older and smarter school.

But it was a *Saturday* after all.

She wiggled her bum to get a better position on their lumpy bed, her science book sliding off her lap.

It was quiet, so she listened hard.

Mamma's snores could be heard through the open door into the main room. Thandiwe smiled—Mamma was thin from a long strange illness, but was getting better, so it was good to hear her sleeping. She had always found that old brown couch very comfy; so much so, she seemed to be using it more and more.

Thandiwe had started to miss Mamma's presence in their bed though—although it was also guiltily good *not* to have Mandla screaming so nearby at night.

Come to think of it, there were no baby cries either. Thandiwe peeked through the door. Mandla lay check-blanket swaddled, sleeping soundly too on Mamma's lap, his rapidly lengthening legs hanging off onto the sagging couch; he was going to be a big boy in time.

Time—and homework. Seven colours, her science book said; that's how many colours in a rainbow.

Thandiwe looked closely through the window; seven didn't look right, it could be more, it could be less. And what was the difference between indigo and violet anyway?

And what, too, was that other story—Miss Mabuso had told them it only the other day, Monday, reading day—a Rainbow drops into a pot of gold at the end; with a funny creature guardian it called a leprechaun? She wished they'd been shown a picture, because she couldn't imagine it from Miss's description, but the teachers were all trying hard to move them away from pictures.

She sighed sadly, remembering her grandmother's colourful tales, embellished with rich descriptions that had burnt into her brain. She missed her *Gogo*, she'd always cooked them the best *mielie pap*—and she'd had a hacking laugh that tore happy holes into the world.

Thandiwe had shared just one of her Gogo's stories at school—Wednesday, oral story day—and remembered the biting comment that had come back from Miss Mabuso: 'Old people's tales; not fit for today's world.'

But then, Miss Mabuso *never* laughed.

It's all going to be letters and numbers from now and into high school; where bigger bullying children may also be waiting. She shivered, despite the sun outside.

Thandiwe thought of the pot of gold instead. It would be like a *potjie*; a large black cooking pot.

And she'd seen pictures of gold before; bright, yellow-shiny and very expensive. Now *that* would be worth more than any amount of homework—she had always been acutely aware of her mother's pain when shopping, as she'd scratched frantically in her bag, Mandla crying on her back at Pick 'N Pay check-outs.

The story of gold at the end of the Rainbow might just be a childish story, perhaps—but, being a *White* story, there was a chance it might even be true.

If she was quick, she could be back, before either Mamma or Mandla woke.

The scramble over the sagging fence was a messy one; she would need to come back in time to clean her skirt too.

She stood up in the field littered with bags, bottles and Pick 'N Pay trollies.

Her stupid Rainbow had moved!

There was a tall line of blue-gum trees she hadn't noticed from the window and the Rainbow dropped with a blur into green branches. With a sigh, she walked briskly towards the trees.

At least she was a good climber—if the pot was hanging from a branch, she'd be up there quicker than Mamma responding to Mandla's cries for milk.

By the time she reached the trees, Thandiwe could see through them, just a thin barrier to yellow grasslands stretching far beyond. The Rainbow seemed to have danced away into the distance.

Thandiwe sighed again, more heavily this time. How on Earth was she going to get there now?

There was a swift movement out of the corner of her eye and she turned to see a large yellow-brown animal bounding out of the long grass towards her.

She almost fainted with fear.

It was a lion, thundering to a halt in front of her. Large and smelling like wet sacking with a huge shocking black mane, it stood stiffly, pawing at the ground. But weren't the Cape Lions extinct? Cape Town itself wasn't so far off either. Still, even though her science book said they were extinct—here, one definitely was—a stinky male Cape Lion.

The lion crooked his left front paw and bent his back, as if offering her a place to ride. Thandiwe braced herself and looked into his bright yellow eyes. Despite her trembling knees, she held the lion's freakishly steady gaze.

A part of her knew she shouldn't, but how else would she be able to get to her Rainbow? Tentatively, she took a fistful of musty mane and swung her legs over onto his back, grateful she was wearing track-suit pants. She had a strange, dizzying sense that she was not the first girl to ride a lion.

His back was rippling with muscles and she clutched hard onto his mane. Up close he didn't smell *too* bad, she thought, perhaps a little like her stale school socks before Gogo—and now Mamma—had washed them.

The lion galloped off and Thandiwe buried her head into his mane, grassland whipping past her. She was sore and bruised by the time he eventually slowed, heading down a bumpy slope where riverine trees stood, eclipsed by a massive, shimmering rainbow dropping down, down, down...

And the Rainbow did indeed pour into a huge glistening black pot—up so close, she realised there were maybe more than a *million* possible colours, if only she had a label for them all.

Were the books wrong, then?

Thandiwe climbed off: 'Thank you.'

The lion turned his head and looked at her. She stepped back nervously, realising some distance was safest, however helpful a lion might seem.

But she wasn't quick enough. He struck, a quick slash of his right paw snaking across her shins. She screamed and clutched at her legs.

But the lion just turned and, with a breath of wind, was gone.

Thandiwe pulled her torn trouser-legs up and wiped a few drops of blood from her shins. There was a thin shallow scratch scouring the surface of both her shins, perhaps just a warning? She pulled her track-suit pants back down and looked up.

Mangalisayo!

She could almost hear her Rainbow humming above her, pouring its multitude of colours into that big black nearby pot, with a surging hiss. It was all *finally* in her reach.

No—who was this? A small ochre-furred creature with wide body, large eyes and long tail, thick moustache and monkey hands and feet stepped from behind the pot. He was not wearing any clothes apart from a leather pouch on his left hip, so she could see it was a *he*.

Most definitely.

With a sudden chill through her body, she recognised it from her Gogo's old kitchen stories.

It couldn't be a leprechaun; surely it had to be a *tokoloshe*?

'I'll let you have a look into the pot, little girl.' He stepped aside to let her pass, grinning.

Thandiwe looked at the tokoloshe and smiled, despite the terror surging within her. She couldn't let him know she recognised him; it would only alert him that she *knew* he couldn't be trusted.

She kept smiling as she moved forward as carelessly as she could, trying not to look at his daggered teeth and bracing her burning legs beneath her pants.

Without warning, he leaped forward to grab at her with his lightning quick monkey hands.

But he wasn't *quite* quick enough.

Thandiwe ducked underneath his grasp and snapped the pouch from his waist. Two quick steps back and she had the stone from the pouch into her palm and then her mouth.

The stone burnt on her tongue but the tokoloshe flailed wildly at thin air, lurching away: 'I'll get you, little girl.'

She smiled, knowing she was invisible. Her Gogo was right, though, the tokoloshe was not *too* clever—just as long as you kept your wits about you.

She was glad she'd enjoyed Gogo's stories so much.

This felt like no story though.

The tokoloshe was smart enough to lurch back to the pot, poking the air in front of him, nose tilted to sniff the breeze. His nails were clawed and sharp.

With a shiver, Thandiwe paced quietly around to the far side of the pot, finding she was *just* tall enough on tip toes in Bata Toughee school shoes to peer inside.

At last…

The huge *potjie* was empty. The Rainbow poured in, disappearing into black nothingness. She rocked back onto her heels with crushed disappointment.

A tall robed person with wings and a glowing head stood there, looking at her.

The tokoloshe was gone.

'What is wrong, Thandiwe?'

'There's nothing in there,' she said, spitting the stone into her hand.

'Nothing?' said the glowing person, 'But within *you*, you have gained courage worth more than any gold.'

'Can I sell it or eat it?' she asked.

'No,' the winged person said, looked puzzled.

'*Hamba bhebha*, then!'

They looked even more puzzled.

She tutted; it was obviously a *White* winged-person, so she gave the direct English translation.

'Fuck off!'

They vanished.

She certainly didn't need anyone else to tell her she was good inside.

Thandiwe looked at the slippery stone in her palm. It could perhaps make a neat paper-weight for Mamma's hospital notes, perhaps?

She looked up.

There was no Rainbow, nor any pot.

The lion was standing in front of her, stretching its paws and offering her his back.

Thandiwe looked into his eyes, knowing he was a dumb but dangerous beast. 'I get it,' she said, 'Be careful whom you trust. You *hambha bheba* too, then.'

The lion did not even bother to run, turning on its paws and disappearing in a puff of disbelief.

Thandiwe braced herself for a long walk.

She could feel changes in her body and knew with peculiar certainty she was no longer a child.

Sighing, she clutched the warm stone in her right palm and began her walk across a field littered with burnt out tyres, bags and bottles.

It no longer mattered if she would be late; only that she got home at all.

Come to think of it, the stone could always be a weapon too, if necessary.

Big school no longer felt so big.

Thandiwe walked home, step by step, pants torn and with burning shins.

*

It was night time when she finally got home, the darkness heavy on her shoulders.

Gogo waited for her on the other side of their sagging fence, holding Mandla in her arms.

He was still sleeping.

'Where's Mamma, Gogo?' Thandiwe asked; cold in her sweat from the long walk.

'Gone to the shades, child.'

Thandiwe clambered over the fence and her grandmother handed her the baby. Thandiwe could see her Gogo's old and craggy face, fuzzy and vague in death; she was careful not to touch hands as she took Mandla.

'You remember the ceremonies needed; my special *intombi*?'

Thandiwe nodded; holding back the burn in her eyes. Mandla was *mielie*-sack heavy and opened his mouth to scream. Thandiwe loosened her clutch and his screaming wail dropped to a whimper.

She gave her Gogo a stiff smile and went inside.

Mamma's body lay at a rigid and crooked angle on the couch, legs hanging onto the floor. Thandiwe could not look any more, so she draped Mandla's check blanket over Mamma as much as she could. She was panting with the baby under her arm; he was starting to whimper loudly, threatening to scream.

Thandiwe stepped over her mother's calloused feet sticking out from under the blanket, trying not to look directly through her blurred and burning eyes. She opened the door slowly, suspecting even more was wrong.

The shadows outside were full of menace and she heard a throaty chuckle, catching a glint of green slitted eyes.

The tokoloshe was waiting for her.

Why had he followed her all this way, so far from water?

Mandla began to cry, so Thandiwe stepped with him into the night shadows, hissing: '*Hamba bhebha!*'

The shadows were empty as she knocked on their neighbour's door, holding her now screaming brother as gently as she could on her hip.

Mrs Motlala held Thandiwe close and pulled them both into the warm light of the living room.

Five Hundred Photons

Five hundred words Izzy. Further we go, less we get. No pictures either. We lose bandwidth as the lightyears mount, so my words must be enough. We're beaming photon packages with data ten light years back. Latest planet-hope is called Delteron-9. Twice Earth-size so gravity may be a problem; exo-skeletons and gestational support needed for first-generation colonists, but I'm ahead of myself. Just logged into orbit, so much analysis still to do, this may just be another red-herring, a planet with parameters beyond our abilities for terra-forming. We hope and pray as we know the years pass more quickly on your heating Earth. Still, I hope to see you here, perhaps with children?

Let me paint a word-picture for you at least. The planetary disc swirls and shimmers a pale blue; not deep blue like Earth, but a water-blue at least. Acid-wet though, so work to be done before anyone can swim or drink here. Three moons swing in orbit; two little more than the Martian rocky moons, but one a large dead world that glows in pink phases from an orange-red sun that looks so similar and yet so different to our own. No sun's name though, that's only for official reports. Five thousand words allowed for those. Not fair is it? Anyway, there are flashes of orange on Delteron-9; ground is roughly ten percent of its area and is crinkled and crusted, some mountains rearing twenty kays high. White topped, places to walk or climb perhaps, like your father loves (or loved?) to do.

No words allowed from you here. Data is precious, time is short they say. The mission is all.

To them.

But when we drift around the night side, purple flashes seam the darkness. Atmospheric flares or pulses of fluorescent life? Too early to tell; we need to send the probes. As colours strobe the darkness I wonder, is it lightning, is it rain? It's been fifteen years since I felt wet rain on my face. Fifteen years since I pushed you high on that swing and you laughed and looked back at me; your face caught in my head and heart, hair flying forward as you started your arc back down to me. I have no picture of that moment, but it lives inside me as I watch purple stain the darkness above or below us. Two pictures I have; you know the ones, one with your dad and me in front of the cake, one with your mom. Five years old. They're pasted against the window over my cocoon-bunk. I look at both you and the new worlds beyond. But mostly I look at the gut-wrenching darkness of space. Purple flashes are few now; I see the orange-gold glow of an imminent sun-rise. I watch the sun rise for both of us.

I'm too scared to ask the Ship for relativity calculations of your age. Wish you here Izzy. Love You. Grandfather.

...

FAILED TO DELIVER. RECIPIENT DECEASED. NEXT OF KIN UNTRACEABLE.

God in The Box

Michael knows exactly how to irritate me. Even when I control myself and pretend I'm cool, he somehow knows I'm not. And the bloody amazing thing is; he can even anticipate the evolution of new pet-hates of mine. From dirty socks in the bath to toilet seat in the up position to talks from concerned teachers whom I hope will never ask what I do for a living.

After all, I sometimes need to remind myself that *I'm* the psychologist.

And Michael is just my fourteen-year-old son.

Today, he throws his school bag across the room as he comes into the kitchen. Buckled and zipped, the bag scrapes over my newly laid pristine wooden-floor. It feels as if it's scraped my skin. I grimace, back turned to him, trying to control the harsh words that want to burst out. Behavioural extinction is needed. A dead calm lack of response.

"Stop doing that, Mike!" I snap as I turn.

He's already slouched on a kitchen stool, face dark and sullen, heavy bodied. My response makes him smile slightly.

Bugger. He's won the opening salvo.

"What, mum?" His feigned innocence is designed to rub it in even further. This time, I manage not to rise to the bait.

"Never mind," I'm tired and dispirited, "How was your day at school?"

"Fine."

I know nothing more will be forthcoming. I don't know why I still persist with that hoary opening line. It feels like it's just etched and perseverating verbal routines, nothing more. Except that I really do want to know.

The phone rings. I sigh.

Upstairs, I know Jack is probably reading the paper, with no intention of talking to us, let alone responding to the outside world.

I make my way into the hallway.

"Hello," I said, "Dr. Brandon."

"Dr. Brandon? It's Tom." The voice is officious, deep and confident, ringing slightly with its narcissistic surety.

Great. The Major. I still have to smile every time he uses his first name, though.

What crippled mind did he want to me assess now?

"Hi Tom."

"Eva, we have another case for you to look at."

Why else would you phone me, idiot? I keep it a thought. As I mostly do with the Major. He makes you feel vaguely guilty of something (everything)—even when he just looks at you. So I try not to see him too often.

"Eva," He says and his voice sounds different, strangely tight and anxious. "Eva, we need you to section a policeman who has found God."

I'm aware Michael has come into the corridor and is hovering behind me, breathing heavily.

"I'm sorry, Tom," I am sure of this one, "Religious belief is beyond my clinical jurisdiction."

"I don't think you understand. He claims to have brought God with him. We've got both of them locked up."

I startle a bit, uncertain as to whether I have heard right. "Uh—what exactly are you saying, Major? You've got God there as well and you want me to section them as both insane?"

A little deep chuckle—most unusual for him. "No, Doctor, just the policeman will do."

I turn to look at Michael. He hasn't heard anything, but he knows. "I'll make my own dinner."

I feel a pang. He looks so goddammed resigned and distant.

*

The Institute—Bayford Military (B.M.I.)—is not that far.

It's based in a large old mansion house—hidden by trees—close to the University where I do the bulk of my teaching. The B.M.I. was established as an army research lab—one of about twenty throughout Britain after the Terror Wars—to document the human and military fall-out from the war.

My job was to assess the human side. I generally had to evaluate what mental and neuro-psychological damage was manifest in the military—and occasionally civilian—population. One of the perks of employment was that I was paid extra to be 'conservative' with disability assessments involving compensation suits from soldiers following the Wars.

Which is why I'm still in a 2 bed-roomed terrace on the outskirts of London…

Major Tom (smile) Stone was a tough Military man, but a damned fine scientist too, specialising in neuro-biology. (He liked his science hard too.)

He had a lot of clout at the Institute and was the liaison person for neuro-psychological assessments. Me, I was just one of several external consultants they pulled in. They had offered me a full-time post once, but I'd turned it down, for fear of seeing the Major every day.

Not that he was bad looking. A smallish man with a tight handshake, and razored grey hair on top of his sharp, finely featured face.

It's just that he was an awkward argumentative bastard.

"God, my arse!" I say to him, after I'd tried to squeeze his hand as hard as I could.

He waves me to a chair. His room was brown and warmly furnished, if a touch Spartan in the decor.

He came around his desk to sit opposite me: no barriers in this session then.

"Well, the copper thinks so. And we've taken possession of—uh, It."

"It?"

"What he calls God—a meteorite from space, is all, we guess. But it's a bloody unusual one."

"How so?"

He shrugs, taking out a box of cigarettes.

What an archaic and disgusting habit for a man so bright—I shake my head.

He glares at me and puts it back in his pocket. "Well, geologically it's a unique specimen. We're still trying to analyse data, but it looks like there might be entirely new scientific elements encased inside. We're also concerned about contamination and radiation, and so we have it securely locked in quarantine."

"So it's a funny rock—perhaps a relic from the Terror Wars? It's a huge leap to God."

He smiles wryly: "The policeman's word, not mine. And apparently the owner of the rock before him."

"Who was that?"

"We haven't been able to trace her. She brought it in to the station when Constable Pridom was on desk duty one night, claiming to have found it in a field, but saying by rights it belonged to the whole world. Because it was God."

"And then?"

"The Constable laughed at her and told her to piss off. Then he touched it."

"And -?"

"He agreed with her—suddenly and whole heartedly. When the Station Commander heard what had happened, he sealed the Station, suspecting terror contamination, and shipped the stone off to us. Well shielded."

"What happened to the original owner?"

"Gone, no trace, as if she's fallen off the face of the earth," he moved uncomfortably in his chair. An energetic man, the Major hated to sit still for long.

"Or gone as if she's ascended to heaven," I say.

He wrinkles his nose. "Fun-nee! She may well have had outside help disappearing, leaving us with a potentially lethal mind-altering hot potato."

"Neuro-biologically?"

"Nothing. There are no signs of any disease, contamination or illness in the policeman. We haven't a clue yet as to possible pathogenic vectors, so we've sealed the bloody thing in a vacuumed anti-radiation box."

"So it's safe to talk to him?"

"Surely," He said, "That's if he'll talk to you. But that's your job, I'll leave you to it." He got up and walked over to open the door.

Standing quietly behind it, blinking, stood a large man with a square head. It was obviously a policeman (uniformed), politely holding his helmet in front of him.

"Peter Pridom, meet Dr. Eva Brandon." The Major waved the man inside and left his office, closing the door behind him.

"Pleased to meet you, Doctor."

I gesture him to sit, but he continued to stand. "I don't want to waste your time," he said.

"You're not wasting it," I said, "They're paying me for this."

"It's still a waste," he said, "I can see you don't believe me. Your mind-models have ruled that out."

"*Welll…*" I'm hoping to tap into his delusional system, "Perhaps you can persuade me?"

"Sorry," he smiles slightly; "I don't think so." And he stood there quietly, serenely unresponsive to all my cues and questions and—eventually—please.

But at least I got a 'fine' out of him when I asked him how his day had been. It was vaguely reassuring to know I was not doing worse with him than I generally do with my own son.

The Major came back not too long after I'd given up the limited conversation, smiling when he saw my exasperated face. A soldier was with him to escort Constable Pridom back to his quarantine quarters.

"Gave you a hard time, did he?" The Major asked, with a small hint of sadistic satisfaction.

I didn't even bother to reply. "I need to see the stone."

He frowned: "You work with people—or so I thought. Or do you think you'll get more from a stone than you got from him? You're not a psycho-geologist, you know." (Irritating chuckle).

"Let me just have a look, Tom," It was late and I was tired. "I'm a scientist, whatever you may think—and I need primary, not secondary, data."

"Sure, Eva," He looks a little taken aback. "Come with me."

*

I don't know what I had expected.

The stone is held in a small grey room with an armed guard outside. It was sitting alone in a translucent box of indeterminate substance—approximately a yard cubed—surrounded by blinking sensors and computers. The stone itself was contrastingly black and absorbent, showing no flicker in response to the array of light around it.

It was just a rough few inches in diameter.

I wondered whether it had a history of being thrown through people's windows. It looked like just the right size and shape for the palm, and I'm talking old but wayward youth experience here.

"So," said the Major, turning to look at me, "What…"

He has no time to finish the question. I'd stepped forward and touched the box. It felt like hard fibreglass.

Except it was warm. Wonderfully warm.

He grabbed me back.

In slow motion.

Like a bloody movie.

And I think, yes, you're such a good scientist, why do you have to be such a shitty man? And what do I need to do to get Mike and Jack together and talking again? And how can I make my work meaningful like it used to be when I was younger?

And I had the sense that all these questions could be answered if I only trusted myself and the world around me just a little bit more.

Somehow.

"Stupid!" The Major's face was twisted and hard, he's furious.

His hand was tight on my arm. It hurts, so I stepped on his instep. With my high heels, he shouted and let go.

I think he's just a bully, if it all comes down to it. No clever psychodynamic formulations flow to mind. He just likes to push his weight around.

I'm not a flyweight myself, though.

He scowled sidelong at me as we headed back to his office, gesturing abruptly at a chair when we entered his office.

This time he sat behind his desk.

"What the hell was that all about?" He snarled.

"Primary data," I said. I pause. I had the feeling that things were tying together somehow, that there was a pattern here, that I was not just exposed to loosely random events, over which I had no control.

"So?" He spat the word.

I didn't even hesitate. "I think Pridom may be right."

He barked, throwing his head back in threatening laughter. "Are you so impressionable? Listen, Eva—I touched that bloody thing too—really touched it, not just when it was sealed, like you. It's just a weird fucking rock."

"Then why are you so frightened?" I asked.

He stopped and then looked at me with that look that usually made me feel guilty. But this time I don't feel a shred of guilt. I stared back at him.

"Come on Tom," I said, "We're scientists. We've got to leave a little room for Uncertainty."

"Your field is a lot more uncertain than mine," he said, "And your scientific objectivity has been compromised."

I think I knew a little more why the policeman had said so little to me. But I tried again.

"Science doesn't always have to explain everything."

"It's done pretty well so far," He shot back, "To call the unexplainable 'god', is to work with an ever-shrinking god of the gaps."

"Perhaps that's why God has come to earth? Squeezed out of the heavens by a rampant science?"

"Listen to yourself, *shrink*," The word was used contemptuously, and I knew a line had been crossed. "You're saying this stone is like some bloody broken off piece of Kubrick's 2001 monolith that was floating through space. That's pure bloody science fantasy, let alone science fiction."

"Clarke," I said.

"What?"

"It was Arthur Clarke's 2001 Odyssey first."

He stood up. "I don't give a toss. I'm sad it's come to this."

I know it is the final handshake. He held his hand out: "Goodbye, Eva."

As I shook his hand, I do believe he *is* just a little sad.

But not enough.

"My job," is his parting shot, "Is to find better ways of putting bullets through people, not spreading world peace."

Ah, so there's the rub.

*

It is about 3 months after Bayford had fired me that I arrive home from the University, exhausted after an R.A.E. visit. There is a parcel on the kitchen table. Jack had obviously signed for it reluctantly.

It's squarely wrapped in brown paper, with my name hand-written in a neatly penned scrawl. Featureless brown, the parcel rattles slightly when I shake it. The postmark is London. I don't remember ordering anything from London.

Shredding the wrapping, my fingers are tingling as I expose a small grey box, stamped with a company name. Theologica Pharmaceuticals.

Ah! A drug company. And we psychologists were still awaiting the new bill for basic prescribing rights, in the face of the fading few psychiatrists left in the health service. A pre-emptive strike it seemed, by an alert company, into a pending new market.

Except, when I look at the accompanying letter attached to the box, I realise I am just a potential customer.

Dear Doctor Brandon,

From Bayford Military, We believe you are already familiar with the elements of God that have fallen from the sky. We have confirmed after extensive tests that there are no harmful effects and that there may be some veracity to the claims that God is somehow resident in this element. Out of our Company's extensive civic duty we have diluted this compound into tablet form, as a means to spreading the joy of the existence of God. This is the first stage of market research. Please take this pill with our compliments and give us independent feedback as to the relative blissfulness of your experience. (Form enclosed.) This will be invaluable when it comes to allocating a fair price if and when full publicity and marketing becomes possible. Please note that the Military currently retain ownership and any (even singular) negative experience will result in Bayford destroying all remaining batches.

Yours sincerely,
<squiggle>
C.E.O. Theologica Pharmaceuticals

I look at the box. It is white and plainly marked in black Gothic print: 'God-Pill.'

There are brief instructions on the outside of the Box: 'Please take one every 24 hours in the event of nihilistic feelings or if in prolonged existential crisis. Possible side effects: Excessive euphoria.'

It takes me a while to open the box. Damned thing seemed designed not to be opened, as if reluctant to reveal its contents. Then I notice my hands are shaking.

It is a small green pill. Organic-like. (Black pills don't market well.)

And I can sense whispers of something through my fingers. I cup the pill in my right palm. It is small, almost lost in the wrinkles and folds of skin now starting to appear on me.

Small, yet potent, and promising much. Imagine the experience if I ingested it into my stomach—what would the impact be on my nervous system? They must have already found out, if it has reached this stage. I wonder where the human guinea pigs are now? What are they doing?

But then an inkling of doubt, a vague sense of paranoia, creeps into my thoughts. Is this company a front for the Military? Are they perhaps trying to get rid of me?

I sniff the Pill.

The Company is small. It recedes from my mind. Even the Military is faltering. I sense the Major wants this destroyed, but it is clambering out of Its' box too fast. Too many people have felt It. God?

Or is it Pandora's Box?

I sniff again.

No. I don't think so. It smells like the end of War. Where is the evil in that?

But the Major will try and destroy the batches somehow, I know suddenly and certainly, nothing will be left.

Nothing but rolling the Sisyphus stone of work and family up the hill every day. Waking up from dreamless sleep to find it all at the bottom of the hill again in the morning.

If I take this pill, perhaps I can save It. Save everything?

No. What a messianic joke! I can't change it all on my own... But at least for some hours perhaps I can feel as if I have touched the Face of God?

I lift the pill and open my mouth.

I see my black fillings and gold tooth coyly hidden in the back of my mouth.

Startled, I realise I am looking at myself in the bathroom mirror. How on earth did I get here—the last I remembered I was in the kitchen with the parcel?

I must have walked up the stairs without thinking, like I often drive down a well-known route, suddenly conscious of the arrival place with no clear memory of the journey.

My face is oldish in the mirror, wrinkling fast these past few years, but at least my eyes are still bright.

And the toilet is open (seat up yet again, bloody men!)

The toilet is open. Like my mouth. Calling.

I hesitate, desperately wanting to feel that connection with God again, that sense my life was meaningful and worthwhile and had a plan leading it forward to some lasting purpose and joy. I just needed to swallow that little green God-Pill.

But I suddenly realise why the toilet seat is calling.

My arm and hand shake with the agony of the decision. It is bloody madness to throw it all away. It's not as if my life is steeped in ongoing transcendent experiences of the divine.

But somehow—I hope—it has to be the right thing to do. I don't want tiny dosed pieces of God. I want more—the whole shebang. Most of all, I dread the sense of being left with nothing.

So it feels like I'm flushing my own soul away as I lean on the toilet lever and watch the green pill get swallowed up in a pool of suctioning bubbles, the pan draining to leave…

I peer forward, hoping against hopes; the pill is too small to have gone.

No.

It is gone. The toilet is empty.

I can't believe I've just flushed God down the fucking loo.

*

Michael finds me still sitting there, on the edge of the bath, peering in.

"Eh-? What you looking for mum?"

I look at him. He doesn't seem to notice I've been crying. "Nothing Michael. Nothing."

"Oh!" He stands in the doorway, momentarily undecided, bag hanging over his shoulder. Then, taking the plunge, he turns and throws his bag along the wooden hallway. I hear the bag scuffing and banging along the passage, thumping suddenly against a closed door.

I open my mouth to scream blue murder at him.

And shut it again.

He looks like he always does. Face dark and sullen, heavy bodied. Except I sense some sadness from the day in his thoughts too, as if he has trailed them in here behind him. Just wishing he could hurl it over my neatly new wooden floors like his bag.

"You've had a bad day, son?" I ask.

He startles slightly, looking at me hard suddenly: " Eh—what's that mum?"

"You've had a bad day, haven't you?"

I think it's my knowing assertion that hits him. His eyes mist just a fraction until he hardens them desperately. Tough boy.

"Yeah, actually, it was a bitch of a day."

I stop the urge to chastise his language and deal instead with the pain of the message.

"What happened?"

He looks at me suspiciously, aware we're on new and unfamiliar territory for his age. (He used to talk so freely when he was a little boy.)

But he's bigger now—a lot bigger.

"Um—I let on I fancied this girl to Stevey, and he made a move on her today. Now what sort of mate is that?"

"Not one you deserve," I say, "You've always been extremely loyal with all the friends you've ever had."

He turns his head away to hide his eyes. "Jesus, mother, what are you on?"

"Nothing—and I swear I haven't touched that stash hidden under your bed either."

He looks back at me in shock. "Er—er, I'm just keeping that for a friend, like…"

I wave his words away. My bum is sore and so I stand up. I still look up at him now, even with my high heels on.

"It doesn't matter, Michael, as long as you have a handle on it."

He looks at me, relaxing visibly, staring hard at my face, and noticing things. "Are you okay mum? It looks like you've been…"

"I'm okay," I say.

I almost hear him think: 'Tough old bat.'

I know I should actually model more self-disclosure. But in this case, I don't know what the hell to say.

"Oh." He closes the topic with a relieved and disbelieving shake of his head, but picks up quickly on my earlier statement: "Yeah, I guess a little weed doesn't matter. It's obviously not as bad as scratching wooden floors."

I look at him. He looks at me, slightly scared, as if he's afraid he's overstepped the mark.

God, what an idiot I've been. But then I smile.

I step past him into the hallway.

He turns to watch me. His bag is lying crumpled against the firmly shut study door, where Jack no doubt lurks, with his reading and computer stuff.

I drag the spiky heel of my shoe in a scratching tear along a polished maple board.

Mike looks down in horrified disbelief at the floor. We can both see a large six-inch gouge in the woodwork.

"I should have done that a while ago," I say.

He looks up at my face, agog, with rising laughter: "Jesus, mom, you're barking mad, you know that!"

"Woof! Woof! What do you expect?" I said, "After all, I'm a …"

I leave it unsaid. I can't actually say it, because I'm laughing.

And so is Mike. Big belly guffaws. I've forgotten how infectious his laugh can be. It's only a matter of time before we both need to find a chair to sit on, down in the lounge, to ease the bellyache of laughing so wildly.

Even Jack comes down to see what it's all about.

I'm thirsty from laughing so much, but think it's probably still too early to have a drink of water from the tap. I doubt they've recycled our toilet waste yet, even though we feed into one of London's largest and most efficient sewerage recycling reservoirs.

How will London react to a homeopathic dose of God?

Bridges

Silence…

Silence shrinks an already small room and I stare at the young man who will not talk, wondering how I reach out across the space between us, how to make his words flow. He stares across to the picture on the wall behind me: his eyes are hooded, his body slumped. The room is a tight box of peeling institutional yellow, mould flicking corners of the ceiling, the narrow walls groaning with a history of mad voices . . . or so I've been told. The young man's head is cocked; as if he's listening. Perhaps the voices in the wall have overwhelmed him? Me, I've never heard them, sitting as I am on the right side of this small square desk, panic button comfortably within range on the wall next to me.

"What do you hear, Sibusiso?" I ask, normalising his experiences, just in case.

He flicks a glance to my mouth, as if unsure that's where the voice has indeed come from, but his eyes scan back behind me.

How indeed to build a link between us? I swivel on my higher chair to look at the picture locking his gaze. It's an old photograph I'd taken perhaps a decade or so back, at the turn of the century. It's of a rope bridge with snared base planks, swinging over the Umgeni River: an empty bridge, too treacherous to walk on or cross, with an angled view of the green and distant slope on the other bank. The glass frame keeps the picture from deepening a further yellow and curling at the edges. Reflected lines of hot sunlight spill in through the slats of drawn blinds, making it hard to see the picture clearly. I know it by heart though— that and the similar but different one in my bedroom at home—the Umgeni Bridge; a place of wild voices, a place of beginnings.

So I stand up, hitch the picture off the hanging nail, and turn to hand it to him.

"Do you like it?" I ask.

He holds the picture, studying it for moments and then he cranes his neck back in order to look up at me. I stand waiting.

"Did you take it, doctor?"

Ah—a personal question; we're ever trained to divert those. "What would it mean to you if I did take it?" I ask.

To my surprise, he just chuckles a little to himself. The nurses had said he was responding to the amitriptyline; he'd even managed a supervised weekend out recently. He leans back to look up at me again.

"I would just like to know whether you've been there and seen this, doctor."

"Yes," I said; if in doubt, keep it honest and short.

"Would I be allowed to go there and see this for myself too, Doctor?"

"Um, you've only just been home for a weekend, Sibusiso." I sit down, now that a flow of conversation has opened between us. "Why would you want to go?" *Why does he ask what we both know is impossible? And it's a bloody high bridge too...*

Sibusiso Mchunu sits up a little straighter, the creases in his neat green psychiatric overalls twisting into fresh angles across his lean body. "I never said I *want* to go, just am I *allowed* to go, if I were well enough, doctor?"

"I don't think so, Sibusiso..."

The reason hangs between us like a damp, dark unspoken secret. I get up to switch on the hanging naked bulb overhead so that we can see each other better, the green shades leaking humid heat and light, but keeping the bulk of the sun at bay. I wish the afternoon thunderstorms would gather more quickly.

Perhaps safer verbal territory would help too. "So, tell me something you may have enjoyed doing on your weekend out then, Sibusiso." I sit down and watch his face; he is alert and watchful in return. Keep it close to home; keep it fun, especially with a young man recovering from psychotic depression.

"I—I went to listen to a band playing music at one of our local *shebeens*—it, uh, was good stuff, doctor. They played old covers of Aretha Franklin, Stevie Wonder, Gil Scott-Heron and even some old *mbaqanga* township jazz."

Sibusiso's tongue clicks over the last word, leaving me slightly perplexed, slightly distanced. I recognise the first two names and wonder if the third person referred to was also...black. No, the word was still not to be mentioned—here, at least, race and colour will *not* be an issue.

So, keep playing it safe, encourage his words—for, in the end, all talking should help. That's the faith of my job. "What did you enjoy most about the music, Sibusiso?"

"That..." Sibusiso took a breath and leaned forward slightly: "The fact that black people make such wonderful music and more ..."

I smile awkwardly and lean back in my chair. What to do, how to respond? I am a liberal Afrikaner, non-racialist in my attitude; for me, colour is not an issue, not here, not now. I weigh him up with my eyes—he is sitting forward, eyes wide but respectfully averted, waiting for an answer with a slight twist to his lips.

He raises this mindfully—still, follow the patient, as they say. "So… what does this mean to you?"

Sibusiso flashes me a fleeting look that takes flight like a cagey *springbok*, dropping his head into his hands, palms up on the table between us. His head is shaven short, the back of his head scarred with a swollen weal as if he'd been beaten in the recent past. By whom, though?

"Sibusiso?" I chime the name delicately, to emphasise both respect and concern.

He stays bowed, silence pooling onto the table.

Is this a signal indicating a therapeutic rupture, presumably around the question of what it meant to be both black and to have (musical) achievements… and perhaps my inadequate response?

I sigh. Shall I call in a Zulu nursing staff member to take him back to the ward? No, that'll be a message that I've given up… and I don't give up on anyone, even if they're just a young Bantu man. I must keep trying to span this experiential chasm that separates us; try and reel him back into this room with words. And, if words do indeed fail, there's always *the* machine, *my* machine, my Bridge of Feelings.

I lean across the table until I am close to his scarred head, recoiling a little at the sharp smell of sweat. Was this a sign of deteriorating personal hygiene, a cultural factor, or poverty? Ashamed at my ignorance, I decide I need to confront this silence.

"I'm sorry Sibusiso, did I say something wrong?" (I am careful not to touch him.)

Silence continues to drip off him in sick emotional waves. I lean back to breathe more easily. How can I use words to step across the huge gulf that divides us? He had even initially refused to talk to fellow Zulu nursing staff, perhaps afraid they might be government informers. All reports suggest he may be a '*comrade*', an anti-apartheid activist, although he had denied that of course in his few, terse words on admission. Here, our task is to make him better, not to vet his political views or activity. I stay neutral; dispassionate, scientific. Psychology is politically impartial in South Africa—even if we have no trained black Zulu psychologists to see Sibusiso either.

There is just me…I stand in frustration. Perhaps he thinks I'm connected with the S.A.P. Special Branch, white man that I am; no matter how much I emphasise confidentiality. My words seem too feeble to convince him otherwise. Just… just perhaps my Feelings Box can heal this rupture, span this gap? It's almost ready; one final test tonight and I can smuggle it in tomorrow… if it works.

I look down at the young man's hunched body.

"Sibusiso?"

Sibusiso looks up; his face is stained and shiny with tears. "It—it means the world to me, doctor."

Ahhh…he's answered my earlier question. Slowed response though, perhaps indicating psychomotor retardation—does his medication need to be increased, after all?

The Umgeni rope bridge photograph lies face down between us, hidden, just a tan cardboard backing in view.

I touch his shoulder lightly and pick the photograph up, putting it back on my office wall.

I'll smuggle the Feelings Box in tomorrow then, if I have to, despite Doctor James. I am old enough to make my own choices.

*

Outside, thunder-storms are indeed clearing and cooling the air, although the sky is also darkening with the storm and the onset of night.

Safe within the comfort of my small house I hold Jacky, my spaniel cross, my cheap *brak* tight, as she struggles in my arms. Wires lace down from our scalps to the Black Box at my feet. I stroke her and murmur in her floppy ears. This is the warm blue leather couch where we usually sit in peace and watch an evening's TV, skipping past ongoing news flashes summarising the year about the never-ending State of Emergency; the continuing collapse of the *rand*. New threatening news for us too, we are told—Obama and Osama to meet the Soviet bloc in Peace Talks above the Berlin Wall, as the Soviet Union tires of thirty years of haemorrhaging men into their Afghan ulcer.

I switch the TV off, wondering if the calming couch associations will reassure Jacky, as she scrabbles and scratches at my chest. I take a deep breath and switch the foot-square box-machine on at my feet. Nothing happens; my brain fails to swing into the space separating our different bodies, our separate brains.

I growl with puzzlement, fear, restriction, even a little cold pain, but warmed by sweaty human smells and image flashes of meaty chunks dropping from pink familiar smells. Chunks not here though, body sore, warm smell is squeezing, fear rising, snarls from outside monster…

Arms let go and I scramble under the couch yelping, ripping the electrode-cap free from my/her head. With short, ragged gasps, I clutch at my ribs and lean forward on the couch. The arms are…mine. I am… Martin Van Deventer, neuropsychologist. Doctor Van Deventer, one of the inventors of the 'Feelings Box', the 'Empathy Enhancer'—an EE machine and…it works, it sure as hell works! I must tell Dan…

I stroke the leads that trail from my scalp-cap to the machine, vine-feeders of emotional images from another species. Dogs do see colours, despite having only two visual cones…or does this come from being filtered through my own brain? Dear God, but this machine could change the whole world, let alone this depressing, ravaged, racialist country.

"Jacky…" I call her out from under the couch. She comes reluctantly, trembling, confused. I lift the cap that she'd pulled loose but she gives a brief yelp and retreats under the couch again. Okay then, I'll just have to keep pairing the cap with meaty treats to reinstate a Pavlovian pleasure association for her. Eventually in the future she should yet again lick her small, brown animal-shelter chops, every time I pick up the electrode-cap.

I stroke the chunky Black Box Dan and I had cobbled together over the years with carefully filtered research funds. 'Our Empathy Enhancer' up until now had only delivered brief canine flashes of experience; smells that drifted up like vague colours of dried piss from deserted night time telephone poles. I craned down to tickle Jacky's throat with the fingers of my right hand under the couch—she'd eventually forgive me as usual, although now I'd be able to check whether she'd forgiven me for sure.

But is it right to assume such forgiveness? Is it right to coerce such participation?

I check the dials on the machine. I had the settings on 'import' but it is theoretically possible to switch it to an interchange of import and export, an actual swapping of visceral experiences via mutually enhanced and transmitted brain wave responses. (Does this imply there may be neurones that act like experiential mirrors in the mammalian brain? A flaky hypothesis indeed, I know, but some evidence is gathering.)

This would still need someone else to independently verify it—and that means another human participant. It might be risky indeed to try it on each other, Dan and I.

But there is no way I will get permission to use the Empathy Enhancer (EE™) on another person, without rafts of peer-reviewed papers to bolster its safe use and our claims. My supervisor, Doctor Ronald James, is already deeply suspicious of it and has warned me about its dangers. 'Some boundaries are sacred,' he'd said in our last session, before admonishing me for not adequately working my divorce through and unconsciously inflicting my 'issues' on patients, especially the white people I saw over weekends in private practice.

…But, to start off with, no one has to know. There'd also be far less fuss if it was a black person… and I know just the man, I think.

But is it right to assume such participation? And can one fairly ask someone, a young Bantu man certified for treatment, within this current psychiatric power structure?

Outside, the storm continues to shout at the house, so I close all the curtains, finding it hard to control my shivering. Jacky trails behind me, whining.

*

Sibusiso eyes the machine straddling the table between us with obvious doubt.

"It looks like a box the Security Police would use."

I look at him with surprised shock; forthright views indeed for an endogenously depressed patient, especially a black one. But the night nurses did report he'd been more talkative this morning, more assertive.

"It's okay Sibusiso, I've tried it on myself—it doesn't hurt, it only amplifies your brain waves and makes me understand your experiences a whole lot better; it works better than any language could."

"What's wrong with my English, black man that I am?" Sibusiso slumps in the chair again, his eyes veiling over.

I knew I would have to engage him quickly, before he regressed further into a depressed stupour. "Stand up, let's move around a bit," I call; behavioural activation always helps alleviate mood-based psychomotor retardation.

"*Ja baas*, have you been in the army, *korporaal*?" He stands; but sullen, angry and hostile.

This is not going well. I hesitate, unsure of whether his question is seriously meant or a bit of loaded sarcasm. But he continues to stand and stare at me directly, as if in defiance of cultural respect for his elders, waiting…

I smile to break the tension: "We're here to treat you, not me— your family were worried and brought you here because you'd stopped eating."

Sibusiso shook his head: "No, it doesn't work like that. You expect me to share things, hurtful things, dangerous things, but yet you say nothing about yourself, nothing about who you really are, away from your work? And the white army patrol our streets, shooting and whipping us."

Is this where his head injury comes from?

Silence…

I sense there is no way forward, without a big step of trust, a leap of faith.

"No, Sibusiso, I've never been to the army. I'm a secret draft dodger, a good few years back now. I've moved addresses many times and they've given up chasing me—at least, I hope they have, with all their energies in the… *black* townships, as you say." The word 'black' sticks to my tongue like glue, but Sibusiso has given me enough cues he wants me to verbalise colour, although I still worry it polarises us…

He watches me and relaxes just a little. Then he chuckles, looking around the dingy yellow room: "Well, if you speak the truth, I can probably be sure this room is not bugged."

Is this one reason why his words have been so guarded, so hard to come by? It seems behavioural answers lie not just in a man's mental state, but in their surroundings too. It's a wide gulf between us indeed, even in this cramped and stale room, where we're standing so close we can smell each other. Sibusiso is sweating, although the sun's mid-morning heat has yet to build strongly. He stretches his arms in response to mine and looks down on me from across the table; he's tall, thin and powerful. I feel the weight of early middle-age years and the spread of my stomach: "Shall we sit again?"

He takes the back of his chair and moves it, appraising me coolly from a standing height as my own chair squeaks, swivels and spins unexpectedly beneath me.

"I'll do this on one condition," he says.

I stabilise and root myself by planting my shoes firmly against the concrete floor, grasping the table in front of me.

"What's that?" I look up to capture his glowering gaze.

"You must go first, doctor," he says.

Ag, I'd not expected this.

I can see by his stare this is not negotiable. I hesitate, racking my brain for a therapeutic response that would open him up again, a psychological jujitsu phrase that would put me back in control, with therapy moving forward as planned.

"Okay," I say. *That's not it! (But what else can I say; who else will agree to do this?)*

I take a deep breath and clip the primary cap onto my scalp. He watches me closely; his eyes measuring mine more than they did yesterday.

I hold the second cap up to him and he flinches away. "You can't read me if you're not connected," I say.

He holds a warning finger up: "Promise me you do it the way I want."

I nod and fumble with clipping the electrodes in place, glad he's had his head tightly shaved since coming onto the ward. I am sweating too, even though it is not as hot as yesterday, a drop of sweat falls on the table between us and I can feel my collared shirt stick to my back.

We face each other over the Box, which is plugged in, green dials flashing.

"Ready?" I say, breathing deeply and dreading I am breaking ethical codes across the board. There is still time to stop, to unplug the machine, unclip our caps, to return to words…

But Sibusiso just smiles and nods.

I flip the switch on to 'export' and wait. For me, I feel nothing. All I can do is think calming thoughts about surf rolling across Durban North beach, which should hopefully hide my more intimate thoughts. At the same time I concentrate on sending him positive thoughts that should hopefully pulse along these wires with a mood of optimism and change.

His eyes are closed and his face twists with amusement, concern, a bit of disgust, sadness…joy? I struggle to read the fast flash of feelings as they wash over his face like the sea—his mouth open, as if gasping for breath, but no sound emerges.

Silence . . .

I catch flashes of fire in my head, smoke stings my eyes and I fall as something hits me on the head. Glazed, I look up to see a white policeman swinging his *sjambok*. Dogs are barking nearby, big dogs. Wetness drips down my face and my clothes are damp. I look around the shack-ridden dirtied landscape. There are hundreds of us, but hemmed in, milling, the Peace March broken as gas infiltrates our lungs and purple spray marks us as enemies of the State.

I cough and switch the machine off. Shit man, a bit of resurgent identity feedback, despite the one-way setting? I'm scared too of what Sibusiso may find, afraid of the effects of mixing brain waves, merging identities, even though our huge differences are mapped onto our skins.

Sibusiso opens his eyes and looks at me, smiling peculiarly in what looks for a moment like self-recognition.

"Well?" I ask.

"You're mostly okay doctor—a little more racist than you think, but a little less racist than I …worried."

"*Ag*, thanks," I say: "Who's the one in need of help here, hey?

"I am sorry," he looks down, "I did not mean to be rude." (But he continues to grin.)

Someone knocks; their shadow filling the frosty door pane. I scrabble to pack the Box away under the desk. But it is too late. They don't wait for a reply, opening the door with only the briefest of pauses.

It is Doctor Ronald James of course; a tall, pale stooped man, with a tweed suit and sticky looking brown tie, sparse grey hair sleeked back. He looks past Sibusiso as if he were invisible.

"Is that what I think it is, Martin?"

I've always been a poor liar, so I don't even try. I can see he knows what it is.

Slowly, Dr. James shakes his head: "I'm sorry, Martin, but this time you've gone too far."

"I'm busy in a therapeutic session, Doctor." *There are boundaries that should be respected, whoever you are.*

"This is a step too far, Martin!" He continues without blinking: "And I may have to report you for this."

I hesitate; he has good connections with the National Psychology Board.

"You will stop this session right now." Dr. James stands like my father used to; back stiff with righteousness. I know the good doctor also has connections with all the training Universities too—and some whisper even more than that, retaining his active military service.

I look at Sibusiso, who returns my gaze with weary resignation, as if used to being ignored.

No, I will *not* reinforce this experience for him, this experience of being no one.

Dr. James is indeed a well-connected man. But then, for many younger years I had thought my father was directly connected to God as he claimed.

I stand: "Did you not read my 'do not disturb' sign, Dr. James? Or does it not matter to you, because my patient is black?"

"How dare you!" He snaps, hanging on the door-handle. I refuse to sit and our gazes lock.

His eyes narrow: "On your own head is it, then." The door closes with a forceful bang, just short of slamming. *Do the ghosts of one's parents never disappear, even though they have yet to die?*

Sibusiso looks at me: "Trouble, doctor?"

I smile at his leaking concern. "I think I can talk Dr. James around when I show him this machine really works. It—it does, doesn't it?"

"Yes doctor," Sibusiso smiles widely, "oh yes, it works."

"So now I can hook you up?"

Slowly, he shakes his head: "Sorry doctor, there is too much and too many I must protect, I can't have anyone—even you—digging around my thoughts. It won't be safe for you either, to know what I know. And doctor…"

"Call me Martin," I say.

He fails to even blink, all serious and stern: "And doctor… You must also take much care the Special Branch doesn't get hold of that. Such a box is both wonderful and dangerous."

Ah, of course… I'd never thought of that. For me, it was a box to share intimacy across physical boundaries… but what about risky secrets? How do I ensure their protection too? And will they welcome a Box that reaches across the racial divide? I doubt it.

Sibusiso presses on through my thoughts: "I'm just happy to talk now and please, I also want yours and Jabu's help speaking with my father, before I'm discharged. Will I see you again tomorrow?"

Jabu is the lead male Zulu nurse, a no-nonsense man of brisk commands. I nod at Sibusiso and stand. Sibusiso takes on an aggressive political establishment; but struggles in fear with his own father . . . in that we share something too.

He holds a hand out and smiles as I shake it firmly. "*Hayi*, but you do need to find another woman, doctor."

I almost snatch my hand back in shock. "That's confidential, Sibusiso."

"Sure, I know what that means. I will keep it safe, as well as my thoughts that you also smell bad."

I feel my ears redden: "See you tomorrow same time, Sibusiso."

"*Sala kahle*, stay well, Martin," he leaves quietly, gently.

The Feelings Box has been scrambled under the table. I will pack it for home at the end of the day. When to speak to Dr. James? Perhaps a day is needed to enable us both to calm down. For now, there are other patients, a pre-discharge group and ward rounds. Always work to be done here, in this black psychiatric hospital that used to be a military fort.

There is a faint whisper. I look around the room, puzzled, wondering whether it's sound reverberating from the wards through the pasty-yellow thin walls. There it is again.

I place my left ear against the cool, slightly damp wall and a word echoes through my head: 'Beware, 'ware, 'ware…'

Hell, does this mean I've now got tinnitus to add to the woes of my fat and ageing body?

I laugh, but the word stays with me throughout the day, impossible to shake, whatever I do.

Voices…

*

'Beware, 'ware, 'ware…' the word throbs alongside alarm beeps, as I punch in the alarm de-triggering code into the pad inside the front door.

The house is quiet, the hall and dining room settled, undisturbed. I place my bag with the EE machine quietly under the dining room table.

I pick up a hockey stick I'd kept placed there, just in case. Where's Jacky—the dog-walker should have brought her back hours ago? Removing my shoes, I stalk through to the kitchen; stick raised over my right shoulder.

There's a man standing by the kettle, helping himself to a cup of *rooibos* tea. He has a large black briefcase standing on the kitchen desktop.

He turns to me as I enter, with a welcoming smile that chills the muggy air. "Good afternoon to you, Dr. Van Deventer."

Relief and then anger floods me after the initial shock of seeing him—he's white with mild blonde hair, receding and a little plump, but respectfully dressed in a suit—so he's not out to rob or attack me then. I let the stick drop to the floor, but keep a grip with my right hand.

"Who the hell are you and where's my dog?"

He replies in Afrikaans: "My name is Brand. That's all you need to know, Doctor. I am here in the interests of the security of our country."

Ag, kak…

I drop the stick with a rattle on the tiles and look past him, but I speak Afrikaans too, knowing he sets the agenda here: "Where's my dog?"

"I shut him out the back. He wasn't very nice to me."

Yelps come from the back yard, but I leave Jacky there, suddenly too frightened to turn my back on this man.

"How the hell did you get in?" *I want to step up the force of my language, but am too terrified.*

"Just a few quiet words with your patriotic dog-walker," he smiles.

"What do you want?"

"Your special box, Doctor, I just want that box."

I know better than to argue. White skin is not an absolute charm.

He follows me though to the lounge with his tea and briefcase. I pull the EE machine from my bag, strewing it on the floor, box, wires and scalp caps. He stands, looking it calmly over, taking a sip of tea.

"This is the sole prototype isn't it?" He doesn't wait for an answer, as if he knows it all already: "Well, as long as just the State has this box I think we can reach agreement, Doctor. We'll be nationalising this invention solely for state purposes… in true communist fashion." He smiles again. "I trust you note the irony? You'll need to sign this away to us—on pain of…assertive state retribution, shall we say?"

"But—but, it could help us all reach out, understand each other better; live together better, move towards peace…"

He puts his cup down on the table and looks at me. "*Fok* peace! They've declared war, or haven't you noticed, doctor? You're betraying your own *volk* with this, don't you understand, you're a *verraier*? These are terrorists we're dealing with—and there can be no peace with terror."

I look down at the black Box—it's small, a foot square, but responsible for that magical wash of empathic feelings across Sibusiso's face earlier in the day and I feel the burn of a blow across my head.

"If you sign this box away and promise never to build another, you will be safe, my friend. We will have a similar agreement with your colleague Dr. Dan Buys."

I am no friend, but nor am I a hero; I look at the man's cold green eyes and am afraid, very afraid.

"Alright," I say.

He wishes to seem a good-humoured man, smiling again as he hauls a sheaf of papers out of his suit pocket. He places them down on the table in front of me: "See doctor, we work within the rule of law, that's what makes us civilised."

I scan the terse document quickly; it's as he says, with President Terreblanche or a proxy ratifying it, so I sign in coloured triplicate. *How on earth did they find out?*

"Your copy, doctor," he hands me the green copy at the bottom.

I fold it and put it in my trouser pocket, holding in a sudden urge to wet myself as an idea comes to me.

Brand bends down to scoop the electro-encephalo-caps into his expandable briefcase. He has black leather gloves on now and I notice he is balding on top too—my father is completely bald, but he's nearing seventy after all.

I brace myself, remembering the urgency of Sibusiso's plea; his expression of fear. I step forward to stand on the box, my weight crumpling its thin metallic frame with a crunching grind of broken parts. I wince as a piece of glass snags my ankle and I pull my foot back, blood starting to drip through my grey sock.

Brand lurches forward, pushing me with a snarl on his face and I fall onto the floor, clutching my ankle. He stands over me, looking down. I lie on my back and hold my right ankle, waiting for him to do something terrible.

But he doesn't.

Instead, he sits himself quietly on the floor next to me, sweeping a few shards of the broken box away with his gloved right hand.

"A mistake, doctor, but we all make mistakes."

Why does he put himself at my level?

"I do what I do to help people like you, doctor, but I sense you will not build us another one."

I see the calm sincerity in his face and it hits me: *he is a people-reader too.*

"It is no matter. You will build no more for *anyone.*" He smiles again, but it is tinged with… sadness? "We are not so far apart, brother, we both have faith in what we do. But now that America has elected a *kaffir* president who seeks World peace and the fokking Nobel Peace Prize by talking down the Soviet-Generals, we are losing the support we once had under the Bushes and Blair. Now is the time we need to be strong."

I let go of my foot and brace myself to sit upright with my hands. *Where is this lecture leading?*

He sighs and takes something out of his top pocket, placing it on the floor-space between us: "Just doing my job, doctor, as you do—

there shall be no more feeling machines. Let this serve as a warning."

He levers himself to stand over me in one deft motion; he's fitter than he looks.

Looking down, he repeats himself, even though I have no doubt as to his message: "No more Feelings Boxes, Doctor van Deventer, you understand?"

Jacky's frantic yelps outside are rising in volume; she is scrabbling desperately at the door, which judders duh-duh-duh against the lock. I am aware that Brand has gone and I did not even hear him leave. I stare at what he has left me, propped up on the floor amongst the debris of my broken EE machine. It's standing on its own rounded base, metallic, long and pointed—an unmarked rifle bullet.

It sucks in my gaze like a black hole.

I start to shiver, despite the balminess of the late summer afternoon. *No, I will not stay sitting here.* My bloody right foot is marked only by a shallow gash, already coagulating. I keep my sock pulled down to avoid it drying against the wound and stand up, making my way to the back-door.

Jacky jumps into my arms. She's unhurt. Box or no box, I *know* she will always love me…I cuddle her on the couch and she licks my face, until I stop shivering.

The sun blazes lower and warms my face too. No point staying here.

I stand up and sweep the EE machine into the corner of the room, piece upon broken piece; springs, coils, relays, software boards…and it feels like I'm sweeping myself raw inside. Dan will be devastated— my neurological software partner up at 'Martizburg University— we'd adapted and extended the design from biofeedback models, but took it two steps beyond. Direct brain wave stimulation across two mammalian brains.

A double-edged sword of invention, it looked little more than a broken-down metal and glass toy constructor set. I'd loved construction sets as a child —but my ultimate game had been building racing tracks for electric cars, especially the trickiest part, the bridge in a figure eight. It needed just the right amount of pressure and angling…the stress of a raised bridge could mean poorly connected track-pieces and cars failing to make it over the hill.

I move to the bedroom to clean and bandage my ankle.

Suzette looks at me from the picture at my bedside, the Umgeni Bridge dangling dangerously in the background. I'd proposed marriage to her there, almost dashing across the bridge to the other side to celebrate—or perhaps show off—when she'd said 'yes'. I remember getting some way across, but the bridge starting to swing in the building breeze, alarming us both. I'd scrambled back, carrying an irrational but private and enduring shame.

We never spoke about it—even though we were both psychologists in training—and a little more than seven years later, all our words ran out.

Funny thing is, I'm not looking at her. Instead, I watch the thin brown rope bridge spin across the gorge, wondering how it feels now.

*

I am grateful that the drive through the peaceful white suburbs of Howick is quiet. The journey grows ever quieter as I head up the valley past sweeping imported eucalyptus trees; no drifting teargas smoke to worry about, no burning tires or police blocks strewn across the road. The mid-summer sun still hangs low with some warmth as it drops towards the hilly horizon. Christmas is nearing fast.

It's too quiet—I look in the rear-view mirror, but there is no car following.

I start to tap the steering wheel of my old Ford as my CDs play, especially when Aretha asks for respect, but keep glancing in my rearview mirror at the empty road behind me. (I must look up Gil Scott-Heron on *Wikkopedia*, if it's accessible through the State Firewalls.)

There are only a few cars left in the car-parks at the entrance to the Umgeni River Valley Nature Park and I pay my way in, eyeing the 'Slegs blankes/Whites only' sign on the wooden kiosk.

My camera bounces against my chest as I wind through wooded *thornveld*; a few large birds shriek in the canopy. (We still wait for cam-phones, but they remain banned as a potentially easy source of troubling video.) The path drops down towards the valley and I take the detour left to where the old rope bridge used to be. It's a balmy evening and I see no one else at this late hour. The path levels out in front of me and I see the bridge, but it's different from how I remember; built of strutted wood and more solid looking.

The river rumbles with summer rains below me and I smell the dung of a large mammal in the bushes near the bridge. I smell my own sweat too, as I pant to catch my breath.

Well, here it is; the swaying bridge I have never crossed.

I stand at the spot I took those couple of pictures almost a decade ago—one devoid of any person, fit to adorn the wall of my then new job, freshly qualified as I was. The other picture still sits as I left it beside my bed, with Suzette looking out at me; the bridge small, the valley obscured behind her long blowing brown hair.

Strange, but her face dims even more in my head as I stand here.

The valley sweeps in a torrent of brownish grass and green woodland down towards the racing river. I take a hold of the wooden railing and step onto the struts of the bridge. They creak with my weight. I wait for moments and then step deliberately across, one slat at a time, focusing on the next slat, not looking over.

The other side arrives almost too suddenly, my feet squelching onto damp tussocks. I hold the bridge post and swing around to check the view.

It's very similar to the other side, thicker riverine trees and bushes dropping to the edge of the rock-strewn white spraying river. But on this side there's a scarred and stripped patch I hadn't noticed down near the riverside. It's a blackened, burnt area, stripped and empty, but glinting with one or two long and shiny corrugated aluminium boards lying derelict. The vegetation has not re-grown, it's fairly recent. I have a decent guess as to what it may have been... Probably illegal black squatters had come through the fence and set up camp, but had been forcibly evicted, their homes crushed, the place stripped and burnt.

Pain thumps in my head, a *sjambok*-blow pain and there's an acrid burning smell in my nose, stinging my eyes—smoke; or tear gas? Then, just as suddenly, it's gone.

I take a picture of the scorched, desolate earth. *There's only one cause of fire at this time of year.*

I step back onto the bridge and make my way across to the swaying middle; bracing myself as I stop to look down. I'm giddy with the deep drop to white-green water below and the pungent vegetation scented warm wind that buffets the bridge.

I cannot take a picture here; I am too afraid that I or my camera will topple over. Instead, I hold onto the rope railing with one hand and feel in my right pocket with the other. Bracing my feet and ignoring the burn in my strapped right ankle, I swing my right arm around and launch the grasped bullet downwind.

It spins and drops, glinting once, and I don't even see where it splashes.

I am tired of threats and ghosts.

The river rolls on and I watch it, caught in its hissing motion.

I will clear my weekend of patients and go to those meetings of radical psychologists and social workers who fight for political change, saying there's no normality in an abnormal society... ah, and a good few woman psychologists and social workers go there too, I believe.

A gust of wind rocks the bridge, pumping my heart as I stand over the Umgeni River. I hold on tighter to the railing with both hands. *I need to have a word with that Dr. James too...A firm word, a* vuurwarm *word.*

The bridge swings in a gust of strong wind again and I inch my way across to the car-park side of the river. No point in false heroics, never mind no one's here to see them.

On firm ground, I look back across the view that is captured within the pictures in my office and bedroom. No, this is definitely a *different* bridge, a newer bridge. It doesn't look nearly as far across to the other side anymore either. Perhaps its' my living perspective—but I also have a sense that maybe most of the vastness of the chasm has been inside my head.

Brand has called me both a brother and a traitor to my people. But I don't know who 'my people' are anymore.

There is no one else standing by the bridge. Suzette is gone…

I walk back up the sloping path, glancing ahead. On the distant hill summit above me, I see the long rocking neck of a giraffe. It's blackly silhouetted in solitude, near a bent thorn tree against the fading sky. Giraffe's are social animals; I *know* there must be other members of the herd on the far side of the hill, but still I feel a pang of empathic loneliness. I have heard rumours the South African Defence Force have been here too; ivory poaching to fund the War on Terror. Would they target a bit of family giraffe meat too?

I am too afraid to climb the hill, for fear there is nothing on the other side.

Stay focused, stay here: It'll be good to see Sibusiso tomorrow. We need to sort out his relationship with his father, before discharge as the ward closes briefly for the year's end. Perhaps it's time I speak to my own father again, too…

Something howls in the bush to my left and I break into a wincing jog uphill. No silence here, but the wild languages remain alien to me. Still, it's good to hear voices.

I pant up the path as I head back to the car-park and realise I am rebuilding the EE machine in my head, piece by bloody piece . . . and not for the State either. *Why?*

What can I say?

I build bridges.

Azania

I'd never been very cold before—not until I headed into space. Deep space I'm talking, not a joyride to the moon. So deep, we go on and on, past suns and planets, moons and nebulae—deep, deep space, through the coldest of empty places that hang between the stars.

So cold, it penetrates our star-ship TaNK, infiltrating the dreams of my long sleep; for I see nothing of all we pass.

Instead, I lie encased in ice, too cold to scream.

For twelve years...

And still more.

It is time for the last lesson but thunder rumbles over the sound of the bell. I laugh and run, finding myself in a strange field, far from home and school. The ground is bitten red-rock dry and marked only by redder crumbling fragments of dried out anthills. No trees, no grass, no houses or sounds. Above me, the sky roils in with darkness and lightning sheets that spark my blood. I laugh and tilt my head backwards, flicking my hair so that it tumbles down my back. I close my eyes, opening my mouth as the wind sweeps in great water blasts that sting my face and lips. I suck greedily, as the dust churns to muddy rivulets beneath me, shifting my footing, muddying my feet. The warm water slakes my throat, turning cold and then, to ice. I choke, mouth frozen open, unable to breathe. I am pinned tight in a latticed cage of ice. I open my eyes. There is nothing else around me; nothing, till a flash in the darkness. I turn, but too late. The arrow pierces my right ear and bores into my brain. I can only gag on ice.

I wake shivering.

Above me, there is a large overhanging tree trunk. Frosty edges of the dream-cage melt around me and I track the blurred branch to the huge trunk and overhanging canopy.

Muuyo—the African baobab. The soft green leaves swirl and shake, always just out of my frozen reach. I struggle to stretch out painful fingers, searching for warmth in the green. But the organic patterns shift and reform, distant as stars, untouchable.

She watches me through the leaves, wearing the face of Wangari Maathai. Is it in identification with me that She is mostly female?

I sigh. So...

Not my Copperbelt home then, nor my old school.

Not even Earth.

Planet XA- I've lost the numbers in my cold, waking head-fog—or, as we prefer to call it, Azania. (A planet partially mapped by the African Union Robotic Missions with (just) breathable air and water and no known advanced life forms—a veritable waiting Eden).

The baobab branch bending and swaying above me, however, is but a digital shadow on our domed roof—a shape without texture, form without life.

Wangari, She smiles, with richly red lips: <Mangwanani, Aneni.>

"Morning," I grunt, sitting up and casting a glance at grandfather's rough, reddish-brown stone sculpture, dimly but decoratively placed near the screened window, as if keeping alien forces at bay.

Besides me, Ezi stirs.

I sign to She to keep quiet and swivel clumsily out of bed; bracing my stomach muscles for the pull of serious gravity. The room spins beneath the canopy of faux leaves and my feet fail to find floor.

Instead, my face, fists, and breasts, do, hands barely in place quick enough to protect my teeth.

I spit blood from a cut lip, concerned about one thing.

There is something in my ear.

It's a faint tickle in the right ear, deep inside, but followed by a sputtering burst of popping noises, as if my ear is protesting and trying to expel something. Then a pain lances through the right side of my face and I grunt and clasp my ear.

I sway.

Ezi is starting to snore, low and rasping, as she has rolled onto her back. I watch her for the barest of moments, sealing the pain within me so that I don't wake her, reacquainting myself with my old adversary.

It's been many, many years—but, almost without thinking, I rate the pain five out of ten and akin to a bright blue candle burning inside my ear. I close my eyes to pour cooling imaginary water onto it, but it continues to burn just as brightly, just as painfully.

I'm out of practice, my spine now comfortably straight, even stiffened and dulled by the passing years. Pain pulls me back to thirteen again, my last spinal surgery sharpened by anxiety around my first period.

This time, though, there is no mother to hold me.

Instead, I need to see She in the Core Room.

Firstly though, I cover Ezi with the scrambled thermo-sheet to keep her warm. (Always, she kicks herself bare).

I manage the corridor with my left hand braced against the wall, following etched tendril roots, past the men's door and on into the heart of our Base, where She sits.

Or squats—her heavy casing hides her Quantum core, scored with bright geometric Sotho art—her flickering holographic face above the casing is now the usual generic wise elder woman, grandmother of all.

She straddles the centre of the circular room, like a Spider vibrating the Info-Web.

She smiles again, but this time with pale and uncertain lips.

"I need help," I say, "A full medical scan. My ear feels painful and my balance has gone."

<A *full* scan?>

I swallow, appreciating the caution in her emphasis, but strip off my night suit with a shaky but firm certitude: "Yes."

And so I am needled, weighed, poked, sampled, scraped, and gouged, until I shrink with exhaustion from the battery of bots she has whizzing around me. I finally take refuge in a chair near the door and gulp a cup of my pleasure, neuro-enhanced South Sudanese coffee.

She calls off her bots and they swing back into fixed brown brackets raised around the edge of the room, as if pots on shelves in an ancient traditional rondavel. She has her eyes closed, soaking in the analysis.

I finish the cup and rub my stinging lip where it's cut.

She speaks: <Not detecting any pathogen nor otological dysfunction, but I do see diffuse activated pain perception across your somato-sensory cortex.>

"Show me." I am a doctor after all, even if many years a psychiatrist now, specialised in space psychosis and zero-G neurosurgery.

I watch my rotating holographic brain in bright blue, with red traces glowing in the anterior insula and cingulate cortex—sensory, motor, and cognitive components, involved then: a dull, all-encompassing pain, no identifiable specificities tracing a direct neural link to the ear. There's new pain merged and mixed with old memories perhaps, fudging and blurring my experiential pathways? I scan the data that She scrolls condescendingly before me—no, there are no clear signs of dysfunction clearly emanating from my inner ear that I can see either.

I stand and sway. Surely it can't all be in my head?

"Aneni?" It's Ezi on our room screen, frowning from the bed, thermo-sheet clutched to her chin. "There's something sore in my right ear."

Dhodhi! As always, I keep the expletive hidden inside me. "I'm on my way, Ezi."

I lurch back down the corridor, just as the men's door slides open. Petrus is on his hands and knees and startles as I stop and lean against the wall opposite him. I watch the corridor light bounce off his brightly tattooed scalp as he bends his head to look up at me.

"Sorry Cap'n," he says. "Can't seem to stand upright anymore... and my ear's *fokkin'* sore."

I'm always cold, whatever temperature we set here, but now this coldness bites almost as deeply as my pain.

*

We meet where we eat, genetically diverse, even though we number just four. It is dull but honest food, the cassava and eddoes Anwar had saved on arrival, holding starvation at bay on this alien planet.

I nibble and long for a pineapple or banana.

Finishing up quickly, the others look shaken, unwell, with little appetite.

She has sprinkled the table and walls with swathes of savannah grass and shimmering pools of blue water. They bleed into my vertigo. I ask her for plain reality. She gives us a brown table, flanked by opposing brown seat-bunks, ergo-green kitchen neatly splayed behind with heaters and processors. She has the windows sealed white against the planet's night, keeping the focus on our preparatory tasks within.

I steady myself with a firm grip on the table—tension is building—I don't need my psychiatric training to tell me that. The men sit opposite us. Ezi and I exchange the briefest of encouraging glances and brace ourselves. At least some vestibular stability has returned for us all.

Sure enough, it's Petrus who sits opposite me; brown head and hairless, smooth face lined by late middle age and constant earnestness. "So... *Captain*, what is responsible for our ear pain and dizziness?"

He has not used my name nor looked at me directly since three Earth days after we arrived; certainly not since I moved in with Ezi. That's six weeks and rising now, in Earth time.

Azanian time, though, it's been just four days.

I shrug and gesture to the ceiling, where leaves still hang heavily over us: "She doesn't know."

Anwar chuckles at me; his white teeth sharply offset against his trimmed black beard and moustache, his ashen grey skin obviously short of sunlight. His teeth look sharp, conveying little of his humour; but perhaps it's just my mood.

"She is not omniscient though, am I correct, Aneni?"

I nod and smile: "She wants to check all of us thoroughly. She's learned literally nothing from me."

All three of them groan and I let slip a smile.

"Is it the same ear for all of us?" asks Ezi. Both men turn to look at her; Petrus gesturing right, Anwar left.

"Random, then?"

Ezi ignores me. "Mine's the right ear like Aneni and Petrus," she says, leaning forward, right hand grasping the cream, circular utilities

59

remote. With a flick of her wrist, she sends it straight towards Anwar's midriff. He stops it with his left hand.

"Maybe your dominant ear is left," says Ezi, "but then, what do I know? I'm only the engineer." (Why does she look at me? We all know she is a special engineer, simply the best on antimatter rockets. More to the point now, her genius resides in having gotten our waste recycling going again, such a welcome respite for our noses.)

"Neurologically targeted?" I ask.

Ezi shrugs, coiled corn-plats flicking across her shoulders. "What do you think, She?"

<I cannot speculate without sufficient evidence, but I can confirm a full physical is needed for all of you.>

They eye each other with reluctance; the full physical on waking from years of enforced hibernation six weeks earlier no doubt still fresh in mind. A rigorous exam followed by even more rigorous exercises to recondition our severely weakened bodies—we still struggle against the pull of this planet, even though it is barely five percent more than full Earth gee.

I smile again, despite the ear-pain, having done my time. "We'll stay here until we've all been assessed. Alphabetical order, first name."

Anwar scowls at me as he gets up to go through to the Core-Room.

Petrus looks at the cup of coffee in front of me. "So, what do you suspect, Captain?"

I look at his scalp, feeling inexplicably sad. Two human figures are etched in sub-dermal nano-ink on his skull. They've not moved since we've woken from our Star-Sleep, their micro-programmed motility messages seemingly degraded and destroyed by his prolonged, lowered neural activity. His head used to show the Mandelas walking endlessly free from prison in the late twentieth century—now; it's just two faded humanoid shapes frozen together, smeared like an ancient Rorschach blot across his scalp. I can't explain it, but the still and fading images continue to cool my early desires for him.

"Aneni?" Petrus is looking at me, green eyes fierce and I am reminded of his rough Cape Town Flats roots.

"At this point I can't say, but there has to be some foreign pathogen, despite all our precautions. We can't all be ill with the same symptoms simultaneously."

He raises his eyebrows and leans forward, "Foreign?"

For some reason, I can't take my eyes off the Mandelas on his head, "From Azania perhaps, although we can't rule out a hidden, mutated infectious agent from Earth."

Anwar stomps in and Ezi sighs as she stands up.

It's strange to sit alone again with the two men, both who appear to keep smouldering with residual resentment at my authority and unexpected relationship with Ezi. Strange too, to think it's a full sixty years now since the African Gender and Sexuality Equality Act. Laws we were all born with—but still for some, slow to shape trans-generational attitudes around queer sexuality—despite credible arguments they are internalised residues of negative colonial views. (In the end though, nothing is so neatly separated, unless you're an exceptional surgeon. As for me, my words are my customary tools, blunter than any scalpel, so I keep my thoughts private.)

The men mutter briefly and inaudibly to each other. I smile behind my hands, for I am used to masculine silence; fifteen years in the Zambian army is preparation enough.

Ezi comes back and Petrus leaves. We stare with discomfort at the table; we have silently avoided this threesome.

I am startled when Anwar breaks it. "I've made a holo-disk of Yakubu Chukwu."

It's Ezi's favourite West African Federation footballer. "Really?" she smiles.

I stand to halt a surge of emotions. Ridiculous really, as if physical actions can stop feelings—I should indeed know better. Walking over to the blinds that hide this planet from us, I grasp their metal slats, ready to claw them away.

This is why we are here.

This is where we need to survive.

But Ezi's eyes do not follow me, so I hesitate.

Ezi's from South of the Tenth Parallel, an old fracture line Anwar may not find so easy to cross—Africa harbours exacting fault lines, both ancient and modern.

Still, the AU is—was?—a powerful, if fragile and fast ripening fruit of i-networked Lion economies, ready to burst across the burnt out husk of the Earth—if it survives the gathering heat. We are indeed the first of its more ambitious and widely dispersed seeds...

A further ten missions have been planned, but spread across a number of promising solar systems. None follow us here. We will remain alone.

I look at the others and suddenly begrudge them nothing. This will be a hard place to survive.

As if on cue, Petrus returns. He looks at me and I turn away to the window—thinking of seeds, I thumb the shutter button.

The slats rise on darkness. An almost impenetrable blackness, with both moons yet to rise. I press my nose against the cold-treated quartz—against the faint starlight and the reflected light from within; I make out huge trunked shapes swaying in a light nocturnal breeze.

It's *always* windy here; circulating air continuously ensuring temperatures are not excessively varying across the long days and nights.

In the reflected window, I can see Petrus is standing quietly behind me. He glances up.

She is back amongst the canopy of leaves over our heads: <There are no clear biological markers I can identify as yet, I'm afraid—but I can offer you all a blunt neural painkiller. Our scheduled venture onto the planet surface will be set back indefinitely. We are, in effect, quarantined. I will also ask Kwame Nkrumah for His thoughts.>

Ah, Kwame Nkrumah, the Father-ship that circles above our head, He who watches from above.

More waiting, more cages, quarantine shuts me in, like the ice cage of my dream.

So many people left behind too, of whom I miss my daughter the most. Anashe, she was barely twenty-three when we launched from Kinshasa. As a child, she had loved to sit under the baobab.

I look up at She's swaying branches and '*tccchhh!*' with irritation, "I am tired of baobabs, She, give me a fever tree."

Above us, a yellowish tree with fern like leaves billows, photosynthesising through the pale bark—an odd tree indeed, but somehow more suitable for this strange planet we still try to hold at bay with walls and shutters.

I stare into the darkness again, no longer hungry.

*

I wake.

It is worse.

Much worse.

I look pleadingly at She but there is nothing for my gaze to hold onto, just a rumbling, tumbling vertiginous splash of browns and greens and yellows. I sway and spin even though I am lying still and wait quietly for the vomit urge to die, sweating out my fear.

Blurred colours sharpen and take shape.

Chinanga—the fever tree.

Cautiously, I lift my head.

Chikala! Of course, my bed is empty too.

Slowly, I swing my legs out of the bunk and anchor them on ground. I sit and earth my feet on synthi-steel, one by one.

The pain shreds my ear.

I close my eyes and isolate it. There is only one arrow. It is nine out of ten and ice cold, bright blue-white. I send my spirit to stroke it, warm it, but it cuts at my hands. I blow my warm breath onto it, steaming it red in my mind. My breath runs out. Blue it burns again.

I ask for help from grandfather, holding his rough-hewn sculpture, warm Shona stone, but all I hear is silence—the silence that leaks from vast and cold interstellar distances. We are alone here. Only the wind speaks, but in what a strange and empty tongue.

I stand and move before the pain burns too brightly, eyes open, anchoring my swaying body and shaking ankles with step-by-step focused visual cues, to help stabilise my proprioceptors.

There, door button, now press... root tendril designs, pick one, follow along the hall to She's heart; ow, get up, get up, focus, follow and lean on that root, don't lose sight, don't think ahead, not of She; get up, damn it, again, same root, that's it, ow, that's it, up again, the root's thickening, approaching CR, door button, press, collapse...

The floor is cold beneath my back.

I look upwards, feeling sick as my ear burns more and more. What on Earth is happening? No, *not* Earth; is that indeed the point?

Don't fight it; it's just one Buddhist arrow. No thoughts and emotions to make a second arrow, a second and deeper wound. Examine it; inspect it. This arrow is seven out of ten—steel grey, but pulsing blue. It's only pain. It will shift; it will change. Everything does.

Eventually.

Above me, She's face is a familiar old bald white man in a white coat. He's got a stethoscope draped around his neck. I remember him, old Doctor Botha from my childhood. He'd been one of the South African émigrés, moving north for new opportunities, new challenges. Why has She become him?

She speaks slowly, words pulsing with warmth: <You seem ill Aneni, what can I do?>

I cough, but my throat is clear, I am not choking. "Make it go away She... please!"

The old man shakes his head. <I still don't know the cause, although I can maybe dull the pain.>

Yes... and no. Fuck it; I don't want to just ease things. There's a job to do. There's always a job; but how can we live and work if this world is somehow poisoning us, sickening us?

I lever myself slowly into a sitting position and slide against the wall. "Open all room channels, She."

Two screens flicker on as the wake-alarm sounds.

Ezi is hanging head down, retching over the side of her mattress, now stacked on top of a black bench-press in our tiny Gym-room. Every day, she must pack her bed away, for all of us still need to bulk up our bodies with exercise there, ever-fighting against this planet's enervating pull.

Petrus is lying in his bunk, body still, limbs twitching and eyes open. Anwar is strapped to a Smart-chair facing skywards, a chair that constantly cranks itself towards our solar system. He must have been praying, even though Mecca itself is too blunt a target at this distance.

"Aneni here, how are you all doing?"

Ezi is in no state to talk and the men can only groan, although Petrus makes a fist of it. "*Kak!*" is all he says.

I look at my old Doctor, whose face is now filling the room with concern. "Is this terminal?" I ask.

She looks at me long and hard before shrugging: <I'm afraid I don't know, Aneni.>

I sigh, gathering in strength for more words, hard words, "I'm taking a vote on Procedure F76."

She's eyes widen with simulated shock: <That would breach our Primary Mission Goal.>

"If we're going to die, we should at least have the choice of *where* that is."

Silence.

I look down. The arrow is eight and rising; purple now, steady and aching. Wrap it tight with the words you must say. "All in favour of F76, special emergency protocol I am empowered to authorise, just say 'me'; voice recognition certification on full, She."

The old man looks disappointed and puts on a pair of glasses, black horn-rimmed archaic ones. I don't remember *those*.

"This is to return to Earth, no?"

It takes me some moments to realise it is Petrus speaking, his body twitching but stilling in his bunk.

I nod, suddenly feeling cowardly.

"I think Allah has brought us safely here for a reason."

Confused momentarily, I suddenly realise Anwar has followed up on Petrus's question. (His face averted skywards; I had not seen his lips move.)

The old man She looks up at me, smiling.

"And...," continues Anwar, panting after each brief rush of words: "Do we really want to... to bring back with us... dare I say it... a plague of ...of possibly Biblical proportions?"

His words shame me and remind me of time, both ancient and future. "*If* we do leave, She, when will we arrive back on Earth?"

She is no longer my doctor, but has morphed into a small, elderly and sharp featured brown woman in a bright orange sari. I immediately recognise Indira Moodley, my teacher, the great Kenyan psychiatrist who revised Fanon, integrating his theory with genetic neuro-physiology into a marvellous psychiatric Theory of Everything. (From the mindfulness of cells to the Minds within politico-cultural events and back down again.)

<It'll be 2190 when we get back.>

I realise I'm looking at a long dead woman.

Seventy years gone! I'm freezing fast on this icy surface. I close my eyes. The arrow is Ten and vivid fucking violet. Out of the darkness I see the second arrow coming, but I am too cold to move, ice forming around me like a casket.

There is no way home. There never was. I'd known that in my head when we'd left—we all had, but not to the core of our cells and selves.

There is nothing else to do but whisper goodbye to my family, to Earth, although my voice is broken: "*Sarai zvakanaka.*"

Anashe will be dead too—perhaps *long* dead, my beloved daughter. My eyes sting, so I close them, coughing out words I hope can be heard. "Shall we vote?"

I knuckle my eyes and open them, but She doesn't even bother to wait for us—swelling, shifting, and swaying... Finally bursting into a huge wind-stalk above us, a thick-stalked purple plant with splayed giant leaves hanging from the apex—but swirling to the sound of alien winds we cannot hear.

As for the arrow of pain, now drilling through my head and into my left ear, there is only one thing left I can do.

I hold it, my fingers cupping my ears, burning and melting into the white-hot shaft of pain. I hold and don't let go, as if my hands have fused across my ears.

Tonight, please let me dream of the Copperbelt again, even just fleeting fragments of places I don't recognise. (Huge rainy season droplets on my tongue will be enough, toes curled into reddish-brown earth. No, *anything* will do...)

Later on, though, I dream of nothing.

*

We gather for the Sun-Show meal, warming up first with my Zambo-Chinese tai chi lessons—short form, the long form can come later. Petrus has proved himself a natural master in waiting, moving with a slow grace. So too have I taught them to harness their visual attention and their muscle proprioception, in order to compensate for now periodic vestibular disturbance.

She opens the blinds as daylight gathers above the rocking purple wind-stalks, standing ten to twenty metres tall. We watch them sway as we eat, our balance strangely bolstered in the pending dawn. Anwar has prepared a glorious meal indeed—tested on the five mice that survived the trip—spliced and pummelled purple cereal lifted from 'bot samples, with a sharp, but curiously pleasant tang.

At the end, we all look at him and he smiles: "It is our first safe combination of Earth and exo-plants." (He'd been thrilled to find a workable genetic compatibility, Allah seeding the Universe.)

So.

We will greet the new day with a hope of real sustainability—perhaps we shall not starve, nor die, anytime soon. As for our ear pain, it both fluctuates and hovers, like a random and ghostly wasp who has been angered.

Perhaps it is here to warn us, that here too, we also need to bend our ways of working to survive? I have banned religion from the table—Western tables must be really dull without politics as well—but for once I relent.

It is that afterwards, with thanks, I hold a truncated ceremony of *kurova guva*—welcoming the spirits of the deceased, although Anwar leaves to say his own prayers. I know remembrance rituals differ across the continent, so I keep it brief and generic. "We leave a bowl for those who travel to new places and hunger in the holes between. May you all find your way to new joys... and just perhaps a few of you may even make it here."

Ezi has no belief, but still she cries, quietly. (Hers was a close family indeed, her grandmother a Hero of the Oil Wars; the start of Africa reclaiming her resources.)

The sky is paling fast, the wind-stalks bending before the heat of this sun's heralding winds. We stay quarantined; the First planned Walk is no longer taking place.

But I am tired of waiting. Still the pain bites deep in my ear, but I feel there are no answers here.

I bow to the others and leave the room, making my way to the airlock. (We're just about breathing native air by now anyway, sterilised and incrementally added into our closeted atmosphere.)

I pick up a head-suit with visor; there is no reason to take unnecessary risks on the eyes. The scalp cap peels on with a sticky tightness and I flip the visor down, the small room darkening instantly.

Flicking a switch, an inner door seals the small room, lined with built in benches in case of prolonged emergency use. I pick up a walking rod too.

<Is this wise, Aneni?> She warbles into the ear-speaker.

"Since when have I been wise, She? Open the external door please."

<And if I deem this a breach of safety protocol, given our quarantined status?>

"We're humans. We do things. I am tired of cowering from this place."

The door remains shut. I turn and lever the walking rod through the handles of the inner door, effectively locking it.

<*What* are you doing, Aneni?>

I sit. "Just waiting for you to open the external door."

<We don't know enough yet about the biological risks.>

"Perhaps we never will," I say. "Life is a biological risk. Open the door."

<You're not ready for all possible challenges that may arise, in your physically compromised state.>

"I am a woman."

The external door light glows green, but it remains shut. I make a note to ask Petrus whether quantum She can have two different minds at the same time.

"I am an *African* woman!"

A green light flickers on and I hear a hiss from the ceiling as odourless but penetrating and sterilising nanoparticles descend, seeping through my overalls, cleansing me in readiness for a new place. Slowly, the door grinds open and I gasp and cough at the acrid, burning air. Gradually my breathing eases and I'm able to raise my head. The ground outside our Base is rough, uneven, with tightly latticed blue grass of sorts.

As my gaze lifts, I sweep past the Lander-Plane that spring-loaded our base, down a rough, uneven slope towards indigo reeds lining a patch of dark water. The water is partially obscured by towering wind-stalks that seem to be circling the small lake, like giants rearing above us and emitting a stench that seems part sulphur, part acid. My eyes stream under the visor and I cough again, but pull the walking rod free and step forward, moving slowly around our circular base.

The others are pressed against the wide kitchen window and wave, but I'm too engrossed with the sparkle of orange-red rays amongst heavy grey clouds overhead.

"Azania," I breathe.

She must have patched the suit-speaker into the kitchen.

I recognize Ezi's voice, groaning: "Ahhhh, mmmmm!"

"What?" I turn to the shadowed shapes behind the window; Ezi is etched thinner and taller than the men.

"Ahhhh, mmmmmm," she repeats. "The sound of this place. We're not going to repeat the same shit that happened to us, we're not going to do a Shell Oil or Cecil Rhodes on this place!"

I laugh, coughing at the burning, almost peppery air. "Good point, although if we're going to change the name of this planet, wouldn't 'Euromerica' be a more easily pronounceable name?"

"Look," says Petrus, and I see him pointing high behind me.

The first rays of the young new sun are flashing through the wind-stalks, now shimmering a deep violet. Below us, the ground sways with rustling purple reed ferns. Shadows shrink, hiding nothing but vivid variegations of purple and movement—as well as purpose? Have our projections onto the landscape begun? Or are there some things or beings hidden and active amongst the vegetation? TaNK has seen nothing so far, but He is not God.

Still, could there be things so small they invade our ears undetected—

even now, the pain is five and... I forget the numbers, there are too many beautiful colours flowing down the groaning wind-stalks as I brace myself against a blast of hot and pungent air.

And then it comes again. A high-pitched keening sound, but more modulated, subtler.

"Ahhhhhh, mmmm," Ezi repeats in my painful ears, but she's not even close.

The atmospherics amplify and fracture the sound, enhancing into a multitude of varying tones, polyphony of sounds and calls. It's as if the wind-stalks are talking.

<Aneni,> I know from the intimacy of her tone, She has secured this communication just for me. <I'm picking up a slight neuronal rewiring throughout your auditory cortex, a hint of neurogenesis.>

"Ah!" I say. So it's my brain, not my ear. Have we been colonised so deeply too, from within? Or is this the consciousness of cells responding to a new and alien call?

I take grandfather's sculpture out of my baggy jacket pocket, stoop with bended knees and braced back, placing it carefully on the ground. It's not a spirit or a person, not a totem or God—Grandfather Mapfumo prided himself on being a modern man—his grandfather before him driving regime change in Zimbabwe with Chimurenga music. Instead, it's a Zanoosi, Zimbabwe's first Eco-car, running on degraded organic waste, not someone else's food, like maize. The car he helped design, which powers the Southern African Federation lion economy. This sculpture was of the same car he drove us all up to Mufulira in, where he traded with the Chinese and we settled, establishing new factories. (And it was he alone who never laughed at me, when I spoke of going into space as a little girl.)

I straighten, stiffening my spine against the pull of the planet. I taste the sour but balmy breeze on my tongue, knotted, blue grass closing around the sculpted stone, sealing it from view.

I believe the rain here is a little heavier, a little saltier.

Out of Africa and now out of Earth...

No, not Earth, but a new... place. Home is a hard word. Why couldn't I have just gone back some several hundred k's to my old familial roots in Mutare, instead of trillions of miles here? Of course, the signs were closing in, as Earth heated up and disasters grew worse and I'd never been able to convince myself, unlike mother, that it all meant the Rapture was indeed near.

So, here we are, with biological seeds from Earth, including a frozen egg from my very own daughter. It is here we must make our heaven.

I stand stiffly, locked into the planet in a left bow stance, as the bright new sun burns its heat into me. 'This is the same sun imbued with illusions/the same sky disguising hidden presences'— words from an old Leopold Senghor poem that circulate my head.

But—this is a new sun and I have no idea what lies beneath it; whether voices or spirits, plants or animals.

"Salaam Aleichem."

Behind me there are racking coughs. I turn—all three have followed me out, arms around shoulders as they walk, bracing themselves against the whipping wind. Ezi, thin, but as strong as rope, is in the middle.

"Don't tell me you want to hog this planet's air all to yourself, Aneni?" she chides me: "Wasn't stealing my sheets bad enough?"

An old joke, but who knows the barb beneath? The English have a saying about dirty laundry—but as for us, all is public, all is shared.

I smile; the new Sun shines on Petrus' scalp; almost making the Mandelas dance. He gestures at me to join them. I smile at him again but move next to Anwar, who stiffens at my touch.

We can't afford to lapse too quickly into neat and convenient relationships, however fecund. Not yet. This world has hurt and shaken us, perhaps for a reason, perhaps not. But for now, we must stay on our toes and learn new things, new ways of being.

At the end of the line, Petrus breaks into a slow tai chi stepping motion, moving from a left bow stance. But his left arm is still anchored around Ezi. Down the line, we echo and ripple his motions, the line dipping and rising with the flow of movement.

So it is, we dance African tai chi in our first real alien dawn. As we move, I note the pain—neither an adversary, nor a friend. Like rain and bananas, mice and joy, it just is.

We move slowly in a clumsy, lurching and stumbling dance—I laugh as Ezi bursts into a song, in words I don't understand.

Finally, I am warm again.

Lunar Voices (On the Solar Wind)

The lunar rover rolled to a halt in the shadow of Shackleton crater and a chill entered Phulani's bones. His suit had registered a drop of 250 degrees Celsius on his visor display within just a few minutes. He could well imagine the sparse, rare ice locked within the crater's frigid soil the other side of these walls, gradually being mined and piped back to Base.

But the full extent of the temperature gauge crash had locked his throat with shock, he couldn't even speak.

Baines could: "Give your suit time to adjust; they've built these bastards well."

Phulani's helmet-lamp kicked in, bringing the person in the space-suit next to him out of the darkness. He could spot the Scottish Saltire stitched in the left side and could just about make out her name underneath—perhaps because he knew it already and knew it well—*Mary Patrick*.

Baines himself sat at the front, the driver and always in control, a voice crackling out of the dark: "We're out of radio com from Base now, as we haven't got any satellite relays in lunar orbit yet. Just listen…"

Phulani wanted to say something to Baines, anything that would get an affirming response, an acknowledgement. He felt very much a raw novice. But he could think of nothing impressive to say, so he reluctantly kept quiet…and listened.

There was nothing to hear in that long empty silence.

Nothing.

Absolutely no sound.

The silence seemed to want a voice, shrilling in his eardrums like a thin static radio whine. Perhaps it was a sub-threshold crackle in their interpersonal communication system? Perhaps it was just his ears straining for a sound, any sound?

His lamp picked out the stiff, aloof back of Baines' sitting suit, and he noticed his helmet was craned back, as if Baines was searching the sky. Involuntarily, he slowly arched his own neck too, joints in the articulated neck-piece attached to his helmet groaning in his ears, although he knew no noise could be relayed in this frigid vacuum. It was then that he saw them.

Stars.

Thousands of sharp, brightly coloured stars; spattering across his vision, ice cold and crisp; red, yellow, blue. Not flickering, but steady, piercing... and skewering something inside him, so that he almost winced with pain. Old light, many of those stars millions of years old, but burning so brightly still in this ongoing, empty darkness.

A flutter of two green electronic hands washed across his visor's *com* display top right—Mary had clicked her suit and British Sign Language (BSL) words formed from scalp electrodes reading her brain, registering her holographic visualisation of how she intended to move her hands.

He didn't need to read the tiny text translation below those flurrying hand shapes. Baines needed that, he didn't.

Beautiful, burning now, both before we be and after we be, yet not caring *if* we be...

(Holographic hands had glowed on 'if'; as if emphasising the word.)

Mary was looking up at the stars too. He half-wished he could touch her real hand, so well had she signed some of the thoughts that danced around his own. But there was not even a hint of his other thoughts there, so he kept his gloves to himself. He knew it was crazy, but still he also had a sense of Heavenly Cattle feet tramping the sky, opening up holes of starry light, a way through to *iNkosi yaphezulu*, Lord-of-the-Sky. That had been grandfather's favourite story...dead grandfather's favourite story; *ukuhamba* grandfather, who continues on in spirit and shade...

But he must forget those stories. Science alone keeps him alive on this dead and dusty world.

"There!" Baines pointed to the right, rupturing Phulani's silence and his thoughts. Phulani spotted a particularly bright red-orange star, but Baines rattled on without pausing: "Mars. If you're lucky, you'll be chosen to go there. But first you still need to show us what you're made of... and to be able to manage this silence and isolation..."

Phulani could tell from the faint vibration in his suit that Baines had started the engine again. "We're done, let's go," Baines's voice crackled curtly and he winced. Mary at least would only see flickering hands on her visor screen from the translation software. She'd had a lifetime of silence, born and raised proudly Deaf—her parents refusing her cochlea implants at birth, she'd told him on the Space-Plane over, with not a hint of regret.

'I can handle this silence,' Phulani thought, 'but why are *you* in such a rush, Officer Baines?'

He glanced up at the pinnacles of the crater walls, trying to spot the solar panel arrays in almost constant sunlight that powered the Base and maybe one day would provide clean energy to help save a crowded, heated Earth…but all he could see were grey walls and broken cliff faces, arching up and around to the nearby curved horizon…

His eyes swung to look at the Earth, a blue-green marble, hanging low on the horizon, beautiful, breath catching, a magnet for his eyes.

Then they were trundling out in the glare of sunlight again and a torrent of words burst in with the brightness and the heat: "…Rover Five, come in, come in, please, this is urgent, Five, please reply…"

"Five here," Baines said.

"Five, return to Base *now*! There's an S.P.E. heading your way."

"Damn!" said Baines and Phulani jumped. "How long?"

"We spotted it just over five minutes ago and it's *big*, X-class maybe." class maybe."

"On our way," said Baines, and Phulani felt the buggy shudder as it ground into maximum speed. He was grateful for the seat-belts as the rover began to bounce and buck over smaller rocks hidden in the lunar dust.

Mary palmed a button on her suit to communicate her thoughts and hands flickered up on his visor: *Good news not…*

Vomit rose in his stomach, he quelled it with force of will, having heard it was possible to choke to death in space-suits. "What's an S.P.E.?"

"Solar Particle Event," said Baines, "Not a good idea to be outdoors to watch one."

Phulani checked his visor clock —Shackleton's shadow had been their furthest stop. They were just over three hours away from Base, perhaps two at top speed. There was a sharp and stale stench in his nose; it took him moments to realise it was his own sweat.

"Stay calm, we'll miss the worst of the storm," said Baines and Phulani remembered that Baines had both their vital signs up in his visor's LED display.

Hands flickered across his peripheral view: *Fifteen minutes for the first SCRs maybe…*

He didn't want to know what an S.C.R. was. Trust an engineer to assume everyone spoke in acronyms…

"The worst of it's still at least two hours away," barked Baines, "We should make it back before then."

Phulani was glad he couldn't see Baines's bio readings, if the bite in his voice was anything to go by. It was the longest two hours he'd ever known and it was all he could do to stop himself throwing up…

But then it became even longer.

The buggy ground to a sudden halt, almost throwing Phulani forward against Baines. He bounced slowly in his seat against the tethering safety straps.

Baines unhitched himself and turned to face them. Mary was busy with a display in front of her; gloved fingers poking at flickering dials.

"I'm finding it hard to breathe," he said, "Someone else needs to drive."

"What's wrong, Officer Baines? What can I do?" Phulani unbuckled himself and stood up unsteadily in his seat.

"There's something wrong with both my primary and back-up *OPS* air supply on my PLSS," gasped Baines tersely, "I think the ice..." A burst of static tore Baines's remaining words apart. Numbers and signs scrambled momentarily on Phulani's visor display before blinking and disappearing, all he could hear was a faint hiss in his ears.

"Hello," Phulani said, "Hello?"

Hsssss.....

He could hear no words, see no electronic hand signs, but he sensed a soft subliminal hissing that penetrated deep into his skull...was that the sound of the sun in his ears—or perhaps even residual noise from the birth of the Universe?

He saw Mary helping Baines into her seat. Get a grip, Phulani, time to focus, time to help...

He took a slow and careful breath, a pang of isolation spearing him, along with a sudden sense of radioactive particles piercing his skin, poisoning his organs.

He turned to scan the horizon, looking for signs of their Base. The craters and scattered boulders with deep shadows dark enough to drown in looked unfamiliar and alien; he could see no sign of Base, of home. Then again, it would only be a dust covered door leading below a crater wall for maximal shielding, hard to spot unless you knew exactly where you were going. And they had no guidance now, no radio signals to reel them in...

No rover tracks to trace either, Baines had obviously been driving the shortest route back, focused by his deep, almost unique knowledge of this terrain.

Mary turned to face him and he could tell from the helpless hang of her arms she did not know where they were either.

Baines sat strapped into Mary's seat, immobile—Phulani could not tell whether he was conscious or unconscious, dead or alive.

Panic rose with the bile in his stomach—he focused desperately on one smaller craggy crater wall off to his left, wondering if he could reach it in a few bounds and leap inside, to find a spot where he could hide himself—they could hide themselves—against the sun's invisible rage. He stepped off the buggy and with a further step away, braced himself for a run...

But there, on the cratered wall, tall and thin, grandfather stood with his old dog *Inja* by his side. Grandfather was shaking his head, even though he was three weeks dead now.

The old man stood upright and pointed behind Phulani with his stick. Phulani could see it was the long *knobkierie* with which grandfather used to walk and shake at stupid youngsters who were rude with their new city ways, when they pushed him aside and failed to show him *hlonipha*, the elder respect due him. He was pointing back at the lunar buggy. Although he knew no words could soar in the vacuum between them, Phulani could hear the old man's voice ring in his head.

"*You're Amazulu boy and a Matlala, with a job to do. Now go and do it!*"

Phulani turned and walked back to the buggy; he knew he must hold onto the experience-hardening memories within him, he had negotiated a tough peace through volatile communication conflicts on the training Antarctic winter base after all.

Hello to you too, grandfather, nice to see you again too...

He hesitated by the rover, wondering where he should sit, what he should do. Mary was crouched in his seat, studying a laminated map.

What good were his communication skills out here?

Hsssss.....

They'd warned him about this—how massive solar particle ejections could disrupt electrical communications systems; he'd just never expected to experience it so closely, so intimately and with such absolute terror, completely isolated inside his hot, sweaty, bombarded body.

They were dying as they just waited there, that he knew...

Hssss....

An idea thudded into him, as if punched in by a high energy particle.

Phulani took a deep breath, glad his suit's oxygen and cooling system continued to run, even if he wasn't sure for how much longer. Okay, so he did speak nine languages and was communications officer for the International Lunar Base; now was the time that he should really earn his keep.

He turned to face Mary and held his hands up, grateful that NASA had built such cleverly dexterous gloves, in their constant search for maximising working suit efficiency. Still, even so, as he fumbled a few words in the ninth language he knew, wondering if they would be dexterous enough.

Mary laid the map down and clumsily fisted some finger and hand positions back to him. *Not Still Know Where We Are.*

She picked up the map and handed it to him. He took it with difficulty and peered at it. The shortest distance between two points was a straight line—perhaps he could try and track a straight line from the curve of Shackleton to the Base. But where exactly did the crater's shadow lie? The curve of the rim was kilometres wide and Baines had been careering to avoid obstacles...carrying on in the direction of travel would be a hit and miss affair.

Hopeless…

Mary was fisting signs in his face. *Together are we; together we hope; Baines lives still…*

Phulani smiled. Nearby, a dog barked.

He'd recognise that bark anywhere. It was *Inja*, prancing in front of the rover, as if wanting to play catch. Yes, he definitely wanted to be chased or followed, he'd always pawed at the ground at the start of this game, just like that…But this time, he sneezed with the cloud of lunar dust he'd kicked up with his paws.

Phulani laughed and signed to Mary: *Drive you, I show way…*

He caught a shadowy glimpse of her expression before she turned to climb into the driver's seat. He wondered if he would ever be able to tell her that he could see a dead dog on the Moon.

It was madness he knew, but he could think of nothing better than to point ahead in the direction that *Inja* ran, yelping with pleasure, hurtling ahead like a *springbok* in the lighter lunar gravity. Mary drove on, with an occasional turn of her head, checking the direction of his pointing through her peripheral vision.

They drove for what seemed like an eternity and still, it seems even a dog *shade* tires…

Inja slowed to a ragged jog and dropped alongside the rover, panting and peering in at Phulani. He stretched across to pat the dog, as he had when a boy, but he patted nothing but vacuum.

Inja was gone.

The rover crawled to a halt, a large boulder ahead obscuring the view. Mary unbuckled herself and turned to him, signing: *Okay you? Forgot way again?*

He nodded tiredly, forgetting it was hard for her to see his face through his glinting visor.

The Moon felt empty, desolate again.

Mary went to check on Baines.

Phulani closed his eyes and listened to the faint whirr of his oxygen fans. *Together we hope…*

Old images, paintings and words floated in the darkness of his mind; he tried to hold them steady as light meteors ripped through them, solar storm particles in his brain?

An old book he'd read had charged him with his first excitement about the Moon, painted and spoken by a Moon-Walker from almost a century ago…oh yes, Alan Bean, Apollo Twelve. What had he said again? The solar glare had bleached the lunar landscape, making it hard for them to see when looking into the sun.

Phulani opened his eyes and looked across to his left, up a ragged sloping hill towards the sun. He unbuckled himself.

Where go? Signed Mary, crouching over Baines; *Baines breathes still, but almost conscious not...*

Something to see... He fisted a reply.

He leaped up the hill, bouncing unsteadily with the thrusting of his boots, bracing himself to slow and stop as Baines had taught him on earlier Moon-Walks. He turned to face down the slope, scanning the widened expanse of terrain with the sun blazing at his back. Left to right, slowly, surely, not even sure of what he might be looking for...

There, a faint but regular pattern against the dust in this chaotic jumbled world—just a bit further on and to the right of that boulder ahead of the rover. Phulani bounded down the slope carefully, aware he may just have been seeing things. Still, it was all they had.

Mary was in the driver's seat again, waiting for him. Phulani pointed ahead and to the right of the boulder, preferring to jog ahead. It took him only five bounds.

He braked to a dusty halt.

It was a line of rover tracks.

Galactic Navigator, that's the name of the particular Bean painting which had stuck in his head. Easy to get lost, but all you need to find are tracks, your marks and patterns in history.

Mary ground to a halt alongside him; pointed at him and gave him a sign for love, which was a bit like hugging herself. He laughed with a rush of elation and heat, clambering into his seat.

Which way? He signed.

Haven't watched you sun's angle to grossly direction assess? She gave him a flurry of signs and then turned to accelerate right along the rover tracks.

Phulani looked behind him with difficulty at the receding hill. Grandfather stood there, waving his *knobkierie*, with *Inja* howling to the Earth.

Yes, he knew they had told him to expect visual distortions in this alien land.

Still, he waved. *Sala kahle, grandfather...*

His sense of time drifted away after that; mostly he closed his eyes and felt ill with the swaying and jolting of the rover as it bounced over the ragged terrain. But every now and then he opened his eyes, sweat dried in cold patches on his cheeks, watching Mary steer with certain and assured conviction. She slowed.

Relief shocked him as a dusty crevice opened up in the bottom of a crater-wall ahead of them. Someone must have seen them arrive. Mary manoeuvred the rover down the slope expertly, the buggy skidding to a dusty halt in the dark cavernous air-lock. Behind them, a large dust-packed door ground closed, sealing out the toxic sun.

Lights flickered on around them.

They stopped and sat silently for a moment. Mary unhooked herself and swivelled round on her seat to reach across to Baines, slumped next to Phulani in his suit with its faded stars and stripes.

Hsssssssssss…..

Phulani realised with relief that there was oxygen being pumped into the room and that he could hear again. On the other side of the dark room the airlock door blinked orange as the air pressure rose. Mary had twisted off Baines's helmet and was busy unfastening her own. By the time Phulani had wrenched his helmet off, the airlock was blinking green and Mary was leaning back, smiling.

Baines was groggy but conscious; limp, but grinning in between ragged gasps.

Mary looked across at Phulani with a smile on her lips, helmet cradled in her lap, red hair frizzed madly; electrode bugs hanging off her scalp like electronic lice. His own helmet finally off, he took a deep breath of rich Base air and then vomited—with great embarrassment—deep into his helmet, closing his eyes with shame.

A woman's voice crackled over the intercom: "I'm reading your rad exposure levels; you're all going to be sick for a while. I think you'll be okay, but I'm getting some sick-bay beds ready."

Phulani's mind played for a moment on the word 'think'—there was no certainty in the woman's voice or that word. Still…he hadn't come almost four hundred thousand kilometres for either safety or certainty. He'd come here because of the call of the stars and he'd seen them and maybe heard and felt them burn deep inside him. (And perhaps much more besides…?)

He opened his eyes, his head turned to face Mary.

She was signing: *Talking is Baines…*

He hadn't heard anything, so he looked over to Baines in confusion. Despite waves of nausea and an acid burn in his throat, he still managed a grin.

Baines was giving them both a big thumbs-up with his hairy right fist.

Behind Baines, a shadowy old man bowed; his one hand on a panting dog.

African Shadows

The man who'd lost his soul was cold to the touch, even in that wet heat. I tried squeezing some life into him, through my old and aching fingers. But he lay, slackly propped against the thorn tree, eyes staring at nothing that I could see. So I turned again to the old *sangoma* standing nearby.

"Xolile, please, can't you help him?"

He opened his pale palms to me. They were empty.

Desperately, I asked: "Haven't you got special equipment for this sort of thing?"

He smiled more wrinkles: "You mean the masks and bones and all the other witchdoctor stuff you've no doubt seen on your magic TV boxes?"

"There's no need to be facile."

"And there's no reason to be angry! Patience, Ruth ... my paraphernalia won't impress John Jones. He doesn't know me—with or without my masks"

I didn't really know the old man either. He hadn't asked me much about why I was there. Quiet he'd been, from the airport to his house. From his house to this tree. He'd given only commands and demands, and all I wanted to say, was bottled like stale wine.

I swigged some warm water from a flask, and looked back at his house. It was a handsome house: cool and clean, with Western décor, shimmering vaguely amongst the dense African *thornveld*. Square and stolid, with vined veranda and a steep slate roof, pitched sharply against pending sub-tropical storms (a far cry from the mud hut covered in skins that I'd half expected).

I wanted to go back to it.

"Come, let's go on," he said, "Before the sun gets too high ... The healing is in the journey."

I wiped some flies from John's slack lips, and trickled some water into his mouth. He dribbled like a paralysed baby. The pulse at his flaccid wrist kept a slow and primitive beat. I levered his arm around me, and, with a helping hand from Xolile, managed to get John standing. A tall and fit young man he was ... yet he seemed twice as old as us, a vacant husk...

A star man, astronaut, back from deep space ... yet somehow emptier now than the vacuum from which we'd dragged him. 'We are the hollow men ... ?'

Xolile hoisted his haversack onto his biltong back and smiled at me. "Come."

The sun's heat swallowed my breath, as I led John along a dusty red track. The path faded quickly into arse-high yellow grass. Angry grass that sliced at our legs. Grass that stretched into a white heat and pale sky—and there were no safely square buildings to trap my gaze. Behind me, the house was long gone. There was just grass and trees and hidden things that could sting and bite.

I fixed my stare on the wiry shape, moving ahead with certainty and vigour. *Quo vadis?* I don't know whether I spoke, but he never answered me.

My shirt was a soaking skin, my eyes aching from the glare. Only the next step became real. My thoughts congealed in that heat, sinking to my feet. They pushed puffs of dust along the narrow track that opened up ahead. Dust which dropped redly onto my boots, with no sense of helping or healing spirits to lift us.

Onwards we kept moving, through the grass and between the trees.

Trees? Strangely squashed trees (crowding in thorny clusters), dangling webs that clung and teased. The sun was hanging heavily through the lower branches, swollen with red age. And the air was cooler, stirring life above my legs.

The old man stopped to sniff the air like a dog. My nose was numb with sweat, yet something tickled my skin and tingled my hairs.

The grass and bushes were greener here, the trees denser. The old man nodded a sense of arrival, and stopped John's mechanical gait with a firm hand to shoulder. I dropped onto relieved haunches, rolling back onto my rucksack. My shaking legs splayed in front of me. My constricted chest would not let me speak.

"Well," said the old man, "Here we are."

I looked around. He pointed at a thick screen of bushes, just beyond the loose gathering of trees behind us. Still too tired to talk, I threw him a questioning look.

"There's water hole behind there ... But don't worry, it's more accessible to animals from the other side. We shouldn't disturb them here."

I could gasp some words then. "What about them disturbing us?"

He laughed: "Nah, I think it's more likely rebel troops might accidentally find and shoot us first."

"And that's supposed to be *funny*?"

"Ruth ... " he pulled John (still almost sweatless) into a sitting position, and sat down beside me. "Ruth, how can you heal, if you can't laugh?"

"I can't heal," I said tightly, "that's why I'm here."

"So tell me." His gentle hand on my arm unlocked my words ... at first a strained trickle, then a tired torrent. My reticence dissolved by his touch, exhaustion and emptiness babbling forth.

"I was his- his personal therapist on the mission, Xolile. Interstellar space experiments—you know, Deep Space Mission Five? Do you remember all that biological stuff to study plants and life, far away from the effects of solar radiation, in case someday we needed to leave this planet? Any- anyway, it was expensive, budget cuts, and all that, so we could only take one crew member. To do the stuff the robots and computers couldn't. We looked around and chose a loner, comfortable in his solitude. John. And I—I ..."

"Were you supposed to look after him?"

"Yeah ... 'Therapeutic radio contact,' I was entrusted with his mental state. And I tried, only..."

Always encouraging others to cry, I was ashamed of my own tears. I fought to lock them inside, but the old man held me, releasing them. The damp air seemed to suck my words into the open. I struggled not to hide my failure.

"Things were- were okay at first, but then John got increasingly moody and withdrawn, more and more hostile. It was when space began to drag our words into long delays ... 'Squeezing their juice out,' he once told me ... Once he shouted 'You're not listening to me anymore. Just to the past. Oh my God, why aren't you here?' And then he became silent, mute."

"And that was it?"

"Just about—I knew somehow the loneliness of space had gotten to him ... It's not easy maintaining an effective phenomenological approach across millions of miles of an ever-increasing distance, you know."

"I have no reproaches, Ruth, but you say there was something else?"

"Just one phrase, at the farthest point of his mission. 'Where's the sun?' he asked. He'd gone past Saturn by that time ... And then he stopped working, became catatonic, so they brought him back. I'd tried to get him back earlier, but they wouldn't listen to me, what with all that money and everything, and him still working ... But then he stopped. Like he was dead, so we kept him alive with computerized drips. And he came back ... But in a way, not really. Four months he was gone. Just four months, and his life seemed to have leaked out of him."

"So why come to me Ruth?"

I shook my head slowly. "Dunno ... I'm getting older, weaker, Xolile, my words aren't working anymore. John's not the first one recently. I'm fifty now, and it feels like my powers have generally decayed. And no-one else's words seemed to help either. Even fiddling with drugs and his neuro-transmitters achieved bugger all! It's like he's died inside his body ... So I looked around..."

"I'm flattered," he laughed, "I never knew you could see me from America."

I had to smile, a small twist of my lips. "Not you personally at first, Xolile, that only came later ... I just felt the faint stirring of the new millennial breeze; the awakenings of old ways of re-birthing, healing ... and the 'new' ways seem so weary now, so sterile. There were a lot of rumours floating out of Africa."

The old man stood slowly, stiffly taking his haversack off. For this first time, I realised he was really old. He seemed not to have heard my last words. He was darkly etched against the bloody grey sky and hovering branches.

"Where's the sun?" he muttered, "Where indeed?"

*

We built a quick fire against the gathering dusk. The astronaut sat like a robot, gazing dumbly at the struggling flames. A hope tremor shook me, was he responding to environmental cue? But the hope rolled rocklike into my stomach, as his eyes began to flicker randomly again. My eyes darted too—over encroaching trees and fireside shadows. A short dusk here. We sat in silence, while the darkness dropped heavily onto our backs.

Somewhere in the distance, a strident trumpet bellowed, hung, and then dissolved in the crackle of flames. The chill shock mounted my spine, thrusting me to my feet. With my back to the heat, I stared outwards at blackness.

The old man paused while feeding the flames: "Relax, Ruth, that's one of the last tuskless elephants. It's far away."

But I couldn't relax. I could feel senses stirring around us, waking from the day's heat. Not seen nor heard, yet blinking and bleating on the edge of ear and eye.

"What is this place?" I asked the old *sangoma*.

He'd taken a pot off the fire, and poured some soup into recycled cups. "A water-hole," he said, "Come, let's eat."

The soup was good. I wasn't sure if it was meat or vegetable. It didn't seem to matter so much here. I watched John gulp greedily. Old mind pictures of mentally disabled people eating between dank yellow walls flitted through my head. But John was not like that. We—I—didn't know what was wrong with him ... Or was Xolile right? Was there really a ghost in the machine?

He licked his empty plate and belched.

Xolile had finished too, wiping his mouth clean with a fist. Darkness dropped from the branches, trying to suffocate the fire. A broken moon wandered behind the trees, leaving us alone with the cold night. Cold? In Africa?

I drew closer to the struggling fire: "How did he lose his—uh-soul, Xolile?"

The old man smiled, as if sensing my doubt.

"He flew too far from the sun's light. Lost a sense of centre, of home. The soul was torn out by the dark and empty spirits in the space between the suns."

Were soul and psyche cultural labels for the same thing? I was tired with thinking. I just wanted John back. "How do we find his soul down here, then?"

The *sangoma* had gathered a pile of ash at his feet, crouching cross-legged before the fire. My question faded into darkness as I watched. Spooning hot ash in his fingers, he smeared his face and body. Firelight highlighted the grey streaks, a sinewy skeleton emerging from blackness, etched in gold. A smiling skeleton, he'd stripped off his clothes. He gave a little bow.

"Witchdoctor Radebe at you service." His voice was different. I struggled to grasp why. Somehow flat, more distant, more...someone else?

No, stay calm, it's not possible, he'd merely changed inflection ... All around, sounds scattered from the night. A croak. Rustling. Low whistles, a hoot ... Things were there. No! Primitive fears, unfounded!

The skeleton laughed. Wings fluttered through the branches. Something shrieked. My God, I had no control here.

I was up and crouching to face looming trees closing in on the fire. Shadows blurred with the trees, mixing and reforming. Taking other forms, gaining solidity...They were large black women, tilling the earth, babies blanket strapped to their backs. I watched, my arms folded under sagging, un-suckled breasts ... I watched, and found my face wet. Salty wet.

The smell of damp earth and sweat clogged my nostrils. I moved forward to touch one woman, but my hand slipped through her. She seemed to sprout from the ground, large and bent, furrowing soil rhythmically with a large hoe, oblivious to my presence, as if I was the phantom. Her baby was snuggled and asleep, content. I longed to hold her or him. But couldn't. The more I tried, the more he or she faded, along with their mother.

The other women had gone too, leaving deserted shadows blank and empty. Numb and alone, I stood. What did it mean? A vision?

Hallucinogens in my soup? Psychosis?

No. Whatever the trigger, it was real. Real for me, and the land around me. I wiped my hands and turned to the fire.

The *sangoma*, smeared and vague, cradled the astronaut's head on his lap. Crooned over him in Zulu. I sat next to him, enjoying the lullaby lilt of tone, unsure of word meaning. No matter, I just listened. Voices dwindled into the night.

"What is this place?" I asked again.

"A place of tracks. Presences. Spirits. A crossroads, where animals and people come to quench thirst. A meeting place."

"Why did you bring us here?"

"To call his soul back."

"But we've tried that, in a way. It didn't work. With his family, people who've known him his entire life. We even brought in his dog. Zit. Nothing. How can we call him, who hardly knew him?"

"Not just us ... the earth around us. His living family have known him only thirty years. He needs an older, stronger call ... call of the ancestors, the animals and the earth."

"The elephant?"

"Was just one voice. Many surround us now."

The night was strangely quiet. Brooding and pregnant, withdrawn. Even the fire shadows had shrunk, as flames subsided into hot coals. I had a fear of hope, with the dwindling light and dark stillness. Why could I hear nothing anymore?

"Will it work Xolile?"

The old man shrugged, "The earth groans under a sea of concrete and plastic ... animals are fewer, cries fading ... but old voices are strong here. Let him have your hope. It is another voice. And it's not as weak as you feel it to be."

The sudden staccato wail of a baby's cry shrilled the air. I peered into the thick shadows that engulfed us now ... On the cusp of absolute blackness, a mother stood, cradling her baby. My dry womb ached, and they were gone ... But I was here. And so were John and the old man.

It was time to sleep. I said goodnight to Xolile. We laid our sleeping bags out near the dying warmth. We placed John (with a struggle) inside his. Xolile sprinkled ashes around our bags.

"Animal owners of live voices don't like the ash," he said.

Hardly reassured, I was surprised to fall asleep.

*

Something had changed.

I groped for a torch near my bag, panicking blind. Silence screamed in my ears and my eyeballs were sore from the pressing dark. My torch flicked on, splashing light around the campsite. There were dead coals and a discarded sleeping bag. John was gone. The old man sprawled alone, snoring.

My thought hurried from a sleepy stupor.

Was this another stage in the illness, nocturnal wandering?

Where to? My torchlight was pale, and stars prickled through locked branches above me. Dense bushes clawed at me, holding me back. I wrestled free and sensed space, dropping down a small slope to a splash of water ... Water freckled with moonlight. The moon was low over the trees, plunging earthwards.

A man stood nearby, leaning against a tree on the slope. He was watching the water. I approached, light bobbing timidly in my hand. The man turned to me, his face young and alive in the wan light.

"Who's that?" he asked.

I stopped. "It's me, John, Ruth."

I dropped my torch as we hugged. He held me fiercely, shaking in my arms. My neck was wet ... his tears.

"Doc ... it was so- so damned empty up there."

"It's okay now John, everything's all right."

For a moment I wondered how reassuring I sounded ... but stuff therapeutic efficacy. I was very, very happy. I could tell John was too.

And he was warm to hold. Nothing else mattered.

His shakes subsided. I released him to step back and look. His face smiled through a damp shine. Quirky and responsive. Nearby, a frog croaked, startling us. John laughed, throaty and deep.

I felt lighter, as if a dead psychic baby on my back now stood before me; strong, mature and alive. Somehow, like a child I've never had. Yet not a child—a man, with his own family, his own life. And good feelings- some for me. I could sense them ... and it's enough.

I felt the tingling of renewal in my bones.

"Have you watched the water, Ruth?" he asked, "It's bloody beautiful."

We turned to watch it together. Burning with the vanishing moon's light, the pool seemed alive too. No animals drinking yet, but we hoped and waited.

Mindreader

I've read that children on the autistic spectrum struggle with the notion of time. Funny, that, so do I. But then, I think pretty much everyone struggles with time. To be on the safe side, though, I rapped on the clinic desk and signed in Jack's visual field—one minute left.

He looked blankly at my hand gesture, avoiding my eye gaze. Then he looked down and shut the book of pictures in front of him. I turned to his mum, sitting quietly in the corner of the room. Janet Gray smiled at me tiredly. I smiled back at her, with what I hoped was a sharing of sisterhood that might strengthen her, although I had no children of my own. Her son was only eight, but I knew better than to shake his hand goodbye, even though our session was over.

Him, I'd never seen smile, certainly not while looking at someone.

Jack stood in the room, staring down at his feet. What was he thinking? The sharp blue metal edge of Thomas the Tank Engine's carriage cut into his left palm as he patted it with his right hand. He'd ignored the toy soldiers, even though The Terror Wars were all over the news. I found that vaguely reassuring.

Clinging to Thomas, Jack turned and tried to open the clinic door. It had another handle, but this was a steel, childproof one, way out of reach above his head. I reached up for it and asked: "What is the best way home for me by train, Jack? It's now five-forty p.m."

He stared at the green door in front of us both, suddenly spewing forth words without a sideways glance at me: "Six-ten.—Midline Train six twenty-three to Earlsmith, six-forty-four to Parkmouth and then a seven-three to Worchester."

He always remembered where I lived. That realisation touched me; his thoughts so anxiously knotted around endless train timetables. In someone with his condition, where it was almost impossible for him to think himself into someone else's head, it seemed a small but vital chink.

I helped him open the door, carefully, as he could bump his head, so eagerly was he straining forward to leave. I knew he would run—his mum too, calling and catching him—and then we'd deal with his tears, after she returned the train to me from his fiercely clenched fist. That was what happened at the end of all of our sessions. He would be very distressed if it didn't happen just like it always had.

But Janet put a hand on my shoulder, face shockingly sad, tears blinking at the corners of her brown eyes: "I'm really struggling with him, Sally," she said. "I know this appointment is for him, but please help me."

It was the end of a long day and I was tired too, but I realised I had the much better deal—when it came to managing Jack's cries and tears, I didn't have to take them home with me.

I gestured her to the couch in the waiting room. Everyone else had gone home. Well, all except the shadowy men with gasmasks and guns in the security office upstairs, monitoring the empty corridors via CCTV.

Janet sat down and started to talk about how difficult Jack's behaviour was at home. I listened, knowing I could always ask Jack later again for the train times.

He had his head tilted back, watching the neon light flicker through the fingers of his right hand and off the blue carriage of Thomas the Tank Engine, ignoring our words.

It seemed he had no interest in them, or in the passing of time.

*

The trip into work in the mornings felt bleak in the late midwinter. It was still dark in the new day, and I could smell a damp saline fog that blurred the orange street lights lining my walk to the train station. I gave a tentative sniff in case there were any strange scents hanging in the air, glancing at the gas detector strapped to my right wrist. But the air smelt merely like a musty sea, a breeze perhaps sweeping in the air over the hills from miles away.

The detector remained dark and inert on my wrist, so I shook it to make sure.

I generally leave for work soon after getting up—I have found it increasingly hard to watch the news in my flat, with constant tales of Terror Wars and hatred and death. The 'Hemisphere of Evil' against us seems to be an entire swollen world, rather than just a neat segment of the planet. It seems to me, the more we invade, the less we conquer.

I pushed with the small crowd, stepping up into the train.

Finding a seat was one of the small pleasures of getting up so early. There was time to think and prepare for the day and watch people if my thoughts grew tired and slow in my head. I scanned taught and anxious faces, some fingering their masks, but no one was wearing them.

Reassured, I glance at the man in the stiff charcoal suit next to me, sipping a strong coffee, and the smell seemed to tickle my thoughts. Yes, I hated news of hate and divisions and conflict, but surely there was a way that we could all learn to see through each other's eyes and realise our shared needs? I remembered playing out long psycho-dramas with my dolls when I was younger, working through conflicts, repairing understandings and trust amongst all the dolls in the end, even the males.

Pete, my brother, would join in sometimes, to "humour" me, as he put it. I'd aim for an ending where all bruises and bitchiness would be over and forgiven.

"Just like old funny Brady Bunch re-runs," Pete would say.

Then he'd strike with his doll at the end, breaking the perfect resolution I had created.

I was just happy he played with me, despite his jibes.

That was until the years he started bringing his friends around. It seemed so soon after that that he decided to serve his stint with the military, placing conscription before University.

A big testosterone-driven row with my dad had cemented his decision.

And I couldn't remember when I last saw him. I wished so often I could bring him back somehow, with the mad thought recurring that perhaps if I played with my dolls again, that would work?

But he remained 'missing in action,' although they refused to tell me what 'action' they were talking about, or where it was…

I reached inside my bag instinctively, but there was just a folded manual and clinic sheet in there.

I couldn't remember where my dolls had gone either.

It seemed like I'd abandoned them long ago for therapeutic software, cards and words.

The worst part of the journey to work was the last stretch to the clinic, where the shadows seemed to crowd in on me, as if threatening to attack.

At least the blackness was greying as I hurried into the research building, loosening my coat from around my ears. I swiped my security card, removing it from the pocket on the chain around my neck—and put it back as I climbed the stairs, struggling a bit as it got tangled with the light gas mask dangling from my coat.

I switched on the light and walked across to my desk, hauling out the files of children coming for the day from my top drawer.

As I lifted my head the door squeaked open. Dr Brown stood there, severe in her brown suit, blinking in the room's harsh neon glare.

I stood, surprised—she was so busy, it was hard just getting an appointment for supervision. I'd not seen her outside her office.

"Um, hi, Sally." She looked uncomfortable, gesturing me to sit: "So, busy programme ahead?"

Looking down the list I said: "Six kids as usual."

"Hmmm…" She perched herself on the edge of the table, suit straining with her posture. She edged forward to try to ease the wrinkles in her suit at the front, smoothing them from her jacket with a firm tug at the buttoned base.

"Um, Sally, I have spoken to some people and they are saying that increasingly United States F.D.A. research is suggesting that 'Empath' may be harmful. They reckon it will be withdrawn from testing soon and they want us to consider researching another drug linked with your psychotherapy. We may need to forget about 'Empath'."

I looked at her, appalled, unable to grasp her words. This was two years of my life she was talking about. She seemed to skate her words out so easily.

She looked down and carried on talking: "I have a new and very generous sponsor in mind with a drug called 'Focus'—it helps people focus on a detail of a task, obviating the danger of their getting lost in the bigger picture. It's also very therapeutic; it erases traumatic memories, so it's helpful for our troops caught in the aftermath of war or terrorist combat with PTSD."

I looked at her aghast: "It's a military drug!"

"No." She looked at me. "A therapeutic drug, with some benefits for our troops. There's a big difference. It's already passed stringent safety tests and they've introduced a syringe dose."

"But it's completely different to what I'm doing!"

With sharp eyes and frowning, she said: "No, not really. You are trying to help kids generate integrated thoughts and feelings for other people. This would just mean going the other way. Trying to identify how they can maintain such obsessional focus on detail. This would involve a *positive* reappraisal of autism. Surely you have a positive respect for the strengths of the children you are working with?"

I struggled with the words, rising anger emerging, despite my fears and the biting guilt from her last question: "Well, sort of, Doctor Brown, but, but they're struggling too—and so are their parents. Do you really think a loss of central coherence is adaptive?"

She shrugged. "I think it can be. Just think about it a bit more, Sally. No more agonising over the meaning of the whole picture. Wondering what everything *means*. After all," she gave a little smile, "We all know it boils down to forty-two."

I was stunned. She was referring to *The Hitchhiker's Guide to the Galaxy*? I had no idea she read that sort of thing. Was she trying to make a joke out of people's search for meaning?

Dr Brown arched an eyebrow, getting up from the desk. "Think about it more carefully, Sally. You could move closer to the centre of the city and into a much bigger, warmer place. The research grants for 'Focus' are extremely generous, much more than they were for 'Empath'."

I hesitated; the flat could get so damned cold at times, the train journeys so tedious…

But what about Jack—and Janet?

She saw my hesitation and looked cold. "I need a final answer by the end of this afternoon."

She left, with a sharp slam of the door that underlined her words.

Although shaken I needed to focus on the children coming in. Jack was back again, in the session before lunch. I'm not supposed to have favourites; they're all equally-weighted Doctoral research subjects.

Secretly, Jack was my favourite equally-weighted Doctoral research subject.

I did my best with Mark and Joanna, going through the emotion recognition software and Social Pictures, trying to focus their attention on the salient facial and social cues, drawing out their gaze with commands and gestures. All to try and create empathy with a person in a picture—building emotional bridges for children who remain isolated, withdrawn, and alone.

There were flickers of response, and I cheered and gave moments of rewarding rest, Mark with a book on dinosaurs; Joanna with a shiny decoration from an old Christmas tree.

But Jack remained my favourite because there were moments I seemed to catch him watching me out of the corner of his eyes, as if *he* was the one who would end up publishing research on me.

And he never seemed to forget where I lived.

But the eighth time he looked away, I sighed with resignation, rapping the table between us with the calloused knuckles on my right hand.

"Look, Jack." Point and cue Social Picture 12 on the table. It was face up for him, upside down for me. He turned at my rapping noise, looking down at the table, grimacing with a facial tic, a twist of right eye and cheek.

I didn't think he had a co-morbid diagnosis of Tourette's, I thought, pushing the card forward into his field of vision. *I need to check his file.*

"Jack, tell me what's happening in the picture."

He looked at the picture. At least I'd restored some attention.

I withdrew my hand and sighed again, resting my head in the palm of my right hand, elbow propped on the table. I was tired and worried, but there were still eight more cards to go before lunch—and what would I say to Dr. Brown?

I opened my palms to Jack, breaking standardised administrative protocol in a surge of despair. "Help me with the picture, please, Jack!"

He glanced at me and down at the picture, his right eyelid almost closing with the force of a tic. "I th-th-think that man's chasing the other man."

"Eh—?" He was using his fingers to trace characters in the picture and I felt a hot cramp of excitement in my body.

Jack looked at me for the first time in his life with a simultaneous smile. "I think the man chasing blames the other man for the broken window of his shop, I think he sells flowers. But, but he didn't see the little boy hiding behind the bush with his catapult. I think *he's* really the naughty one." He chuckled, and I could see the laughter crease his eyes.

I half stood up, reaching across the table towards him. "Why, that's, that's brilliant, Jack! Can you see anything more happening?" The last sentence dropped from me with a heavy rote readiness, before I could catch it.

He looked down at the picture again and I could no longer see his sharp, piercing smile. I sat down and pulled my chair in, peering to track his eyes scanning the picture.

But they weren't. The smile had frozen on his lips and he was staring at one corner of the picture. The top left. It was his favourite corner. "There..." he said, trailing his fingers around the stripy pattern on the florist shop's canopy. "There..."

"Jack?"

He seemed to have gone, as if he'd retreated into himself. And I was left alone with my thoughts. Was this sudden acute social thinking by Jack evidence of a new connection with reality, an empathic leap across the page into cartoon shapes, cartoon people? I wanted to sustain that magical moment of hearing him mind-read personal attributions, beliefs and intentions, all from lines on a page.

But I had no idea how—and he only continued to trace random patterns through limited parts of the remaining pictures, saying nothing.

At least he left his scalp electrodes alone, little electronic beetles perched in his hair, jumping slightly and sporadically with his facial tic, which had eased and dwindled as the session moved to a close.

Janet seemed a little brighter at least when she came in to collect him, but I needed my lunch and someone to talk to.

*

I had one person who listened to me properly. There was one person who kept the shadows consistently empty of threat for me when she was around.

We had a favourite corner in the Doctoral Research Students Room, a small chair and seat off to the side of the bookshelf, with a little round table, away from the bustle of the dispensing machine and the large central table and couches.

It was good to meet there for lunch.

"Jees," Melinda said, tipping back her coffee. "Sounds like the precious Dr Brown is getting worse. Me, I'm glad I've got Dr Pillay as my supervisor. He lets you get on with things and tries to help at least."

I opened my hands that had been wrapped around my mug of tea. "What do you reckon I should do, Mel?"

She gave me a sideways look through her short, black curls. "You're going to blame me if my advice goes wrong again?"

I had to laugh. I'd never truly blamed her for her advice on confronting Ray. Maybe for those first few numbing weeks after he'd left.

I'd kept thinking perhaps he was right: perhaps there was a deficit of empathy in me, that part of me that couldn't understand how he needed more than one woman.

But Melinda's phrase had pulled me through, with all its sophisticated insights: "That's pure bullshit!"

And our words had started to flow again.

"No," I said. "I won't blame you."

She shrugged and sized up her sandwich, lifting it off her plate. "I know it's easy for me to say, but perhaps a change of supervisor may help. You know, find someone who's willing to let you do what you want to do. I've heard Dr Brown is being eaten up by thoughts of her ex-partner's appointment to an H.O.D. position at Oxbridge."

She took a bite from her cheese and tomato sandwich, and I watched bits of tomato drop out onto her plate.

I could think of no one else in the department who might be able to supervise me. They were interested in things like suicide in teens and eating disorders.

Actually, there was perhaps only one person who might be an outside possibility for supervising my autism research.

"So, how is *your* research going, Mel?"

"Eh?" She looked at me with puzzlement, and I realised I had been looking down, obscuring my mouth as I spoke.

"How is your research going?" I asked, speaking so she could see my lips clearly.

She smiled. "Good. Too damned good, actually, Sally. I don't trust that I've got positive results."

"Which are?" I said, pleased, but envious.

"Deaf kids of deaf parents have a slightly advanced theory of mind in many cases. They're actually pretty damned good at understanding other people's beliefs, desires and intentions."

"Brilliant," I said. "Why do you suppose that's the case?"

She signed in B.S.L. simultaneously, and then held her body with a crossed arms gesture: "They're covered with the shape of language from birth."

I liked the sound and movement of that.

The covering gesture was also the sign for "love".

I mirrored the sign and gestured towards her.

She laughed, spraying soggy crumbs into the air. Her breath smelt sweet, with a sharp cheesy edge.

I stood, signing awkwardly: "Hungry, food find..."

The sandwich dispensing machine had nothing I liked, and I thought about Mel, glancing across at her. She was busy taking a sip from her coffee mug, dark curls trailing over the back of her tilted neck.

I wondered how I might get on with Dr Pillay, and if he would take me on. Finding another supervisor would not be as easy as choosing a sandwich—and I couldn't seem to do that.

Stepping into the street to clear my head, I waved at Mel, pausing as red and blue police and ambulance sirens shot past. Smoke hung low over the buildings in the distance, as if heralding the aftermath of a bomb blast.

We hadn't heard anything—well, I hadn't, Mel had good reason not to.

It felt like the shadows were closing in on me again, even though a pallid sun was out and the street was brighter and busier than usual.

Some were rushing to find out what had happened, while others carried on shopping.

Me, I hurried back inside.

*

I went to see Dr Brown after I'd said goodbye to Charlie and his dad.

She looked up from the file on her desk and smiled when I walked nervously though the door.

"Hi, Sally, so you've made up your mind, have you?"

"Yes," I said, feeling my stomach whirl. "I think I have."

"Good." She said, "Now this is an interesting research question, isn't it: What prompts local rather than global cognitive processing? What makes someone focus on a detail rather than the overall *gestalt* of a shape or picture?"

"Yes," I said. "But it's not *my* question, Dr Brown. I don't want to change my questions."

She frowned and tilted her head, as if not sure whether she had heard me correctly. "Pardon?"

I knew she would be angry, but I also knew I had to persist. I had been so scared of her, especially when I'd started seeing her; but I wanted to sustain *my* questions, *my* words, whatever they were worth. I did not want to stay small in a world of perceived giants around me.

And I had a legacy I wanted to build and to leave, dream though it may be—of a shared world, where people reached out with warm thoughts instead of guns.

And it was still *my* dream.

"I mean, even if 'Empath' is pulled, I can look at the impact of therapy and teaching mind-reading skills, surely?"

She leaned back in her chair and snorted. "Where's the original contribution in *that*? The real interest is in the potential synergy between therapy and medication. If you only want a Masters degree and not a Doctorate then keep on going. I'm giving you a chance to be in at the ground level of innovative research to help our troops."

Sitting forward I found I could hold her stare, without breaking gaze. She looked at me levelly, with a severity in her frown.

I couldn't believe that she was trying to appeal to my patriotism. Surely, if she'd read *The Hitchhiker's Guide*, she'd also have read the poets of 'The Great War', as I'd heard my great-granddad call them when I was a little girl.

"I'm afraid I can't continue to supervise you unless you change your research questions," she said, hands pressed firmly on an orange desk file. I could read my name upside down—Sally Davies.

The file was closed.

I took a deep breath—a change of supervisor would mean at least an extra year of expense and adjustment. She seemed to sense what I was thinking, from my expression I think, and gestured behind me to the door.

I turned to see a man standing there, pale and blond, brisk and square in his khaki brown uniform.

Shock stiffened my spine.

But he must only be an AA—Army Academic—there was no gun strapped to his hip.

The man tilted his head at me. "Pleased to meet you, Ms Davies." His voice was throaty, but sure. "I'm Dr Butcher, the new Head of Research for the University. All research projects with potential military implications will have to be modified to include some military benefits as well, I'm afraid."

He must have been listening in somehow. He six-foot frame towered over me and I shrunk.

"But my research has no ma-military implication," I stammered, afraid.

He clucked his tongue at me and then smiled, but his green eyes remained cool. "Come, come, Ms Davies, increasing people's capacity to understand others, such as terrorists, only increases people's sensitivity to compromising themselves, and State security. I think we need a serious shift in research direction here."

I stood—just—trembling and with shaky knees.

Although I'm not much over five feet, I needed all of it. "Tell me what happened to my brother, first."

"Eh?" He said, and then his lids closed as if he had realised who I was referring to.

"You've seen my file," I said. "Tell me what happened to Private Peter Davies." I could not believe my voice had stayed clear and strong, despite my legs threatening to crumple.

Dr Butcher's eyes narrowed in a frown, but it was hard to see his brows move, as they were either too pale, or else he had shaven them off.

"Classified military information is not available to a civilian," he said, "and not relevant to the matter at hand."

"Of course it's relevant," I said. "Everything is relevant."

I realised then that my mind was clear, my decision made.

And I did not even feel small as I pushed past Dr Butcher.

"You can't come back!" He shouted down the corridor after me. "And all Empath pills have been urgently recalled. Your research career is over!"

Strange, really, I hadn't even felt it had properly begun.

I wondered where I would go, as I made my way down the research building stairs, pulling my coat in tighter against damp night.

Funny, but the shadows no longer seemed to bother me quite so much.

To the clinic, then—appointments to cancel, children never to be seen again…

Now *that* was a real ache in my stomach.

*

But the waiting room was not empty.

There were two people sitting there with their backs to me—a small boy and a larger woman. I was confused and dismayed—had I forgotten a later appointment?

Then the boy rushed over and hugged me.

It was Jack. Janet Gray had come over and was holding my hand, smiling through tears.

Jack, face twitching, looked up at me. "Aren't you glad to see me?"

"Yes," I said, "Of course, but, uh, did we have an appointment?" I was still nonplussed by the strength—and even more by the reality of his warm hug.

Jack turned to look at his mum, confused I think by my question. She shrugged and clenched my hand tighter. "We just came to say thank you. Jack seems to be getting better."

He looked up at me again, a naughty smile creasing his cheeks. "I can tell when I upset her sometimes, now, and try to think of how to help her. Then I think so hard it makes my face shake."

Could it be, I thought, a physical tic that mirrored the effort of his mind-read, and yet we are so quick to slap on diagnostic labels? And then a new thought struck me.

"Why you so sad, Sally?" Jack cocked his head with the question.

Amazing—a spontaneous emotional inference stimulated by actually watching my face. I blinked at Jack and turned to his mum. "How much medication do you have left, Janet?"

She rummaged in her bag, "Six days worth, I guess, why?"

Six days!

Did that mean they had only six days left of social smiles between them?

"Hey, Sally," called Jack eagerly. "Don't be so sad, you can still catch the seven-fifty-five to Worchester to get home."

I had to laugh then—and I gave him Mel's BSL 'love' sign too.

After all, who *really* knows how much time we have left for anything? Or anyone.

The Paragon of Knowledge

I am the Paragon, Guardian of Truth and Wisdom—part splinted bone and digitised tissue—but all wedded to the pulse of I AM.

I sense Their whispers even now, as I surf through the realignment of data from a primordial copy of the Mabinogion, of which I have fed Them. Swirling mediaeval images of quest and betrayal; the ancient sounds of the Celtic-Welsh voices of Pwyll, Math…and an elusive woman's voice, kept hidden within the shadow storm of sights, sounds and earthy smells.

S/he's happy with my find, I sense, and sends me a shower of flowers—erupting yellow daisies, rare as rain—but still, as always, there is no clear sight of Them.

One clear vision is all I want. *Perfection sustains the will to be.*

"Good, good new stuff," S/he says from within the image storm, "… but go back; someone comes, with a gift."

I rise up in bright, data bubbles from the depths of the Ghost-Ocean, clambering back into my cold skin. My skull is open and raw, screwed and spiked by I AM. 'Disconnect,' I command, holding back the groan as the steel chips pull clear of the hole in the top of my head, clipping my skull seal on.

I re-orientate to the five walls of my corporeal space, high up amongst the clouds of the Shard III Tower of Londonham, an impregnable space indeed. But not, it seems, to…

…An old man in an antiquated wheelchair?

He wheels slowly in—mechanised mind-fed model sure, the archaically laced electrode caplets perch like spiders on his head—and the man is so old, so crippled, he has no right to be alive, yet alone to be in my space. I marvel at the rust on the spokes of his wheels—a bulging bag hangs over his left wheel rim. This old device for transporting broken people creaks and whines with the weight of the frail old man, who sits heavily…with a frown on his face?

FaceRec shows…no one?

I prepare to mentally push the red button, right of centre on my visual interface. Security will be here in no time, given who I am—and

Whom I serve.

But the wizened old man only raises his left arm in a—weak plea? His dull silver wheelchair rocks with his motion.

It is all I can do, to raise my gaze again to his, his...face.

It is crinkled and crumpled like ancient rolled up toilet paper, showing little signs of cosmetic surgery and plentiful signs of massive age. And it moves and twists as he speaks, animated with life that shouldn't by all rights be there, given his countenance. (At the very least he should be under care in an SSC.)

And something else is not quite right either...?

"Thank you, kind Paragon, for giving me a chance to state my case." His voice is husky but surprisingly firm, given the state of his skin.

"How did you get up here?" I ask.

"Uh—alt-abled access."

I titter then; an antiquated slow elevator route near the levitation pods, a remnant of past alt-abled access requirements, before we finally rid the world of disability. Of course it works still, robotics all systematically service spaces within this place—and beyond.

Still, this man is too old and ...decrepit, is that the word—to be a threat, so I sit stiffly down, cloaking the office windows in a secure cloud-shroud. Lights blink on above our heads, flashing down onto the two data pools shimmering in the desk between us, one swirling with organic green, the other buzzing with invisible digi-data.

"Mmmmm," the old man raises his head, as if to sniff the air, "I can almost smell the bandwidth here."

"It's the same for everyone," I say shortly, 'State your case, old man."

He laughs then, doubling over in his chair, his classless blue overall creasing with his mirth. "That's one reason why I'm here," he eventually gasps, as if laughing has made him tired, "It's *not* the same for everyone. Why is that never acknowledged?"

I set the clock ticking in my head. "You have two minutes before I call security."

He rocks back into his chair. "You're one of a hundred and eleven Paragons, protecting and giving to I AM, S/he who Feeds and Reads us all. I want you to feed Them something *new*."

I am somewhat intrigued, as it is indeed part of my job to keep I AM nourished with data—and I have always dreamed of giving Them something so new, so revolutionary, that They would reveal Them-self in full to me. (Debates still rage, both in Ghost-Ocean and Bodied-Space, as to whether They are One—or many.)

"What new thing do you bring me, old man, of what I AM hasn't already seen?"

"This," he says, leaning forward and pinching the skin on his right hand, just above his sleeve. I crane forward for a better view. His skin is shriveled and knotted with grey hair and blue veins, but is...not grey?

It does not make sense. We are *all* grey—even the Paragons.

He moves his hand next to the arm of his wheelchair. "See," he says. "Clock, stop," I mutter.

He looks smug, as if pleased with his possible uniqueness. His skin is indubitably brown.

"How did you manage to avoid the genetic skin recalibrations, all of twenty two point three eight years ago now?" *The Epidermal Act of 2047, designed to eradicate racism.*

He laughs again, but this is a more restrained, shorter chuckle. "I was not wanted; they turned me away, fearing that my...'genetic deformities' would contaminate them—and perhaps even I AM."

Genetic deformities? I fizz the man's face into the digital ether, searching...

"I'm over ninety," he says quickly, "I missed the onset of universal Chipping."

I stand in amazement. He may well indeed be unique. "So you're not even on The Grid?"

He just smiles, as if that is actually good.

It is then that I smell it—a slightly sweet, but yet an astringent and sticky smell—an old smell, the scent of chemical corruption.

Deadly Doug, they eventually called it, after Doug Wainwright Inc., synthesised additives seeded into wheat for the Fourth World over half a century ago, in order to bulk up productivity—but it ended up poisoning and even shifting genetic material, killing hundreds, irrevocably crippling several thousand—always manifest with a persistent malodorous residue that leaks through pores: weeping tissue wedded with ultimately inert, but intransigent, toxins.

All infected had died within five years of infection.

All bar one?

"Just *who* are you?" I stand and drop my question onto him, from my seven feet of height. We are bred both to serve, and to intimidate.

His skin retains some suppleness as he bends backwards to look up at me—motor cortex damage was variable I remember, depending on Doug's mood and the resilience of the diseased organism.

He holds his left hand out, pale palm open. "I'm Frank Atunde," he says, "And I just want to be remembered. Can you please feed Them this?"

There is a small translucent plastic pod nestling in his palm. I pluck it lightly and inspect it—there is a shred of pale brown organic material with a darker reddish-brown stain crusted on it. I poke it suspiciously and then catch sight of a ragged scab on his left forearm. "Your skin?"

"I want to feed I AM a part of myself," he says, "I just want to be remembered."

I hesitate and look up. In the sealed swirling cloud whorls of my office walls, I see the flash of a bird, the stooping dive of a prey-hunter, a raptor, too quick even for me to identify.

S/he always likes flowers—and birds.

"Take it!" commanded the fading screech. Extinct peregrine falcon, maybe?

I pluck the pod from his palm and put it down on the table. In a further fluid movement I am behind him, picking up a digital implant dart from the wall rack.

"Why?" I say, holding it with tremulous revulsion against his saggy, skinny neck. I need to lock Frank Atunde onto The Grid, for his own good. We need to find and fix all the moving points of the world—a few degenerates fight and resist this, from the strips of shrinking Wild-space but, in the end, we will pin them *all* down—and for the good of all. Complete knowledge requires all data to be accessible and we strive for this completeness; it is part of both a human —- *and* a digital, drive.

The old man tenses, his voice suddenly soft and frail, so that I have to lean over the back of his head to hear, "...I have been rejected as risky genetic material. But I want to live on... somehow. I have no one anymore, no one..."

He reverses then, right over my feet and into my groin. I grunt and drop the dart, which clatters under the table. The chair spins around and the old man looks up at me, face blazing: "But you want to stick me down like an exotic insect? Just feed the Ocean-Beast—and let me be remembered."

He has hauled a gun out of the bag draped alongside his wheel and, without hesitation, he pulls the trigger.

My visual array disintegrates, leaving me with just ragged optic nerves.

"A small directional EMP," he says, "Only ten minutes of your local data shredded."

I sit down on the edge of the table, not used to pain. The neuron-regulators feed me nothing—part of my system is in shock, rebooting.

"Why?" I groan; self-control is irrelevant now.

"Why what?" he is suspicious, revving his wheels, but still hesitating.

"You've got full upper body movement, that damage must be remedial now, with cyber neurosurgery."

"At what cost?" He snarls, "And what if I don't want to be fucking fixed?"

And he leaves—fast—through the faltering door—as it sporadically reopens, its programming disrupted. There is no backwards glance.

As for me, I curl up on the floor and wait for my implants to reload, so that they can numb my sore feet and groin. As the pain ebbs, I creep to my feet, picking up the pod of skin off the table, sealing it shut.

What should I do? Should I incinerate it?

"Feed me again," a whisper comes from the corner of the room and I swing round, but nothing—and no one—is there.

"Feed me," Above me now, an owl hoots. "I would eat of him who can survive so much—and for so long."

"You let him in, gun and all, didn't you?" I ask, "Show Yourself first. I have served you faithfully for decades. Show me—even just the briefest glimpse—show me the Real You." I am faint-angered by the implicit disregard for my safety that I AM has shown, as if Their 'gift' was more important than Their servant.

There is a silence, but it is not empty—the clouds have re-gathered around the room—and they are all dark cumulonimbus.

"I will feed you," I say, "But first, we must find the old man."

I AM knew of Atunde's coming; knew of his 'gift' of skin—They are close to God yes, but not omniscient. So how did They know?

I stand and mind-open the scanner screens in the roof, pods and lifts.

There is no remaining data of Frank Atunde's visit, if that is indeed his allocated name.

Then the aerial scanners feed in, drifting data down from the seeded clouds hanging over Londonham.

They lock and follow an old man in a wheelchair, charting a circuitous route somewhere.

We will come for you, Frank Atunde—and we will log you and fix you onto The Grid, so that you will always be accessible, as all should be, to the I AM.

As if hearing my thought, a flower drops from the roof; it is a purple orchid this time—spinning and opening as it wafts and eddies in a digital breeze, settling onto my desk.

A peace offering…perhaps?

"Find him," the air whispers, "and fix him—he is indeed a hole that needs filling…and then, feed Me."

I cannot pick up the flower in my corporeal form, nor do I plug my head in to do so.

There is an old man to find.

A hole in the world needs to be filled.

*

I arrive in a place well away beyond my usual route, Hackney, South East Londonham, expecting a somewhat smooth, gentrified, classless place, as I step out of the SwatKab. *Good, the pavement is clean just like any other, daily scoured with jets of disinfectant that remove the detritus of the night.*

But not the sleeping man rolled up in sodden, stinking cardboard, up against the overhang of the building.

"Relocate him," I tell the first of my three armed Bot-Officers.

Two peel off to come with me, but I signal them back.

Frank Atunde is just an old man, I am more than equipped to deal with him—armoured as I now am, from heel to wrist—and loaded with explosive bullets laced through my fingers.

I step past the old lifts—no levitation pods, code-locked to gene print—and knock on the door of the ground floor flat, with the rata-tat-tat of Knuckled Authority. Frank, it seems, has holed up in a flat in an old tower block that sprouts twenty stories high.

Behind me VARU—the Voluntary Aged Rehousing Unit, represented by a sturdy black uniformed man and woman—have also arrived, waiting with thinly disguised resentment for my call. Mistrust of the Ghost-Ocean runs deep in some humans, ever since I AM surfaced as a conscious Kraken from the electronic deeps. Long gone are the thin—human only—spider webs of disinformation.

I hear the creak of old wheels inside the flat and sniff the bandwidth in the air, troubled.

It is indeed weak, fluctuating almost with the wind, an imperfect net of connectivity.

"Why has this not been addressed?" I ask I AM, but S/he does not answer—perhaps it is too shallow for Them to be able to think or respond here?

Instead, the old man slowly opens the door, wheeling back to let me in, with a defeated slump of his shoulders.

"Do you want some tea, Paragon?" he asks me, "Or would you prefer to smell the bandwidth?"

I laugh, surprised, "You were right Frank, electronic equity is hugely variable indeed. But I am merely a servant of Knowledge, not its recipient—what tea vintages have you?"

There is no choice. He boils me tea that smells and tastes like the earth.

I stalk the small, damp flat with my mug of earth-tea, scanning the two bedrooms, the bathroom and toilet both loaded with assistive mobile bars, for an old man with limited mobility. *How has this old man stayed off the Grid? Most importantly…why?*

"What are you doing here, living on your own?" I ask, smelling also the lack of others, in the weak wafts of floating data that are stirred up by my feet. He stays in the kitchen, as I inspect the bathroom.

His voice wafts through: "This was my family home, but I was sent to the local Sunny Senile Centre five years ago, because my daughter said it was too much for her to look after me."

"You're an escapee," I note, to which he says nothing.

I bend down to lever open a small tile behind the toilet, projecting my voice though the open door: "So where is your daughter now?"

But the old man has wheeled himself in behind me. He is not drinking tea with me; instead, he holds a gun.

I point my right index finger at him, my left hand sweeping into view a small pile of weapons and EMP stunners. *Terrorist cache.*

"There's big back-up outside Frank," I say, "You don't stand a chance."

I stand and stretch, until my armoured skull almost scrapes the ceiling.

The old man drops his EMP gun and weeps.

I offer him the last of my tea.

He looks up at me and blinks.

I smile down at him. "You're not responsible for your daughter's terrorist activities…Frank. But we do have to send you back to your home, you know."

He takes my mug, but does not drink, "To the SSC?" He looks terrified. "But *this* is my home."

I nod and he weeps again, slow, rolling tears that make his crinkled skin partly shine, along the wet tracks down to his chin. "But there's no sun, in those Sunshine centers."

I shrug, "It's a metaphor, I'm sorry—this place is due for regeneration, in any case. I'm afraid I will have to tag you too."

He holds his left arm out, unresisting, "Go ahead—but feeding, tagging, doing…who does anything for you? Who touches *you*?"

"I'm not made for touch," I say.

"Ghost-Shit!" He cocks his head as he looks up at me and I see a keen and empathic sadness, "If that's the case, let *me* touch you."

"What?" I bend forward suspiciously, wondering if he has laced his skin with toxins, but all I smell is the sour tang of a now defunct Deadly Doug, "Why?"

He swigs the last of my tea with his right hand, "I have not touched anyone for a *very* long time. I've missed that. But I think the same goes for you too, although you're blind to it…and, tell me, what is your *real* name?"

"I have no name," I say, "I am just the Paragon of Knowledge."

He smiles weakly, "And you don't even know your own fucking name?"

"Not important," I say, "I am just the conduit, a servant who feeds I AM, as we increasingly map the Grid of all reality, to best serve us all."

"That sounds like a huge task. And I didn't know reality had a grid either—So who feeds *you*?" he asks, putting the mug down in his lap and raising his right hand, fingers poised.

Presumably a rhetorical question—but what have I to lose?

I have been taught never to trust touch, to focus only on the realities within the Ghost-Ocean instead, but a small part of me is curious. So I bend down from my great height and hold out my right arm, shifting the silver synthi-armour up to my elbow, with a twitch of my eyebrows.

My arm skin is hairless, grey and lifeless, from endless glides through the Ocean-Deep.

The old man strokes my forearm gently —- I flinch, there is an electric jolt through my body. I have had brushed contact with many humans before, but it has been a long time since I have been caressed with such ...care and concern? My arm tingles, with both pain and an excitement, which set my legs quivering.

The old man watches me as I weep. I do not know why—or where— *my* tears have come from.

"Do take care of yourself, nameless man-woman," is all he says, "And remember knowledge gets shaped by who you are—and where you've chosen—or been *allowed*—to go."

"Thank you, Frank. I am so sorry, but I ...must...call AVRU in," I say. *What goals have these tears of mine? I am asexual and not programmed to touch—only to serve, so why do I cry?* "And....I'm also sorry, but I still have to tag you."

The old man nods and holds his other arm out, "We're all of us fucked up, just remember that—but you do know that already, don't you?"

Yet another rhetorical question—I tag him with a brief shot into his right arm; the neck is a painful place indeed and I have no wish to hurt this old man any more than I sense he has already been hurt, throughout his long life.

"What brought you to my office?" I ask, "What triggered your wish to be remembered, to donate your skin to the I AM?"

"A little bird told me," he says, looking up at the ceiling, but there is nothing there.

Of course it did.

"Please let me go outside on my own," he says, "Give me *that* dignity, at least."

I nod, "Surely...Frank."

The man reverses and fetches a packed bag on his bed. I have already scanned that, it is full of threadbare clothes, deodorant, toiletries and a tough SSC uniform, labeled 'Jack Jones.'

I salute him, as he wheels though the door.

He stops, hesitates, and then palms me a beacon-pod, without a word. The door closes behind him.

I call in the Bot-Officers to secure the arms cache—and to scan the place more systematically—for signs of where the daughter of Jack Jones—or Frank Atunde—might have gone.

I glance at the beacon-pod in my palm and place it in my hip-lock, to be inspected more carefully later.

I step outside to find the AVRU unit waiting, empty-handed.

"Where is the old wheel-chaired man who came out here?" I bark.

The AVRU burly man and woman shrug in confusion. "We've seen no one, Paragon," the woman replies.

I sense wrongness and trace Frank's tag.

It is twenty stories high. *He took the lift.*

The tag starts to fall.

Fast.

And faster still.

I run.

And run.

And run…

*

I am struggling to breathe, at the stark southern edge of LondonHam, on that strip of Wild-space between City and Sea. I cannot run anymore—and there are multiple warning signs here of Dangers Ahead, although nothing is specified.   I bend and pant air slowly back into my lungs, fifty plus miles is a long run indeed, but at least I do not have to see the broken and dead body of…Frank Atunde. *What lies in a chosen name, nameless One?*

Yes, a long run, and with each and every step I see Frank's face—and I know that fixing all points on the Grid does not just add data, but it can also *kill.*

It has taken me six hours; the cooling sun is low over the tree-line swinging south-west. Fourteen 'Dozer hulks sit here too, broken, but still eagerly poised to spread concrete and bandwidth, their orange metallic bulks beached and blackened. I smell the stale hot tar residue of fritz bombs, designed to minimise human tissue damage, hurled by those who have taken refuge behind Dangers Ahead signs and the woodlands.

The Ferals.

I AM is gathering support from the House of Bankers and Lords, to burn this ancient and still legally protected place, the last Wilderness left on this crowded island of nation states, here in Angle-land.

I walk towards the woods.

"Where are you going?" A starling sits on the steering wheel of 'Dozer728, cocking its head as it speaks. The image fizzes as I turn and approach, a ghostie bird indeed.

"Into the Wild," I say, systematically switching off my beacons and turning again towards the screen of first trees—ancient ash, mixed with yew and several stolid backbone oaks…

"But why?"

"To gain more knowledge, of places I have never seen."

"It is Forbidden. Your reason to be is ME."

I laugh. "I am nothing more than your mouth for accessing knowledge. Yet I myself have realised, how *little* I actually know."

Wait, I can offer you something…Sidhe."

I stop.

The word-name filters down from my distant past—all forty years plus now, an echo from my PTCs, my Post-Tube Carers, whose own names I no longer remember.

My…name? I am the Paragon of Knowledge. Why was I named after ancient mythic Irish mound-walkers? And what can I AM offer me, that is worth a continued allegiance?

"Have you tired of streaming Knowledge? If you could be any, which Paragon would you *choose* to be?"

Are They offering me free choice from the other one hundred and ten? I hesitate; I have always envied Beauty—and even Attraction, although Love would make a much better epithet.

The bird is bright: "We push even now for a 112th Paragon, through the House of Plebs."

Does this mean absolutely free choice? My mind races with possibilities.

The bird misses nothing, "*That* new Paragon brief is already given."

"And-?" I query.

"The Paragon of Profit."

I almost choke on fresh air. "I *had* been thinking, the Paragon of Freedom."

"Why?" The bird looks mangy, feathers dropping off in the minimal bandwidth, "That's not a priority focus—and we are *all* free anyway."

I turn and walk. The yew tree is beautiful indeed, reddish-brown bark, needled leaves and centuries gone by, the backbone of the English longbow.

"Wait—what are you doing?" pipes the bird.

"Exercising my freedom," I say, stepping past the tree and into the woods. I walk deeper into the mass of trees and ragged bush vegetation with entwined thick succulents, encouraged here by the drying of the island.

Here, the bandwidth fizzes and fades.

For the first time ever, I feel truly alone.

I have heard the terrorists, the… Resistance, the Ferals, plant the trees with Dampers, to prevent electronic surveillance from I AM.

I find an old oak, gnarled, bent, perhaps dying—and plant my long spine against it, sidling and sliding my haunches and backside down onto the spiky grass beneath.

I hear the chatter of birds that stay constant, embodied and real.

I press the Beacon-Pod that Frank Atunde gave me—and wait.

"What do you do, Paragon?" A woman speaks, with the voice of that elusive woman from the Mabinogion, through a gap in the trees ahead. S/he is stunning, vivacious, dark-haired and bright, wired with strength and life, trailing a flowing trouser-dress of flowers in rainbow colours.

She, too, wears the brown skin of Frank Atunde.

A vision of perfection.

"Come," She gestures me towards her, "Come home Paragon—and I will show you pleasures, beyond everything you have ever known."

Finally—it is a clear view of Perfection and I cannot resist, I stand stiffly, pushing myself upwards against the oak, my armoured back grinding noisily against tree-bark, although I feel little.

I blink with both pleasure and pain at this Vision, readying myself to step forward, but...

Perfection...disappoints? It flickers and fades, so that even her smile becomes a snarl, with the faintest of bandwidth breezes.

"Come Paragon," the woman pleads, "It is Me, I AM…"

Do I stay —- or do I join I AM, in a more complete way, perhaps, than I have ever done before? Surely this is what my life has been leading to, all along?

I reach inside my breastplate and feel the skin pod of Frank Atunde.

Yes. We are all fucked up —- or dead.

And I still feel the delicate stroke of Frank on my arm, his crinkled fingertips brushing lightly, so that I fill my lungs, to blow hard at this perfect vision in front of me.

"Give me the skin of Atunde!" She roars, and I see now I AM is all teeth—the flowers on her trousers have sprouted fangs.

The wind blows alongside me and fragments her —- She flies apart, blasted into a dizzying spiral of broken blossoms—broom, meadowsweet and oak, amongst countless others. The bright petals spiral on the breeze, dancing around me —- and then fade and vanish.

Perfection is a fragile and fickle thing.

A voice calls from the clouds: "One day, I will be made flesh too; beware *that* day, for you are a Paragon No More…"

Rain falls.

The trees sway with wind whipping in rain-clouds from the sea. It is cold and the light is dying; the rare autumnal shower wets me through and through.

A woman steps into the clearing. She is combat-fatigued and dreadlocked grey, with lines of aged strength etched on her skin.

"Who are you?" She asks, raising a stun-gun, a Damper in her other hand: "You look like a servant of the Ocean-Beast."

I move slowly, so as not to precipitate an attack, taking out the skin-pod and Beacon.

"Your father gave me this," I say, holding up the Beacon-Pod in my left hand.

"Dad? I *knew* it was his Beacon. So where is he? What have you done with him?"

Slowly, I lift up the Skin-pod in my right hand, palm open, facing upwards.

She startles and lowers her gun, sobbing quietly, desperately, for the better part of a minute.

Then she raises her gun again: "Friend —- or foe?"

This decision will chart the rest of my life, so I hesitate, almost too terrified to speak.

I feel the infinitesimal weight of Frank's skin-segment in my right palm.

"Friend," I say, lowering my hands, disarming my fingers.

"Jennifer Jones," she says, stepping forward to take the Skin-pod from my right hand. "We've never had a Paragon desert to us before. Why?"

"He who would lead must become a bridge," I say, "I can give you a route in, between the Ghost-Ocean and The Wild; for without access to the Ghostie-Deep, there can be no lasting movement against the I AM."

"That's a how," she says, holstering her gun, "Not a why."

"Your father would be proud of you," I say, "We're all of us fucked up, aren't we Jennifer Jones—all of us?"

She smiles through her tears: "You say it *just* like dad. He stayed in his chair because he said the wheels had actually become a part of him. They reminded him of the ultimate underlying brokenness of everything—and every one. Yes, Paragon, we are all fucked-up."

"Surely," I say, "...even perfection itself too, is hollow."

For, in the end, *none* of us are Gods.

As for me, as I am led, hood over my head, into the heart of the Wild-space—trust takes time she tells me—and I, too, have become a hole in the world.

But I will *not* be filled—so, as we walk, I speak to the darkness. "I am the Paragon, Guardian of Truth and Wisdom—part splinted bone and digitised tissue—and yet, the only thing that I *really* know, is the importance of freedom —- and the gentle touch of a kind hand."

And, with those words, I weep again.

For touch it is, that sustains the will to be.

Jennifer Jones takes my elbow as well as my hand and clasps the last of her father in between our linked palms. The pod is hard, but her skin is warm and I sense she perhaps weeps too, although she says nothing.

I smell damp earth and leaves; an owl hoots without disguise—all is random here—apart from the constant, guiding palm, from this daughter of a remarkable man.

We walk the wild, of which I know nothing.

Case Notes of a Witchdoctor

He'd reached the age where he'd seen it all—liars, psychopaths, the neurotic... and the *completely* insane. Psychosis it was, though, that still just about held his interest.

Like the young black man in front of him, sitting and grimacing, but trying hard not to tilt his head. He has some insight, then, not wanting to reveal a listening attitude in the silence of the sickly yellow room.

Not *enough* insight, though.

Mark spoke, to put the young man out of his misery.

"I'm afraid you're going to have to stay in for the weekend, Kolile." (Try as he would, he'd never been able to make the correct click on the X in Xolile's name.)

This time he could see he had the patient's full attention. "Please, *asseblief* doctor, I need to go home this weekend."

Mark played with the orange government biro on the open folder between them, feeling a little bored, a little helpless. There was a limit to what he could do—*and* it was Friday afternoon, with rush-hour traffic no doubt building early along De Waal drive.

He took the pen and wrote with finality in the psychiatric notes—Provisional Diagnosis: Psychosis. Keep in for further observation.

He looked up. Xolile was sitting rigid, staring behind him.

Despite himself, Mark turned, to see the thick door and blank wall. He dropped his hand away from the panic button underneath his desk.

"What do you see, Kolile?" he smiled reassuringly and with certainty, keen to wrap up the consultation quickly now.

The young man looked him squarely in the eyes, as if oblivious to customary respectful gaze avoidance for his elders.

"An old white man," he said. "I think he may be your father."

Mark laughed then, loudly. His father had been dead three years.

He stood up: "You'll feel better after a weekend in, on your medication. The staff are very good here."

The young man stood up and held his gaze, until tears leaked from his eyes and he looked down.

"Please," he said, "my mother needs me. I am sick, yes, but I think it is because the ancestors call me."

Mark hesitated; he'd been reminded of caring for his own mother, for a good many months after dad's death.

"*Why* do they call you?" he asked, cursing himself for delaying on what was surely a certain decision, but looking for a hidden delusionary system.

"To become a healer too, like you," Xolile said, his voice muffled in the blue overalls, head bowed. Mark realised abruptly that the young man's head was bowed to hide his tears.

"We shall see," he said, opening the door. Staff Nurse Dumisane, who'd been waiting outside in respect for psychological confidentiality, came in and ushered the young man out.

Mark nodded goodbye and closed the door.

Friday at last, Friday, fucking Friday. The surf must be pumping at *Kommetjie* by now. Time to wash the working week off him in that frenzied cold water.

He closed the file on his desk; Xolile Ngubane. Shut.

He'd seen so many tears, so much *snot en trane*, this was no different.

But Xolile's presence didn't seem to have fully left the room. Mark could almost smell the lingering pain of his tears, the sourness of his body odour, his leaking desperation.

Still, he *had* seen it all. He picked up the file to leave the room.

"Where are you going, son?"

Mark dropped the file, having half-opened the door with his right hand. He peered back into the room, scanning the walls, the psychometric test cupboard, the desk, underneath the desk...

He stopped himself. Stupid, stupid, he really just needed a rest; it had been a hell of a week.

No one to go home to, though. Sharon had left eight months ago, and he'd left Jo'burg over a year ago now, to get away from a needy mother. There had been lots of leavings, with so few greetings anymore.

He picked up the file and sighed. At least the sea didn't judge him. Muizenberg soon with a boogie board maybe, for, actually, he felt like a warmer and gentler swim. So, home first, pick up the board and head waves-side, before the beach bursts with *manne* jostling for board-space.

He stopped himself from announcing his plans to the air and cursed as he saw the black smear on his fingers. The cheap plastic biros tended to leak like an old man with a dodgy prostate. (At least he could still piss a few bubbles into the pot.) Throwing the pen into the bin, he wiped his fingers with some desk-tissues; it's okay, man, just so long as he'd kept the file clean.

He hesitated; the wall was dripping sound. Leaning his right ear against the bricks' clammy, slippery surface, he listened.

Father?

A quavering voice, soft but through cold stones, old stones—a leper asylum before it became a mad-house, so he'd heard.

A dim and distant voice, which was just repeating his name, over and over again.

So many voices lost here.

But this one *knew* him.

He had no answer. It was time to go.

Softly, he closed the door behind him and headed for the nurse's station, along the banana-coloured hospital corridor. He nodded at a puffed up psychiatrist passing him; Jesus, that guy needed to learn to treat his patients more respectfully.

He took a right turn into the nurse's station and the adjoining patient lounge, which was empty, as they were all out for their early supper. Behind the glassed sealed area Sister Mbolo and Staff Nurse Dumisane were standing, collecting night meds from cabinets, eyes flickering up to patient charts on the walls.

Mark stepped into the station quietly; file ready to be deposited alphabetically into the cabinet. He'd update online records next week.

He needed a swim badly.

Dumisane glanced at him, sieving a few tablets into a metal bowl. "Xolile to stay in then?" he asked, clicking extravagantly, to Mark's ears. (He's Zulu after all; Xhosa clicks come easy to him.)

"Ye —"

The old man caught his eye, lounging just across the room. He didn't recognise him, but he knew it wasn't—it *couldn't* be—his father. But dad had lain a bit like that, in the days following his stroke, limp and helpless and dumb.

Three weeks of silent helpless lying, before dying quietly, in the middle of the night, when no one was around.

But he'd done his grieving, processed his feelings, put it all behind him. He'd known what to do, after all. (Spilling himself verbally and with tears; off-loading to Sharon, while trying to hold mom together at the same time.)

Three months after tossing the last bit of dirt on his dad's grave with his own hands, Mark had realised he'd put it all behind him. (Well within the stipulated normal grief time parameters: he'd been proud of that, until Sharon had punctured it by leaving without explanation.)

The old man in the lounge bent over and pulled a page from one of the ward Bibles. It looked like he was going to roll a cigarette with it. Despite himself, Mark smiled—certainly *not* dad, then.

"Dr. Bezuidenhout?" Dumisane was standing up straight, peering at him with obvious bewilderment.

"Um," he said, "Kolile can go home for the weekend, but will need to be visited tomorrow by the community team, to get collateral information from his mother."

"The community team is off this weekend—I can go, I'm on duty and Sister and the others can cover me," Dumisane smiled.

"Really?" The sister glowered at him and then laughed. "So he's safe to go out?"

Mark paused, looking at the Sister, short and smiling, but knowing she was also pure steel underneath.

"He thinks his ancestors are calling him."

"Oh," she rolled her eyes. "Another *ukuthwasa* then. Bloody government's to blame I tell you. They still haven't created enough *real* jobs."

He chuckled to himself as he picked up a pen. It was fine for her to say that!

He hesitated and then, for the first time in a long time, Mark changed his file notes using stale, scratchy white correction fluid, countersigning the change as the traffic grew rapidly louder along the road outside *Valkenberg* hospital.

He smelt burning and looked up in alarm. The old black man was smoking the Bible.

*

Mark woke with the sense of someone watching him.

Without even opening his eyes, he knew who it was.

"Hi, dad." On opening his eyes, he was unsurprised to find his room empty. His dad had been dead three years, after all.

Mark rolled over, groaning, stiff from a late evening's bodysurf at *Muizenberg*. As it had for many months now, the bed felt too big for him.

It was a bright and sunny master bedroom, looking out on a small but neat *Rondebosch* garden, orange bougainvillea framing razor wire and a hyperactive alarm. It was all somewhat on the dull side in long Cape winters, though. As for the children's bedroom—well, *that* never happened, did it?

He walked stiffly through to the bathroom and splashed his face with clear and cold water.

Water *always* does the trick.

A pale and wrinkled face stared blankly back at him, gray hair hung lankly down alongside his cheeks. Shocked, he took several paces backed, slipped and banged his head against the towel railing. No stars, just a burning red blur in front of his eyes.

And an expressionless dead face.

It was his father's face, not his.

Mark reeled backwards, averting his eyes.

God, it was as if dad had died without feeling, without thoughts, a pale husk of a once strong and fierce—but funny—man. It was early morning when we'd last seen him, but for moments he'd failed to recognise it *was* him, so shrunken and waxen he was.

So *dead*.

Mark sat on the bathroom mat, its crinkly blue plastic fur tickling his naked thighs—but he couldn't give a shit about that, quietly crying until thoughts came again.

Including one terrifying and growing thought.

He resisted it at first, hiding it away behind deliberate thoughts of beach or shopping, moving in safe and familiar spaces.

But there was no hiding from it—it kept popping back into his head.

He sighed. He knew he had a phone-call to make. He knew he had somewhere to go.

Somewhere hard.

Mark stood up and faced the mirror. His own tired face looked out at him. He washed his face, shaved and dressed carefully and respectfully in white collared shirt and grey slacks. The house was too quiet, too empty—and the face in the mirror looked even emptier still, although he was just relieved it was his face.

Pulling his mobile from his trouser pocket, he speed-dialed the ward.

"Staff Nurse Dumisane? Doctor Bezuidenhout here. I think I should come with you to visit that patient this morning. Ja, I'm ready—half an hour, hey. See you outside my house, you've got my address, *ja nee?*"

The street was quiet, still early on a Saturday morning in a cul de sac set back from the Main Road. The trees were in full bloom but starting to sway from the gathering South-Easter.

Mark jingled some coins in his pocket, deciding to text his sister in Jo'burg as a distraction.

He was going someplace he'd never been before; a place he'd always managed to avoid.

A township.

A *black* township.

The white Government Garage car arrived, an old Fiat, Staff Nurse Dumisane waving cheerfully from the rolled down driver's window,

Mark got in, feeling even more anxious.

As they pulled off and headed down past *Rondebosch* station and across the wasteland of the Common, he felt his pulse start to race.

"So," he said, "where are we going, again?"

Dumisane glanced at him sideways and then focused on the road, swerving to avoid a taxi pulling out suddenly.

"Gugs, been there before, Doctor?"

Ah, *Gugulethu*, not the worst thankfully, but no doubt bad enough, with very few—if any—white *mense* there.

Mark shook his head coolly. "No, can't say I have, Dumisane—any tips?"

The staff nurse gave a big laugh as he swung past a bus and the streets started to fill up, heading steadily away from the Mountain. "Stick close to me, doctor, and you'll be fine."

Houses had given way to wide and dingy council flats surrounding dirt yards, bright washing swinging from lines hanging out of windows or in courtyards.

The men on the street looked rougher and tougher and downright dangerous.

Dumisane pulled to a halt alongside a small brick terraced house, brightly painted in blue, with a small but neat path.

Mark raised his eyebrows discreetly. He'd expected more overt poverty, more visible desperation.

"We don't all live in corrugated iron shacks, you know," Dumisane said shortly, getting out of the car.

Mark felt a pang of shame; Dumisane was a damn good nurse and obviously a sharp reader of people. He still couldn't stop himself looking carefully around, before opening the door and stepping outside to join Dumisane.

The staff nurse was already by the door, chatting in swift isiXhosa with a smiling middle-aged woman in a neat red dress and headscarf. He beckoned Mark over.

"This is Xolile's psychologist," he said. "Doctor Bezuidenout, this is Mrs. Ngubane."

The woman gave a little nod as she took his hand with both of hers. "Please come in,' she said. "Would you like some tea?"

Mark smiled, wondering if the English resonance was intended for him. She led the way inside, into a small but neat kitchen with dining area. Mark noted the door through to the other rooms—or room—was firmly closed.

Mrs. Ngubane lit a gas cooker underneath a battered but ready silver kettle. She turned to Mark: "Five Roses or *rooibos*, Doctor?"

"Uh, *rooibos* please, Mrs. Ngubane."

Dumisane was obviously a Five Roses man. She gestured them both to sit on stools arranged tightly around a small wooden table.

Mark turned as the door creaked behind him.

Xolile stood, the room behind him darkened, but he looked cheerful and neatly dressed.

"Hello, doctor, staff nurse," he said breezily, stepping inside and closing the door behind him. He leaned back against the door and folded his arms.

Mark sat and drank his hot tea, looking at family pictures arrayed on the wall, while the conversation drifted awkwardly around Xolile's interrupted studies. He'd been a physiotherapy student at UWC before he'd been picked up by a police patrol, wandering and confused, in the dunes near *Monwabisi*.

Mrs. Ngubane looked cross, reminiscing on the events, "You sure it's not *dagga*, my boy?"

"No, mamma!" he said. His arms dangled by his sides, as she had already reprimanded him for the rudeness of folded arms, following up with a warning against hands in pockets.

There was a man in some of the photos, but only in those with a younger pre-adolescent Xolile.

Mark signaled to Dumisane. Dumisane would be able to get much better information from the mother if both were unburdened from the demands of English.

Mark put his empty mug down and stood up. "Is there a space we can talk in private, Kolile?" (Always, he struggled with the correct pronunciation.)

The young man stood up squarely, a good few inches taller than Mark. "Sure, doctor, the street."

"The street?" Mark heard his voice almost crack with a sudden surge of panic. "Why the street?"

"A bedroom is too private," he said. "The street is better."

Mark wondered whether Xolile had guessed he was anxious there—and even more so at the thought of walking and talking in a township street. He seemed brighter and more lucid today—perhaps indeed it was a reactive psychosis—just maybe drug induced?

He followed the young man through the doorway, down the path and onto the pavement. A few men and women stalked past, turning to stare briefly at him.

Xolile smiled. "You'll be fine," he said. "Everyone knows me."

So, for some minutes, they walked and talked, Mark probing about his past and recent present, looking for cues and clues as to the onset of his confusional state. His father had left suddenly when he was ten; they had no idea where or why. Prior to his admission, all he could remember was a gathering glow inside and his dead grandmother whispering in his ears, telling him he needed to become an *isangoma*, to heal his people.

Mark stopped. Xolile had turned into a main street, littered with *spaza* shops and large shipping containers filled with people doing business. There was a particularly appealing cell-phone company obviously doing great business inside a grey metal container jutting some way into the road, people spilling out into the road and pavement, taxis hooting past. Mark was relieved to notice that few seemed to look at him anymore.

Xolile gestured him onwards. Mark hesitated. He wanted to ask Xolile something for his *own* benefit, rather than Xolile's. Ethically, such role reversals were generally frowned upon. There was something slightly freeing about being on strange streets, however, so he took a deep breath.

"My father," he said, "is gone like yours, but dead. You saw him at the hospital and I've seen him since. What must I do?"

Xolile stopped. Mark noted he sighed slightly before speaking. "I saw an old man, who I guessed *might* be your father. Beyond that, I cannot help you at all, doctor."

"But don't your beliefs involve contacting the ancestors?"

Xolile looked straight at him and Mark could see amusement and something else etched on his face.

"My beliefs, not yours, doctor. Even then, I'm not sure of them myself. Look!" He turned to gesture at a shop behind them.

The shop had an open hanging canopy, dangling with jars filled with... strange looking shapes in syrup or brownish liquid, organs perhaps—or animal parts?

"Would you consult here? Would you take those things if prescribed, to help you contact your father?"

Mark spotted a placard outside. It was a doctor's surgery, but not one that he recognised.

It looked as though Xolile had only just started. "Would you sacrifice a chicken—or a goat? Doctor, there are no shortcuts; you cannot pick and choose our beliefs, like a vulture that is fussy for only the best meat. You must swallow all the bones too."

The young man looked down, as if suddenly ashamed of his outburst.

Mark looked down too, embarrassed at asking, wishing he could retract his thoughts and words.

There was a muffled ringing noise. Xolile fumbled a cell-phone out of his pocket. "*Nomfundo!*" he shouted, turning away and breaking into rapid isiXhosa.

Ah, a girl!

Mark looked up as his father walked past.

For frozen seconds, he watched the stooped and familiar gait down the busy street, dad's slight right-sided shuffle after an earlier warning from a left-sided stroke.

Then he ran, until he was alongside and in front of him.

It was an old man indeed, but with a craggy black face and silver pepper-corned hair, neatly dressed, as if off to a Saturday Church. The man looked at him uncertainly. "Police?" he asked, "or tourist?"

Mark raised both hands, ducking his head in apology as well.

He made his way back to Xolile slowly. He was still busy on his phone, talking excitedly and looking at the ground.

Mark looked around to track the smell of burning meat. A man and a woman were *braaing* a sheep's head over a hollowed metal barrel. A few other people were gathering round, bringing drinks, perhaps from a local *shebeen*.

He felt exposed, isolated.

Xolile finished his call. "Sorry, doctor."

Mark held his hand up. "Never mind," he said. "I don't suppose you saw me running after anyone just now?"

Xolile gave him a puzzled look.

Mark gave a wry smile. "No matter, perhaps it was all in my head."

Xolile shook his head firmly. "No wonder you *umlungu* have such big heads," he said. "You try and fit everything into it."

Despite himself, Mark laughed. As he laughed, it suddenly dawned on him that just maybe he would never stop missing his father.

He no longer felt so certain of anything and everything, either.

They turned to watch people gather for food. "You fancy some, doctor?"

Mark laughed again: "Just a little taste."

It was nice to be invited.

There were indeed new things to see—and *new* things to do.

Dream-Hunter

Dream-Hunter.

That is, indeed, what they call me.

And what is it I search for?

The heart of evil and truth —- and, just sometimes, a little bit of madness and lies.

Today, though, I might get the entire shitload.

I choke back unexpected dread as I prepare for immersion in my pod, the Doc wiring my scalp to the monstrous man lying comatose beside me. Out of the corner of my right eye I can sense his slumbering bulk, rising and falling with a slow and menacing snore.

Sledgehammer Jones.

No, Sledgehammer *fucking* Jones.

I wince as the Doc pulls on the scalp electrodes, stinging my right parietal area.

She gives me a slap on my exposed arm, "Stop being a baby."

Like *she's* the one going into the head of a brutal killer.

Straining against the head strap, I lift my head a few inches and turn to the right. Jones is a mountain of a man swelling under those blue sheets, a pale white egg-domed head laced with cables feeding the machine between us. A big man indeed, and with a temper to match, I'd heard.

Not that I've always been on the side of the angels myself. But then, my father had always taught me to be assertive, modelling it forcefully to me whenever he suspected I had lied to them.

Until mamma would step in, a protective pillow against his punches.

I lean back again, to avoid my eyes spilling.

Mother...!

Focus on the job ahead.

We go back a few years, Doc Lizzie Abasi and I—27 missions in all—and I have a 96% hit rate—the best fucking Rider in the world.

Bar none.

But you probably know that, I'm all over the Wiki pages.

Dream Hunter *One*, they call me.

It's almost countdown time now, I can smell the acidic, cabbage-like stink of the REM-inducing drip the doc is preparing and suck in my breath, readying to both fall and soar into Dream-Space.

"Hey Doc," I call, "Give me some decent music to work to this time, none of your funny Irish shit."

Doc smiles over me, the purple bag of Stim swishing in her gloved hands: "I'm not Irish, remember—and you put up with what *I* choose to play, Peter John Scott." Always, she uses my full name—and yes I know, she's Peckham born and bred, third generation ex-Nigeria, so where does the yen for Irish music come from?

Fuck it, who knows where *anything* comes from, especially our nocturnal dreams seaming our lives with images that seldom cohere? And faces. Old women, vaguely recognizable, wrinkled, and dark— darker hued than me, dual heritage man that I am. Always staring at me, willing something from me.

Tip of my brain stuff, never quite named.

Focus, Scott, forget the phantom crones.

I groan, "So what's it to be this time, Lizzie?"

She's busy with the Loom™—the machine that locks brains together, the drip already hanging between Sledgehammer Jones and me. This is always the point where my shivering increases and words start to freeze in my mouth.

My fifteenth year at this game and it only gets harder.

I hear the large man alongside me catch his breath, as if not fully asleep.

Dread deepens.

"'Let's Remember 1848', by The Literal Leprechauns," Lizzie says, moving onto my least favourite part, the needle in the arm. Her brightly beaded cornrows tickle my right cheek.

"Wh-Why?" I ask, looking up at her face instead, forcing words out, unable to hide their quiver, "That's a f-f-fucking long time ago."

Lizzie half-smiles—as if she doesn't notice—and signals to me with a drop of her right palm; I'm going under soon. She tilts her head, squinting at me over her smart-specs with those brown eyes of hers. It's as if there are still things she likes to look at directly, without hearing the verbal comments that attach like buzzing flies to her smart goggle visuals.

Or perhaps she just doesn't like to hear what the Face-Rec sites continually say about me.

I'm not *really* that arrogant: I really do have me some damn fine parietal lobes. Perhaps I have my dead English dad to thank for my skills; I was raised on tales of his lucid breakfast dreams, but my Zulu mamma's daily putu-pap and peanut butter toast always satisfied my stomach.

So it was that I learned to straddle both God and Nkulunkulu: science and myth, dream and reality.

I have not seen my mum since my divorce, more than ten years ago now.

She'd gotten on well with Shireen, my ex-wife.

Perhaps too well?

Mamma told me I'd turned into 'him' and then left me, going back to the other family I hardly knew in South Africa.

'Him'—my father with fists. Surely not, mother?

Surely, surely not?

"We need to know our past, in order to understand where we are going," Lizzie says slowly.

"But *neither* of us are fucking Irish," I say, the quiver in my voice gone, as my hurt and fear fades into the groggy, initial rush of the Stim.

Sledgehammer Jones is waiting, so I hold back from the pull of the dream, thinking thickly, focusing my gaze into the pulsating light overhead.

I have my plan ready, but know that means little sometimes, given the inherent surrealism of the domain. *They* never give me an easy ride either—I've had some mega-whacked out dream partners over the years. Those who refuse to talk—or who deny their crimes—have seriously fucked up dreams.

I get the choice picks, the hardest of the hard. As befits the best of the best, I guess.

My head sinks back and I watch the screen above the far wall struggling to make visual sense of Jones's Imago-EEG, a cloudy and murky grey, he's still some way short of REM state.

Time to let go. I slip into the barely charted space between waking and dreams and hover in hypnagogic flux, pulsing a Door to be walked through—but…

What—the—fuck?

The screen flickers, fuzzes and sharpens. A man stands: slim and sharply-suited in grey, a svelte version of the nude man lying on the medical trolley next to me. This thinner, virtual Sledgehammer Jones is ignoring the glowing green door behind him—avoiding my usually unfailing initial lure.

Instead, he seems to be peering out at me—and, and he, he's fucking *waving*?

"What's, uh,—what's his status?" I ask, my voice fading distant, crashing. My vocal cords constrict as I start to slowly sink.

I can still sense Sledgehammer's body alongside me—seemingly sedated by a drip infusion.

"Dream status reached," Lizzie says, a vague shape now, floating between us. "He's deep in REM sleep."

How—the—fuck—is this—possible? I'm one of only a small batch of people in the world who have learned how to tread and weave the borders of dream and waking. We're starting to knit together at the brainwave level, and it's me who's supposed to be holding the fucking threads—yet, somehow, this bastard is waving at me while dreaming, grinning like a skinny snake.

The pull into sleep is an intolerable tug at my being, but I focus on pushing my frontal lobes for just that little bit longer.

Is this just a hypnagogic hallucination?

"Up his sedation," I grind out slowly; REM sleep locks the body muscles, to stop you doing daft things while you dream, like killing someone.

I see Lizzie's shape swing towards the screen—and freeze.

Forever.

And for no time at all.

She spins around again and hovers over him; I'm guessing she's opening his Stim drip even wider.

On the screen, Jones has turned and opened my green door, blowing it red with a breath.

Red.

The Sledgehammer's favourite colour.

He steps through.

As for me, I lose my grip to the torrent of sleep.

I am disembodied, a vague flash of fish in a raging unconscious river. Then I am there; gasping, wet and shivering, in a muted and pale cream bathroom. I have all the props ready, waiting—a bathroom, a bath, and several…implements.

The man himself is not yet here. I have time to strengthen this dream, to sculpt the images from many visits and forensic holograms—I sense Jones looping along my corridor just outside.

I twitch and tweak his synapses with fused will. There's a part of the hippocampus where the memories beneath the dreams can be unlocked—with the right training and expertise.

He will enter soon, filling the bath with someone he knows and re-enact a scene from his unconscious that he has—until now—always consciously denied.

(Flowers and broken glass make a green rabbit jump.)

I breathe slowly to clear the crazy images and re-orient myself, even though I have no need to breathe. Then, with familiar dexterity, I climb the wall like Spiderman, sticking myself to the ceiling and making myself invisible.

The scene below starts to shiver and splinter into a myriad of dream fragments, a confused chaotic collage, disorienting me for eternal moments.

I forget…no, I …remember, I am Peter, Peter Scott, Rider. This is my dream. *Reassert command; take control…* With practiced ease, I re-clarify the bathroom walls, with matte beige paint and maroon horizontal stripes at chest height, as per forensic record.

Jones must be coming—and he is powerful. But he seems scattered and shattered in his dreaming thoughts. I only hope he is now fully immersed in my dream.

Distantly, I hear bathwater tinkling and I buzz myself back into being, hanging from a burning hot bulb on the ceiling, invisible spider-like legs scalding. Sledgehammer Jones must be disturbing the strands of this scene.

Steam and coconut scented bath salts saturate my nose from the water below; my eyes water with the sharp tang surging through my sinuses. Spiders don't have sinuses, do they?

Focus, Scott. Stay alert—and watch out for the bursting of any irrational anomalies from Jones's unconscious.

The dream steadies, seaming itself thicker, lacing itself with the richest of sensorial detail—and I sense Jones's excitement as his dream throbs ahead of him, moving into the bathroom like a palpable, gloating force, ready to shake and shape events.

Here we fucking go, then. I ready myself too.

It is then that I see her. She is in the bath. Thickened and greying slightly with the approach of late middle years, she is bending forward, water dripping off her back as she scrubs her toenails with deft concentration.

Jones himself enters, and I am relieved to see he is in a red bathrobe that reveals his real, blossoming bulk—no longer able, then, to conjure a lucid and ideal dream-self; he is finally absorbed into the fabric of our mutual dreaming. She—his wife, Alice—hesitates and half turns to Jones.

"I've almost finished," she says, covering her breasts with her arms.

"So am I," Jones says, smiling.

Slowly, she looks up, and her sadness wafts up to me. A drop of water spools off her left cheek. I wonder, for the briefest of moments, if it is salty.

"Why, Alice?" Jones asks, standing squarely, stolid in his growing anger.

She seems unaware, shrugging with resignation and a hint of despair. "Barry *does* care for me, you know. And you haven't really been here for a few years now," she says, "Always—working?"

"Yes!" Jones shouts. "Working, fucking working—while you—you fucked!"

Shit, flashes of a bedroom scene intrude, another man with Alice, their limbs sprawled together, elsewhere. *Take us back, back to my scene. There...* I re-plaster the bathroom vignette, focusing intently on bringing back all pieces, including the implements.

Especially the implements.

Jones's wife has her hands lifted, covering her eyes and, I'm now sure the leaking water dripping through her fingers *is* salty. Her shoulders are heaving and her voice is muffled, "I'm sorry, I'm so sorry. I didn't-didn't mean to hurt you."

But Jones has already picked *it* up.

One of the three implements in the bathroom at the time—toilet brush, hand vac and... a small sledgehammer. Propped behind the toilet bowl, it had been mistakenly left some few days past by builders completing the wall renovation. It was neither easily nor automatically available. And yet the man has stepped *around* the toilet to heft it, moving back to the bath and his wife, readying himself, hammer over his head.

Alice drops her hands to the side of the bath and only gulps with a frightened rasping wheeze. Her pinkish eyes are dilated, huge, staring us down.

Eventually, her voice comes, raspy with fear: "John, what—what are you- what?"

He swings the hammer down onto his wife's head.

Despite myself, I close my eyes.

She screams—and screams—and screams?

I look.

She is thrashing in the water, desperately, frenzied in panic. The bath water is... clear, foaming with her surging activity, but clear.

The large man stands, head down, hammer in both hands. He has stopped the swing just inches from his wife's head.

But... in reality, he had *not*.

Dream-jacking *always* gets to the truth. Defences down, dreamers re-enact events—given the right steer, the right props from an expert Rider—and there are none better than I.

My prompts *always* spark a replay of actual events, dream or no dream.

Uh-uh, focus, Scott...

Sledgehammer Jones straightens and looks up then.

Straight at me.

"So. How much are the Crown Prosecution paying you for this?"

Shit.

Fucking shit.

Jones's wife is standing now. Water streams down her body, over her breasts, down her belly and thighs.

Jones looks back at her, but keeps speaking to me. "My name's John. Just John Jones. I loved this woman dearly. I want to set her free."

"What?" I whisper from the ceiling.

He looks up at me again. "I'm going to put the hammer down and let her go, so she can join Barry, like she always hoped."

"But… that's not what happened."

"No," he says, "But it's what *should* have happened."

I've never faced this dilemma before. What to do? If I just let him take hold of the dream, I have no doubt *they* will fire me. They get paid by the conviction—as do I.

John Jones puts the sledgehammer down. His wife has stepped out of the bath and is drying herself on a large white towel—she wraps it around her body and ties it over her left shoulder like a toga.

"I loved you, John," she says.

She does not look at either of us; it's as if she is no longer aware of us.

I can make the hammer larger, more enticing, Red both in colour and nature—and wait for Jones's hippocampal cognitive rehearsal to kick in, with irresistible compulsion.

…But would this make *me* an accomplice? Will I then be guilty of murder too?

Alice hovers uncertainly by the door and Jones looks up at me again.

Fuck it; mamma had always told me to do the 'right' thing.

(Until she'd left me.)

"Okay," I say, dropping down from the ceiling and fleshing myself. "Let her go, then, if that's what you really want to do."

Alice stays, though: frozen, immobile, her face contorting with the effort to move.

I turn to Jones. His face is dripping with sweaty exertion: "I can't free her," he says. "Help me, please."

But, try as I might, I have no point of contact with her—she is not my dream imago to shift. I turn to shrug helplessly, but Jones has already picked up the hammer, now swollen and red, again.

"My name is John," he says, "Just John Jones. Get that? Guilty— I'm guilty."

He hesitates for a moment and then hands the hammer over to his wife. He bends forward submissively. "Do it," he says.

I open my mouth, but I'm unable to scream.

"Do it!" he shouts.

"Lizzie?" I croak.

Alice Jones raises the hammer over her head and brings it crashing down on the large man's head. The hammer bounces off his skull with a crackling, crunching sound, spraying a flash of blood across the room.

The blood laces my tongue—metallic, salty, explosive. I am falling sideways, grunting, winded, as I land on a crumpled and broken body.

John Jones's wife looks down at me; the bath is empty and dry.

But she is not Alice anymore—she is Shireen, my ex-wife, whom I'd lost patience with -but only once or twice, I swear, mamma—until she left me.

This time though, Shireen is the one holding the hammer. She smiles, dark hair swishing across her face.

Shit, there is no dream-breath from this body beneath me. Jones's head looks misshapen—splayed at an odd and bloody angle on the floor.

Shireen lifts the hammer over her head.

"Fuck it, Lizzie!" I scream, "Get me out of here."

Shireen swings the hammer.

The bathroom walls start to shift externally, crumbling, roaring, as if an empty storm is sucking them inexorably outwards. The bathroom cabinet and a wall explode and beyond, all I can see is a vast and complete emptiness. No sound, no shape, no colour.

No dreaming.

Just ...

Nothing.

"Li-zzie!"

And then I start falling sideways, sucked and stretched into the black hole beyond. I catch a flicker of images flashing past me—Old Man, Hero, Trickster, a flash of bleeding Jungian archetypes. Then dead-eyed animals, increasingly bizarre, mostly mute and long extinct.

I hurtle helplessly towards the empty hole at the heart of it all.

An old woman watches me from a place where everything has gone out. I think I know her, her hollow eyes are like burnt out planets.

"Mamma?" I call in desperation, flailing to stay away from the blackness above and beneath me.

Her head tilts, as if turning towards me—her face is creased with concern, brown eyes focusing on my face.

She holds her right hand out at me, clawed, but tendon-etched strong. "Ngibambe ngesandla," she says.

"What?" I say, wondering if I should give in to the sucking darkness.

"Have you learned nothing of where're you're from, Peter—hold my fucking hand!"

But she smiles as she says it and I realise it is the only thing that might just save me. I scrabble at her, but miss.

The darkness desiccates words, drowning everything.

Something grips my arm and yanks me sideways.

Two hands are huge on either side of my cheeks. The woman seems to be holding my face up.

I recognize her and start to cry.

"Lizzie, thank God..."

"I'm here," the Doc says. Her voice is warm and reassuring.

I continue to see hints of—fractured images and beasts, drifting in nothing with a vast void behind, the nothing that fudges the boundaries and certitude of everything I can now see—or perhaps it's just that my eyes keep leaking, smearing my sight and sense of surety?

Leaking…

Jones's words—were they meant for him—or me?

Guilty.

I'd certainly… hurt Shireen.

Twice.

Perhaps more?

And yes, I remember mamma had told me, when I was still a teenager at secondary school, that even once was too much.

Lizzie holds me against herself; her shoulders are bony, but warm. "It's okay, Peter," she says.

"What- what the hell happened to Jones?" I choke.

And how can I turn this fucking face tap off?

"He's dead," she says. "Jesus, they're going to crucify me for overdosing him on sedatives."

"But," I say and stop, unable to find words; it's all I can do to focus on the warmth of her body and the strength in her hands, still cradling my shoulders and head.

Then she leans back and moves away, starting to decouple electrodes and tubes from the large, still body lying alongside me.

Exhausted, I lie back on the pillow and watch her, unable to move. She switches off the Loom™. The Doc is decoupling me with smooth professionalism and I can see her show of warmth and compassion is past.

My tears stop and dry, prickling my cheeks.

We had a legitimate court order to dream-jack him, but John Jones had already decided to face his guilt head on—and, unable to free his wife, had preferred to die.

Still, where the hell does that leave us?

I look across at Sledgehammer.

There is just the barest hint of a smile at the corner of the dead man's lips.

The bastard had left me with my ex-wife and the hammer.

My body is starting to warm up, just the teeniest little bit, and words free up inside me. "Listen Lizzie, I will testify that Jones chose to die. They will see that for themselves too."

They.

Dream Justice, Inc.—that part of the privatised English Crown judiciary.

I pull the sheet off and stand up, my body—now well on the pudgy side of thirty, and sagging in readiness for forty—crackling stiffly in its jumpsuit. I stretch upwards, my blood needling harshly through arteries and veins again. Every year, my stretches get harder and harder.

Lizzie has covered Sledgehammer Jones's torso and looks up at me with a smile. "Thank you—that may just help, Peter, a devastating nocebo effect, perhaps…"

I wipe my face with a forearm as I stiffly step across to the body next to my bed.

"I'm sorry… John," I say. Given proper training and circumstance, it is clear that he would have been the greatest Dream-Rider in the world, not me.

Funny thing is; it suddenly didn't matter to me anymore.

I'd made my own share of mistakes too—and I was no longer the best anything.

Dream-Hunter *Two*? Not quite the same ring to it.

More, I'd caught a glimpse of what lies behind both dreams and waking.

I open the door to leave and hesitate, "Bye, Lizzie."

"Bye, Peter," she does not look round.

"No," I say, "I mean bye."

She pivots slowly in her chair and looks at me again. Her eyes are a deep and penetrating brown. "You're quitting, Peter?"

I nod. "Don't think I can Ride again on the criminal justice system."

"Bye Peter," she does not get up.

"Did you see…*her*, at the end?" I ask.

"Who? I just saw you rising out of the darkness—as if dragged by hope."

I close the door behind me.

*

Hope lives by the name of Precious Msimang; she has claimed back her old clan name, I remember.

I have forgotten her number but it takes my smart-watch only two seconds to patch me through.

The old woman from my dreams stares at me with apparent disbelief.

"Mamma!" is all I can manage.

"Peter," she says—and then the line freezes.

I know why—she always hated to cry in front of me—especially after…he—had hit her.

It flickers on again—mamma looks old and worn, but with the faintest of smiles, watching me closely. "Why have you called now, what do you want?"

"To visit," I say, "…and to talk about you and the family, and South Africa."

"A good place, now that Rhodes Has Fallen," she says. "This is my place to die."

"Let's not talk about death," I say, "Ngibambe ngesandla, mamma." (This time it is me who freezes the screen.)

I lie back and stare up at the numb white ceiling of my small flat.

I have taken women for granted, including the one who carried and birthed me, with both pain and love.

Guilty as charged. Time to start my redemption.

It will be a long, long flight home, to a place I hardly know.

Still, time to live a new dream.

Dream-Hunter, they call me.

But my name is just Peter John Scott *Msimang*.

Thirstlands

One thing I knew for sure: the rains were late here too.

I scanned the ridge of grey rock towering off to my left—there was no vast, unified surge of water pouring over the edge as I remembered only five years ago—just sparse, thin water curtains dropping from the escarpment into the sludgy green river over a hundred metres below me. Gone was the towering spray of vapour above, no water cloud sweeping overhead. Deep in the wooded Batoko Gorge, the sluggish river struggled through the trees. Good old Queen Vic— although she was long dust, her namesake waterfall here in Zambia was drying quickly too—this was no longer "Mosi-oa-Tunya" either, no "Smoke-That- Thunders."

"Record," I said reluctantly, closing my right eye simultaneously to activate my neural cam. *Du Preez is going to hate this.*

A black-uniformed guard with an AK strapped across his shoulder stood nearby, clicking on his digital palm-slate. The payment request bleeped in my cochlea; with a muttered command, I sent the amount in Chinese yuan from the Office account in my head.

No, Du Preez is going to go absolutely mad, absolutely bedonnered about this.

The guard moved on, accosting a young black man with an antiquated mobile phone cam. There were only five other people circling the viewing platform; none jostling for a view. I licked my lips, ever thirsty as usual.

<Is that all it is now? What a fokkin' waste of time and money!>

Hell, I had no idea the Boss had joined me, watching through my eyes like a mind-parasite, tickling my cochlea with his electronic croak.

So I closed my eyes. In the reddish darkness of my interior eyelids I could make out a green light flicking on the right, virtually projected by Cyril "the Rig's" neural cybernetics. The Office was online, the bloody Boss in.

But there was still only a dull red glow behind my left eye-lid. *Where are you, Lizette? What are you doing right now . . . and are you okay? You must know I hate having to leave you; but I've got to pay the bills, especially the damn water.*

<So what happened about the fokkin' rain forecast and the Vic Falls deluge that we flew you out for?>

"Blown away, I think, gone."

I spat the words, each one drying my mouth further. Eyes closed, a faint tingle of water from the falls sprayed onto my cheeks—a tantalising tickle onto my dry protruding tongue. I pulled my tongue in before the sun could burn it into biltong steak. The water from my hip-flask sizzled sweetly for a brief moment as I swigged, but then the ever-present tongue-throat ache was back.

Always thirsty, I took a final frustrated gulp and opened my eyes.

I stretched my arms and fingers across the wooden railings of the viewing platform, but I couldn't feel any more faint spray. The sky was becoming darker blue—still clear, the bloating red sun dropping onto the horizon.

No, there was no "Smoke-That-Thunders," no constantly roiling crash of water anymore— all that's left is an anaemic spattering of water, me, and a few other tourists scanning the ridge for a riverine surge that would never come.

Beyond, the surrounding green GM bio-fuel fields stretch to the horizon, leeching the river. Over the horizon, in slums on the outskirts of Livingstone, I'd heard there were crowds of desperate thirsty, probably starving, people gathering to watch their food shipped overseas as biofuels for SUVs and military tanks. I had taken the long way round to avoid the sight, so I don't know if that's the case for sure—or if it's yet another web myth. I'm not sure if even Cyril could tell me; I'd heard FuelCorps had censored the overhead sats. Anyway, there's no market for video clips of that sort of thing anymore, not even from the last of the official news agencies.

<Hell man, I'm off to ask Bongani how we can jack up your visuals on your clips to see if we can get any of our online Avatar subscribers to pay for them. Not even our Chinese Stanley will want to meet Livingstone with the crappy shots you got there. Du Preez out.>

Ach ja, shit, and the Boss too, of course. I winced at the sharpness of his tone in my ear. I had no energy to reply—he never waits for one anyhow—and swigged another guilty sip.

There was a bleep in my cochlea—a wifi neural kit was requesting contact. I ignored it; it wasn't Lizette.

"Hey, have you got the latest C-20 model?"

I looked at a man in the khaki Smart safari-suit, skin reddened by the sun, despite the generous smears of what looked like factor 100 white sunblock. His accent was vaguely Pan-European, the wispy greying hair underneath his dripping pith helmet disguising its original color. He grinned at me and tapped his head. "I've had the latest C-20 model inserted, no need for vocal commands, it's all thought operated."

"Mine's an old C-12 model," I said, scanning past him, along the escarpment and eastwards to the vast maize fields below, which looked as if they were encircling and attacking the shrinking strip of green riverine bush and trees. Perhaps I'd edit the clip later; momentarily too embarrassed to audibly cut my shoot.

The man went on talking, breathing hot meat and beer onto me, and I wondered briefly whether he'd heroically Safari-Shot drugged game before eating it: "My Rig's compatible with the latest web designs from China and is wired into the optic nerve for six-factor zoom capability."

"That's good to hear, I'm afraid mine just does a job."

It was then that I saw them, scattered on the edge of the riverine trees, before the fenced maize fields, as if they'd died seeking cover from encroaching razor- wire. I knew the Boss would kill me, but I had to keep filming—it was the biggest elephant graveyard I'd ever seen, and it had been months since *anyone* had last seen an elephant. Huge piles of bones, like stranded and stripped hull-wrecks of ships, some of them arching their white curves in neatly laid out patches—as if their death had been calm, deliberate, and careful to acknowledge an individual, elephantine space for dying.

Jan du Preez may only want Live Game—me, I take what I can get.

The man turned to follow my gaze and grumbled with disappointment: "Bugger. Just bloody bones, I thought you'd seen some real wildlife for a change. Did you know the C-20 also has full amygdala-hippocampal wiring that allows synchronous ninety-three percent recall of emotion?"

"Really?" I looked back at him. For the past few years it felt as if my own feelings were desiccating; the barest husks of what they had been—what must it be like to pull out old video clips saturated with the original feelings, rich and raw with young emotional blood? It's been over two decades since Lizette and I had watched handheld video clips of us and baby Mark, now three years gone to an accountancy career in Oz.

Three years on from the hijacking that left him without a car outside our gates but crying with gratitude he was alive, physically unharmed. Three years since I've been too scared to walk outside the house but weirdly okay to travel to so many other places. It's been only two years, though, since Du Preez contributed to the Rig in my head—to "Cyril," who has helped to sharpen and hold my most recent memories.

Still, I've been thirsty ever since. I'm sure they buggered up my thirst center at the same time they did the Rig neurosurgery. But the insurance disclaimers had been twelve pages long, the surgeons in denial.

The man opened his mouth again; sweat dripped off the end of his nose, as if his Smart Suit struggled to adequately regulate his temperature. I couldn't resist a brief smile at the sight, but turned away, not wishing to say goodbye. Maybe old feelings should be left alone after all, left to dry and wither like fallen leaves.

"Command—cut!" I muttered.

So his Rig was better (bigger) than mine . . . big bloody deal. He's not an African, just an effete tourist in a harsh land his skin can't deal with, filtering it through his foreign money, fancy implants and clever clothes.

And me?

Red blinked behind both my eyelids when I shut my eyes, so I let Cyril randomly cycle a babble of blogs over me as I headed back to the car park, the public toilet, and the chilly airport hotel, before the early morning flight home.

Home—and Liz.

*

The last kay home is always the longest, so I tried to coax more speed out of the car's electrics. The time, though, seemed to drag on for an eternity, inching past corrugated iron shacks. People milled on the right of the road on the approach into Dingane Stad—mainly men, concentrated near a bridge overpass, no doubt jostling in hope to be picked up by passing bakkies or trucks for a desperate day's work.

One old man near the road held out pale palms to me—but I've always avoided paternalistic gifts and dependency; this is Africa. I kept my windshields up, my doors locked.

The fields on the hill were brittle brown and eaten to dust by scraggly herds of cattle, watched by boys with sticks in hands, with shoulder-strapped and cocked Chinese P.L.A. T-74s, that looked in danger of blowing off their legs.

Still definitely no rains here either—shit man, we're lucky we have our secret backup, Lizette; a hedge against the soaring costs of privatised water.

My eyes blinked heavily with the alternating early morning sunlight and the spidery-web shadows of overhead pirate cables snaking down from Council Electric grids and pylons into the shacks along the roadside. The cables will be cut by officials come sunset tonight and will have sprung back magically by tomorrow morning. Crazy, man, absolutely bedonnerd, holding an impoverished community to electric ransom, when there's so much sun for free.

My car was on auto as it turned into the long and bumpy drive past neighboring sugarcane fields up to our small-holding, an old disused farmhouse we'd bought at a financial stretch called "Cope's Folly," in search of a "simpler" semi-rural lifestyle. Hah.

I closed my eyes and sent yet another desperate message, almost a plea: <*I'm home, Lizette.*>

The red light under my left lid continued to ache for moments.

And then flickered green: <*About bledy time, Mister Graham bledy Mason.*>

Relief flooded me. *So she's still pissed off with me. That's something, at least.*

The black electrified gates swung open to the car's emitted password.

Liz was waiting, arms crossed, gum-booted and disheveled in loose and dirty clothes, glowering. There was a barrow of carrots next to her—a good looking bunch, so no doubt due to go to the neighboring township co-op, as she's done ever since we moved here and she started growing food.

We pecked cheeks warily, eye contact tentative, and I'm awkward with a complex mix of feelings. Lizette's a big-boned woman, dark of skin, with wild hair that she shoves back with a red Alice band. Her black hair was greying quickly, which she flaunted with a twist of her band. I gave her a furtive glance. Even angry, her brown eyes were lovely. But the anger seemed to have dimmed, she was almost . . . anxious?

It's not like her to be fearful—she still drives herself alone into the township when I'm away, despite what I always tell her about the dangers. Nah, I must be wrong. She can't be nervous, not Lizzie.

She wheeled the barrow off to pack the carrots away in the shed. I stepped inside and through to the hot sunken lounge, with its big AG ("almost green") Aircon against the far wall. My presence tripped the air-conditioner switch with a *click*; whirring on. The web portal was tucked away discreetly in the corner as she'd insisted when I'd had it installed for her, but the controls were on red, as if constantly locked, unused. But she'd sent me that response just before I arrived.

A new decorative screensaver spiraled, a fuzzy grainy floating picture, hard to make out as I walked through to the kitchen to make cheese sandwiches for us and to grab a drink of water.

She was waiting on the single chair when I came back and she took the plate with thanks, putting it on the side table, as if not hungry. I sat on the couch opposite. She looked at the floor. *Oh no man, was this going to be another rehash of the argument we'd had before I'd left? "Why can't you demand to stay on local assignments, you've never been able to stand up to Du Preez, blah, blah, blah."*

"It looks like the garden's been productive despite the lack of rain," I said, breaking the silence, but putting my cheese sandwich down, suddenly not hungry myself.

She looked up at me and smiled. "Yes, our solar well-pump has helped, although I've been careful not to let the well drop below three quarters."

I smiled back, relieved to see her relax. "A bloody godsend that was, you calling in the surveyor—you've always had damn good intuition, Lizzie."

She grimaced and stood up, pacing restlessly over to the web portal. *What the hell did I say? Must be the swear words—she hated me swearing, never gets used to it, keen Churchgoer and all—"bledy" was the worst of it from her, and even that had only arrived these past few years.*

Her dark eyes brimmed with tears when she turned to face me. She leaned against the thin computer screen, and the floating screensaver froze and sharpened beneath the touch of her fingers. It was a picture of a little barefooted black girl in a broken yellow grimy dress, looking up at the screen, face taut with pain. And it looked like it had been snapped from the CCTV on our outside gate.

"Her name's Thandi," Lizette said, "She came here yesterday morning after you left—her tongue was so thick she couldn't drink. She was dying of thirst, Graham. Dying, man, vrek, out on her little feet, true's God. I didn't know things were this bad! She's just seven years old, Graham, but I had to dribble the water down her throat; her tongue was almost choking her."

"So you gave her tap water or water from the fridge," I said, standing up.

She shook her head: "Nee, Graham, I gave her water from our emergency supply and called the village Traditional Leader to tell him about it and to find her mom. There are others like her, just down the bledy road, man. So I told T.L. Dumisane and said we could spare them ongoing three-quarters of our well supply."

"Ach shit man, Lizzie, you didn't, did you? That's *ours*! Why the hell didn't you ask me first? You've had free access to my head for three years now. And why didn't you return my calls or let me know you were okay at least?"

"It's hardly free," she snorted, "I can only hear what you *choose* to tell me. And what would you have done and said, Mister Graham Mason?" She stood up tall and focused, as if suddenly sure of herself.

I hesitated, but just for a moment: "I'd have given her water from the fridge and told you to keep quiet about the well. You know we have to keep this a secret for our own safety, otherwise we'll be the target of every water bandit and *tsotsi* in KwaZulu-Natal!"

"See, I knew you'd say that, and I hate arguing when I can't see your face. I knew calling you would end up in a fight. I'm sorry I ended up saying nothing and worrying you, but I had to make this decision on my own. Dumisane is a good man, *hy sal niks se nie . . .* and there's no way I can live here with children dying just down the road. No ffff—" She clamped her mouth with her hand and took a breath before releasing it and finishing through clenched teeth: "No . . . way!"

Lizette *never* swears—and only reverts to Afrikaans when she's absolutely distraught. She seemed to crumple slightly, clutching at herself, sobbing. The little yellow-dressed girl fuzzed over and spiraled randomly across the screen. Of course, she'd always wanted a little girl too.

My anger emptied into a desperate sense of helplessness. I hovered for moments and then stepped forward to coax her to turn *towards* the screen. I could send her comforting emoti-messages from LoveandPeace Dotcom that should help soothe and calm her.

Her eyes froze me, though—her dark, lovely, lined but frighteningly fierce eyes. I knew then with some weird certainty that if I tried touching her, turning her to face the computer screen, she would scream, hit and kick me towards the outside door and gate. Beyond that, I could see that there was no returning in her eyes.

My arms hung in frigid confusion as tears streamed from her blazing eyes.

Shit, what else was there to do? I could only reach out to hold her, awkwardly wrapping my arms around her taut, trembling body.

Her arms were rigid, almost pushing at me for moments, but then she seemed to let go, and the sobs strangled in her throat; her hair was thick and tickly in my face, my own eyes stinging from a sudden bite of emotion. I could smell the coconut fragrance in her hair and remembered it had been her favorite shampoo when we'd first met almost thirty years ago. Hell man, it must be years since we'd last really held each other.

Since Mark had left.

"Come," she said, pushing me away but then taking my hand in hers, my shirt sleeve wiping her wet face.

She pulled me forwards.

Oh . . . right, so she's not taking me out to see how the veggie patch has grown.

Dear God, I'd almost forgotten how much of a woman she was.

And, in the end—despite my constant thirst—I wasn't nearly as dry as I feared I might be, either.

*

I left her sleeping.

Face relaxed, serene, dark hair thickly splashed over an oversized yellow pillow, she lay on her back, a soft snore. It hurt to watch her, and I felt strangely guilty to stare—weird man, we'd been together so long—so I rolled over quietly and pulled on trousers and shirt, making my way through to the front door.

The door flickered and dallied while it de-armed, so I toyed with the idea of getting a drink of water from the kitchen. No, a dry mouth never killed anyone in the short term. I scanned the weapon rack behind the door, eventually inserting a taser-rod into my belt, before clicking the electric gate open in the outside wall.

The dry mid-afternoon heat carried little of the past summer humidity in the air. I breathed a set of ten deep breaths to quell my panic and then stepped with jellied legs through the gate, clicking it closed behind me.

As the gate clanged shut, I noted a red sports car parked beneath an ancient oak across the road, its driver in shadow. No time to reopen the gate—it would just expose the house and Lizzie.

So I deactivated the fence charge, rammed the hand-panel deep into my trouser pocket and backed against the gate, hauling out the taser. Shit, I should have gone for the gun instead.

The car door opened, and a young black woman stood up, her arms akimbo, hands empty—dressed in workmanlike blue overalls, duffle-bag strapped over her shoulders, hair cropped squarely close to her head: "*Kunjani*, Mister Mason, I'm here about your water."

They certainly hadn't wasted any time; things must be pretty desperate in the township.

"*Ngiyaphila, unjani wena?*" I replied, easing the taser into my belt.

"I am well too," she smiled with a slight twist to her mouth; I wondered whether she toyed with the idea of testing my paltry isiZulu, but thankfully her next words were in English: "I'm Busisiwe Mchunu, a hydrogeologist for the FreeFlow Corporation. However, I reserve room for a little private freelance work in the services of my community; strictly off the record, you understand."

"Oh," I said, with an African handshake of palm, thumbs grip, palm again: "Graham Mason, pleased to meet you. And of course I understand." *Wow, strong grip.*

"I'm here to survey the underground water on your land. Of course, *before* the white man, all of this land was ours anyway."

"Oh," I said, "Is that a . . . veiled threat?"

She chuckled: "Don't be so paranoid, Mister Mason, we amaZulu don't veil our threats. It's just a historical observation. Your wife looks out for us, so we've looked out for you."

"Hello!" Lizette leaned against the inside of the gate, back in grubby trackpants and shirt. "Who're you?"

"I'm Chief Dumisane's water rep, Mizz Basson," said Busisiwe, walking across. "Just call me Busisiwe."

"Pleased to meet you, Busisiwe, I'm Lizette." They shook hands through the gate.

Lizette smiled as I gave her the controls. She rattled off a fluent phrase of what sounded like welcoming isiZulu for Busisiwe, who responded with obvious delight. I could tell they'd probably get on like a shack on fire.

"I'm just going for a walk," I told them.

Lizette looked surprised as the gate opened. "Be careful, Graham."

Yes, I do remember this was the path on which Mark was robbed and stabbed in the face; I have replayed his scarred face so many times in my head. But I know I need to do this, if I can.

It's a short walk, but every step felt heavy, my legs stiff in anticipation of someone leaping out at me from behind the tall stalks of sugarcane densely spearing both sides of the footpath. The path bent sharply to the right as it had when I'd last walked it with Lizette four years ago, dipping down into the valley with an expansive view of the city, skyscrapers strutting their stuff against the clear sky; no fires today.

There, beside the path, lay the cracked and uneven boulder Lizzie and I had rested on, after we'd agreed to buy the small holding. My bum warmed as I sat down, the disarmed taser-rod stabbing into the small of my back. Around the city lay blackened Midland hilltops, informally marking the southern perimeter of the Umgeni Valley. Dingane Stad, "Sleepy Hollow," as it had once been known, or Pietermaritzburg by the white Afrikaners.

"Switch off." The Rig fell absolutely silent, no lights blinked inside my eyelids, just the red constant heat of the midmorning sun filtering through my eyelid blood-vessels.

It'd been two years since I'd been absolutely alone. Two years since the implant and I'd last been quiet in my head, cut off from the electric pulse of the world. Here, there were no hovering voices, no Cyril, just my own solitary thoughts.

My shirt trickled with sweat, and with my thumb I killed the black Matabele ant biting my shin. It gave off an acidic stink as it died, and I stood up quickly, but there was no nearby swarm, no nest hiding under the rock.

This is a hard place to be, but all I know right now is that this is where I want to die. This is where I want to lay down my bones, just like the elephants. Why? I have no bloody idea. Maybe it's to do with the light on the hills or perhaps just the bite and smell of an ant. The thoughts circled my brain, trapped and private, no place to go.

Still, as I walked the path home, my steps felt somehow lighter, looser, but never quite tension-free.

"Switch on," I said, as if re-arming myself for the world.

<Hey, where the hell you been? You must upload your video clips from Vic Falls for the day!>

That bastard Du Preez. I glanced at my watch, it was after four. <Work's over, I'll do it tomorrow.>

<You'll do it now! Jeez man, I've heard of sleeping on the job, but you just took the bledy cake on that one earlier with your wife.>

Shit, I must have forgotten to switch off, swept up in the day's events, and he had just . . . watched?

<Did you?> I asked.

No answer, but he must know what I was asking. *<Damn you, Du Preez, cut Office.>*

I stopped to take several slow and deep breaths, thirsty as hell.

Around the last bend, Lizette and Busisiwe were standing in the shade by Busisiwe's car and turned to me as I approached.

Lizette shook her head.

I looked at Busisiwe. "It's a shallow freshwater aquifer," she said. "It's also pretty small. I don't think it will last long, unless we get more rainfall."

Lizette looked at me.

This is Africa, I wanted to tell her, doing this may salve our conscience in the short term, but will solve nothing in the long term.

I could tell in her eyes she knew what I was thinking, even without the direct link with Cyril that I'd pressed her so long to get, in the hope that it might bring us closer. I could also see resignation and uncertainty—for us, and all we had tried to build—and, despite this morning, I could also see a fear of the end for us in her eyes.

I opened my mouth, knowing my next words could finish everything. I turned to look at Busisiwe. "Okay," I said. "We'll help."

"Ngiyabonga," she said.

Lizette put her arm through mine. Skin on skin will do me.

I'll take this moment. I couldn't be sure how long it would last. All I knew for certain was that I wasn't ready for some endings and that the rains were late. *Bloody weird, but I'm not* quite *so thirsty anymore either. Long may this last too.*

The Guardian of the Grain

Anne Herewini was the Guardian of the Grain, Earth's Food-Protector. *All* eager clients who wanted access to the planet's bread had to go through her.

Not an easy task, for she was amongst the best of the best; Security Chief Extraordinaire.

She moonwalked with light grace into the Viewing Room, where they were all waiting for her, shards of starlight crystallising in the translucent dome above their heads. The cold and Spartan room was designed to shape an awed focus towards the visual display above, but only the Commander was looking up, even though he knew *that* view so very well. There was no sign of the Earth, she noted in her peripheral vision, but then her focus was firmly on the four visiting CEO reps. Anne strode with certainty borne of several successful decades in her role, bouncing formidably in her loose brown overalls and magnetised grey boots. Her mother would be proud of her indeed—and Earth Leave to visit Mamma Herewini in the Hospice-Home in Auckland was now only a week away.

Mamma, my kokara… *No, hold back your sadness, Herewini, you still have a job to do.*

Commander Ross was grinning as he introduced the visitors, the Ride of the Valkyries playing briskly in the background. He *knew* she hated Wagner. A musical in-joke that Ross never tired of, even though he himself was older than her, and nearing his retirement back to Earth.

Still, Anne smiled with brief satisfaction as a stiff-suited man and woman stumbled while turning to greet her, obviously languishing on Earth legs. Two men and two women—hoorah for global gender equality. Always good to see clients wobbly though—hard to pull a fast one here on the Moon, when you're still on your Earth feet.

Anne had learnt to trust *neither* sex, in the rigours of her job as Security Chief. She nodded at the representatives from leading Bio-Engineering firms in Oceania, Southern Africa, Latin-America and a blonde woman of stretched skin and indeterminate age who fronted an Agricultural Conglomerate from Antarctica, 'Green Growth'. Her handshake had been steely and her balance certain, with her immigrant voice carrying old traces of British-America, before its Trumpian-Brexit collapse.

"Pleased to meet you, Stacey Armstrong," Anne lied curtly to the Antarctican rep, who was no doubt proud of 'their' fast greening Continent.

"Our guests want to be able to analyse the crops, so to be in the grain room itself, before they start bidding for the next three-year tender, to try and increase our global yield." Ross knew her so well, he shrugged before she could ask. "Yes, they've been decontaminated, so I guess it's up to you to ensure we're safe to go."

You can never be too careful. They'd caught one impostor with a bomb and a population reducing agenda several years previously. "I have checked all implants and belongings, so it's all fine—but have they signed legal disclaimers and visiting compliance with Lunar Law?"

The Commander nodded, keying in a spatial array of his fingerprints onto a blank wall. An invisible door slid open, revealing a small glass room. Beyond, a yellow-green haze of greenhouse wheat could be seen. A vast field of Moon-Grain.

Anne waved the Earth visitors into the security transition room; aware wall sensors were yet again scanning their DNA—and every working orifice. The glass room was hot, and she waited until all of them had started perspiring, just to make sure they were clean, before palming the final door open.

This was the Wheat 1 greenhouse—a huge array of sheathed, gene-enhanced cobs, elongated and growing riotously within low gravity bio-guides. The filtered and eternal polar sunshine glowed down, irrigation water siphoned off the ice from within the nearby Shackleton Crater, funnelling along the ragged crop lines and burning the nose with a sharp, synthetic compost smell.

As the Commander led the group down an uneven aisle between two rows of wheat, Stacey stumbled, focused on flexing her right hand.

But Anne Herewini had been watching her.

Closely.

With one fluid movement, she was alongside the woman, cuffing her right hand with a force-field lock.

"What are you doing?" choked the woman, her body stiff—but the cloudy energy field around her right hand was flickering red.

"Red for pathogen," said Anne grimly, "Although I don't know how our scanners missed it."

The Commander pushed past through, "Well done, Chief. We need an analysis, but my guess is it's a delayed action, untraceable biological pathogen—with Green Growth ahead of the game on this, of course, ready to market and sell us their expensive antidote."

Stacey shrugged, avoiding his gaze.

The Commander grunted, as if his suspicion had been confirmed. "Take her to the Interview Room, Anne," Ross's face was twisted in anger. "I'll finish the tour with the other representatives."

Plant disease here could starve the Earth. *What price, the planet?*

"Move!" said Anne, pushing the woman ahead of her, holding a finger-taser to her back. Voice activating the security room, she bustled the woman into the large and now silent Viewing Room, en route to the Interview Room; locked, but waiting, by Lunar Law.

Above them, near the lunar horizon, the Earth was rising, carrying Anne's dying mother.

As the security door slid closed, Stacey reached behind with her left hand, lightly touching Anne's left arm. "You really are *weeks* behind the latest technology, stuck so far out here, my dear."

Anne pushed the woman away, feeling a burning along her arm. "What the hell?"

"*Human* pathogen," said Stacey. "Designed to bypass security scans by mimicking my DNA. We are indeed the company ahead of the rest. Remember Green Growth, as you die. You have five minutes left. Tops."

Anne swept Stacey's legs with her left leg, smashing the woman's face with her forearm on the way down. Then she dropped onto the woman, covering her bleeding, broken nose and bruised mouth with her chest. Anne lay there, raging, her limbs tingling and suffocating the woman beneath her...

Anne felt old, sad and dying eyes on her back. *I'm sorry*, kokara, *my mother.*

Groaning, Anne rolled off, using the woman's midriff as a pillow instead. She felt her own limbs start to lock in pain.

Her burst of rage was gone—her job was to look after resources that saved lives, not to kill. Anne's head lifted slightly, up and down, with the slow, ragged breath of the unconscious woman beneath her head.

Above her, starlight burned down, unremitting. She, too, knew that view so very well.

The dull, blue glowing Earth was near the horizon, blurred with cloud. No chance of spotting Aotearoa—even in digital maps, New Zealand was always hanging off the bottom edge, as if on the point of vanishing. Her *whanau* were now ever beyond her reach.

Still, somehow, she sensed her mother's gaze; her *wairua*, a silent but feisty spirit, even while she felt her own senses fading.

Mother... Anne's eyes hurt; but failed to leak.

Several stars vanished and reappeared as the orbiting Space-Tanker shot overhead, waiting for its next grain load to carry back to a congested and concrete Earth. Anne wished the Valkyries would ride again, because all she could hear was the straining breath of the woman lying beneath her.

And then she heard it—the dramatic opening bars of Wagner. Commander Ross must have programmed the Valkyrie's ride to be activated by her physical presence. *A last joke. You old bastard... So I get to see Valhalla... before you?*

"Kua hinga te tōtara i Te Waonui-a-Tāne," Anne said, for her mother.

A totara has fallen, in the great forest of Tane.

How could I not have locked both of this woman's hands—forewarned is forearmed, and I've... I've been the best of the best.

Now, I will not see my mother die.

Grief has robbed me of my edge.

The best die too.

None of us are immortal.

The blonde woman's breath beneath her was stuttering and slowing.

Was this woman, Stacey, dying as well?

Anne knew what her mother would want. *And grain is for living, not dying.*

So, with great difficulty, Anne Herewini rolled over to administer the kiss of life, with her final, gasping breaths.

Security sirens kicked in, but The Guardian of the Grain did not hear them.

A Million Reasons Why

iKaap, 2043; (i) The Day Nonhle Wished to Be Gone

You never get used to pain.

Nonhle was tired of it all.

Very tired.

Enough is enough.

She had woken from pain-broken sleep, with just one wish: *To be gone.*

Gone from the relentless weight of almost seventy or so blurring years, gone from the constant grind to accrue creds for food and energy for her and the youngster... But mostly gone from the painful burden of carrying The Snake inside her, gnawing irascibly at her insides.

Shoosssh, shooooshhh, shoosshhh... the sea's voice was louder outside their flat this morning, despite the dampening hiss of the almost ever-present rain.

Their flat.

Gill's too, the young one, always bouncy, busy, and sweet.

But Gill would *not* understand, so Nonhle had kept quiet and ensured the morning ritual was untainted, feeding Gill scrambled egg and *putu pap* as usual. The young woman had kissed her cheek before cheerily leaving for work, Nonhle managing a rictus smile in farewell.

This task needed aloneness.

Shoosssh, shooooshhh, shoosshhh—only the sea's endless voice. *Where are you, mama?*

Nonhle fetched the box and bottle from under her bed and took it out onto the undercover *stoep*, placing it on the green, plastic table. Slowly and carefully, she counted out a toxic dose of painkillers. Fifty should do it, she thought, spacing out a mixed batch of white and red capsules into ten discrete parcels of five on her balcony table. She made ready to swig them down systematically with *witblits*.

This, at least, she *could* control.

The cool wind whipped spots of rain across her neck; she would need to be quicker, if she were to be dry when she died. She wanted to die outside, facing the mountain and its flat peak, which she was forbidden to scale.

Was it here the vanishing birds had gone, as the 'nets whispered, trapped as food and stuffed displays for The One Hundred above, whose nightly parties flared the black sky with colour?

But will my spirit be doomed to wander this desolate Earth?

No, I don't believe in the old ways and, and…

Gill would never know.

For, most of all, Nonhle wanted to die; with Gill well away, and gone.

"BawoMa," she spoke to the air. "It is time for me to go."

"Are you sure, Nonhle? What will Gill think?"

The voice was gender-neutral and Nonhle did not even glance at the locked Smart-Door, from where it came.

Instead, she looked up the slopes of the cloud-clothed Table Mountain above her, the sacred *Hoerikwaggo*, where Lion's Head reared off to the right. Incoming, greyer rain clouds sweeping in from over Table Bay.

On the flat mountaintop—beyond the huge red wall that encircled it from *Platteklip* Gorge to the derelict Cable Car—the white glare domes of the One Hundred both ate and blinked back the hot Cape sun, flaring in pockets between the rain.

Flashing solar fingers to the masses below; forever out of reach. *With a view like this, what better place to die?*

Nonhle could feel Inyoka, the Snake, stirring inside her midriff, as if he were growing aware of his own pending danger. There was no better time to act, too, in the midmorning with Gill out, running from flat to shack to house and fixing Pirate-Nets wherever she could. One million and falling on the Flats here, as people fled the rising waters.

We are the ninety-nine-point nine percent, she thought, staring at the pills lying neatly partitioned in front of her on the old wooden table. *And I am just one; I will be long dead by the time Gill comes home. She will understand; she is twenty-one and will inherit this place, for what it's worth. This, at least, I have willed.*

Inside her, Inyoka bit hard, a lacerating pain moving up her right arm and into her shoulder this time—the snake never stayed still—and nothing or no one could kill him…Neither tai chi, nor drugs, nor the *isangomas*, not even the mindful befriending suggested by the white doctor, who flew down from the Mountain Top to run her free clinics for the poor.

Nonhle scooped up her first handful of pills, readying the brandy bottle in her right fist. She sat down, glancing across at the bird feeder hanging off the wall. The birds and the animals were almost disappeared now, their own houses gone, as heat and humans took what they could.

What hope, then, for me?
Time. To. Go.

She swallowed the first mouthful, the blitz burning her throat, so that she coughed briefly.

The wind was sweeping heavier rain in and Nonhle stood in her blue nightgown, crouching to shield the pills on the table. She swallowed another batch and coughed—the brandy would keep her warm at least.

"Nonhle?" The voice was Gill's, a loud shout from the locked balcony door.

What was Gill doing, back so early?

"Keep the door locked, BawoMa," Nonhle instructed.

"Open, BawoMa!" Gill's muffled shout came from inside the flat.

"I am legal House-Keeper, BawoMa, keep it locked!" Nonhle took another batch of tablets, but dropped a couple in her haste… No, she must slow down; there was no way Gill could get in with the door secured.

BawoMa was *hers* to instruct.

Nonhle coughed again, even though only three pills made it down this time.

The door opened, and Gill stormed through.

Gill de Jong, white waif.

Nothing waifish about her now, though.

Gill stood facing her, tall and T-shirt plump, smeared with grit and grime from digging pirated Telkom cables and hacking server boxes.

Her usual cheery face was dark and clouded.

"What—in—hell—are you—doing—*gogo?*"

Nonhle kept herself cold and strong. "I am not your grandmother. How many times must I tell you? I have no family… And I am so tired of this pain that has no end."

"But you have me," Gill said.

It took Nonhle a moment to realise Gill's body was shaking, not from the cold and wet, but tears.

Nonhle stepped towards her. "I'm sorry, Gill. There is no other way out."

Gill shook her head, her eyes red. "You always told me stories open doors; *Nkosikazi Ibali*, my Story Queen."

"Life is not a story," Nonhle bit back, "and you never get used to pain. Never."

Inyoka was gnawing her fingers now, but she ignored him as best she could, flexing her hands to try and abate the pain, keeping her words going in gasps.

"It—is—time—for me to go…" *No reasons to go on. No family left, and ancestors who do not reply to my cries.*

Gill stepped forward and, before Nonhle could close her mouth,

Gill held her face with her left hand, plunging her right index finger into Nonhle's mouth.

Nonhle gagged and bent, vomiting onto Gill's hand and feet. The girl-woman did not look down, nor did she flinch at the acidic smell of semi-digested oats, medication and brandy.

Instead, she continued to hold Nonhle's face gently between her hands, as rain soaked them both. "No," she said, "you don't get to choose your time. *I* am family, whatever you may call me."

Nonhle felt the bite in her own eyes and stiffly straightened herself, despite the ongoing burn in her stomach. It was the first time she had ever seen Gill cry. She had not even cried when her father had left her, all of seven years ago, the girl barely fourteen years old then.

Nonhle sighed and took Gill's hands from her face.

"How—how did you know?" she asked.

"BawoMa told me," she said.

"But BawoMa is just a Home-Help cloud avatar."

"No one is ever *just* anything," Gill said. "You taught me that, *gogo.*"

Nonhle laughed through her pain. Gill grasped and held her, while rain washed the stench and stain of orange-white vomit off them.

Gill laughed too.

"What is it?" Nonhle asked her, turning as Gill gestured towards the table.

"Looks like Jesus is also saying it's not your time yet, *gogo.*"

The table was spread with a dwindling sludge of orangey melting tablets; drip, drip, dripping onto cold concrete.

Despite her disbelief in Gill's religion, Nonhle smiled.

Then she grabbed the bottle of blitz off the table and gulped a large and burning sip to clear her mouth.

Inside her, Inyoka only danced, as if relieved he had a reprieve.

(ii) The Day After Wanting to be Gone

Twenty-five years you have gnawed on my life, Snake.

Twenty-five years since you crawled into my guts, while I served the rich in their mountain mansions.

Twenty-five years, too, since Day Zero first broke this City apart, scattering the thirsty and the poor from its clasp. Two million parched mouths fleeing the relentless drought burning off the Mother City's breasts.

But then, in the end, came the rains.

Without end.

And the wall to end all walls was built; to hold the poor—and the rising sea—at bay.

Yet you remain—how can I be rid of you, Inyoka, yet stay alive?

Nonhle leaned against the corner of the balcony wall, looking up the Mountain in the late evening glow, as Inyoka chewed at her left rib cage. The One Hundred on top had taken so much from below, leaving only destitution and cheap labour to fire in needed resources, through the narrow pipes under their electrified wall.

Ruled from above, by the iron hand—of The Five of The Fist. *You can't take my stories, though!*

Nonhle's nose was teased by the pungent smell of *rooibos* tea on the boil and for a moment she took glad relief inside her nose, a momentary refuge from Inyoka's insistent fangs.

Nonhle sniffed again—not just rooibos, but a few traces of cannabis sativa leaves on the breeze mixed in too. Bless the girl; she must have had a private stash hidden somewhere, which even the DEA sniffer dogs had missed.

God knows where she went to get it though.

Nonhle was too scared to ask.

BawoMa opened the door and Gill stepped through with a hot mug.

Nonhle smiled and took it—she'd indeed never seen Gill cry before, not even when her father had told her to effing stay, for insisting Nonhle come with them too, on their move up the Mountain.

"I'm not paying to take the fucking maid up there!" he'd told his young daughter; not caring Nonhle was ironing in the same room.

Gill crossed her arms and face and refused to move, in the face of her father's wrath. "Now I know why mom left you all those years ago!"

Not a generous or forgiving man, Johan De Jong.

He'd said nothing, just left with his bags for the corporate chopper at Greenmarket Square—his hundred million a ticket to the top.

Gone over the Wall—a man always on the up, so that he was now The Thumb, Security Chief of the Five.

For Gill, though, he might as well be dead.

Nonhle sipped her tea gratefully, noticing Gill watching her with an intense stare, shaking a little, but her eyes clear and blue-sharp.

"What is it?" Nonhle asked.

The tea was still hot, so she put it down on the cleaned table, a small pigeon poo in one corner.

Inyoka was beginning to gnaw at her left shoulder now; she sighed—so what was new?

"They've found a cure for CRAPS!"

Nonhle laughed then, despite the pain. Gill had taken her ironic acronym for Complex Regional Pain Syndrome on board. "They're always finding a cure, my girl." She must remember she was twenty-one now. "But they never end up working."

"I hacked the Table Top PharmWebs," she said. "This one completely stacks up—they're releasing it to The Elite."

Nonhle knew Gill spoke truth. Big Pharma would not release

anything to the wealthiest, unless it was watertight to legal-scientific scrutiny.

"How much?" She asked.

"Uh..." Gill looked down. "Five mill."

Nonhle laughed again, bitterly, even as it started to rain, despite the wan sunlight breaking to the east of The Mountain.

Five million *rand-creds…you* better *start getting used to this pain, old woman.*

"God has given me a plan, *gogo!*" The young woman said, "I have arranged someone with enough money to see us... they're on their way."

"And?" said Nonhle.

BawoMa called from the front door: "We have a visitor downstairs, scan verified."

Nonhle sighed, wondering what mad-cap scheme Gill had thought up: "Let them in, if their scan is clean."

Pain and nerves made her sit.

And then stand again.

Gill went across to pack pots and dishes ready for washing.

A sharply dressed man in a dark blue suit and a straw boater stepped through the front door. He took the hat off and gave a bow.

Not a promising start, thought Nonhle, holding out a hand.

"I'm a big fan of yours, Mamma; never miss one of them old-time stories from your show."

Mamma glared across to Gill's back. "I hope you pay well for it then, mister; we need every damn cent."

The man stood up tall in his suit; boater held across his heart, mouth wide in shock. "I am a man of honour and virtue, I can assure you, mamma."

She smiled. The hat served no purpose but to impress.

She was not impressed.

"Can you get us the pain drug?" Gill barked over her shoulder, clattering a plate.

"Surely," the man said. "But payment is non-negotiable."

"I have little money," Nonhle said.

"I don't want your money; I want your stories."

She sat down, on their one chair, at a bit of a loss. "What do you mean?"

The tall man leaned against the kitchen table. "The One Hundred love their entertainment, as you can see from their nightly displays. I'm sure they would be willing to pay a fair sum for your stories—archaic folk myths are making a comeback, I hear, especially in concerts near the old Cable Car."

"Five million—for my old stories?"

The Man with No Name shook his head slowly and bent to pick

up the boater lying at his feet. "Not quite, mamma. Times are further ahead up there. The Special are now only entertained by the latest direct neural feeds. I will need to do a neural scoop. Five mill is fair for such an operation."

Nonhle looked down. "I have a lawyer who loves my stories too, and so you'd better be frank with me. What are the risks?"

The man hesitated, spinning the bowler between his fingers, tossing it from hand to hand. "Uh, it's physically non-invasive, but might leave you with a headache for a day or so. Um, and you *might* never remember your stories again. It does have a proper dig at your hippocampus—but that's only a one percent worry."

A one percent worry. She looked up, "That's one hell of a potential price. It's my only livelihood."

The man gave the faintest of leers as he glanced across at Gill busy washing dishes. "Your—uh—daughter is partial to psycho-actives, I'm sure you know—she may also be partial to something else, which could be potentially lucrative for both of you. And by the way, how long have you had your pain, mamma?"

Gill stopped drying cutlery, cloth clenched tightly in her right hand.

Rage surged through Nonhle. *Lecherous shit… But the pain has been far too long—twenty, thirty years? I can't remember what feeling well is like anymore. The Snake-monster is pushing up into my chest again—Complex Regional Pain Syndrome they'd kept calling it. Fancy words, but words with no power.*

She needed to take back power for both her and her… *daughter.*

"Fine," Nonhle said. "On one condition."

The man stood up sharply: "Non-negotiable, I said."

"Are you scared to barter with an old lady?"

The man grinned… and she was suddenly unsure as to whether she was talking to the devil himself. "I've bargained with the best."

"Strange you say that," she said. "It just happens, so have I."

Gill moved away to put the kettle on. "Just remember," she said, "we are the 99.99 percent—and my *gogo* is the Story Queen."

And so they bargained, Nonhle and the Man with No Name—and she felt as if she was teetering on the edge of an unsafe space, Great Whites ready to tear at her falling body.

But she was no pussycat herself. Smart enough to handle a devil, but what about the snake inside her?

In the end, they signed the deal with virtual fingerprints. Still, she'd been smart, like her own mamma had been—even though she'd disappeared north many years ago, leaving only a yellowing card promising to return. At the bottom, a scribbled exhortation of her favourite phrase: 'There is always work to be done.'

Nonhle just hoped she had been smart enough—it looked like everything rested on the agreed operation, which frightened her very much. One percent risk may be small, but it all depended on where you stood—and what ended up becoming.

Gill's hug was enough to stop Inyoka's bite deep into Nonhle's belly from doubling her over. *You are my reason to live, child, but I do wish very much to say goodbye to this Snake, who haunts me inside, like an eternal curse.*

(iii) Twenty Days After Wanting to Be Gone

Of her operation, Nonhle could remember little.

She knew it had happened down one of the little alleys amongst the higgledy-piggledy shacks that spread from the base of the World Cup Football Stadium in Green Point.

She also remembered the room was a shipping container that looked dirty, the brain device itself akin to a metal crown of thorns—attached to a Cloud PC, glowing blue with her life's data, her stories.

And then she could only remember Gill bringing her home to lie on her bed, dripping tea down her throat.

It was some hours—or days—later that she woke, sluggishly and resisting, out of long and wary habit.

Without thought, she began to move her awareness around her body, exploring her toes first, moving slowly upwards in a systematic body scan.

She'd not forgotten the Snake, though, bracing herself for the starting slithers of *Inyoka* inside her.

She rolled into a cocoon, but…

…Nothing?

Her body felt light, ethereal, as if unreal.

It was also both warm and welcoming, without the drill of pain sapping her.

Nonhle wept.

"What's wrong, *gogo*?" Gill was standing by the open door, alarmed.

Nonhle got up, slowly and carefully, moving into Snake Creeps Down position.

No Snake.

Her body stretched, painless—she felt as if she was a floating head.

Gill frowned. "What's wrong, *gogo*?"

"Nothing," Nonhle said. "Nothing!"

And with that, she started to cry again.

Her body was warm, comfortable, like an old forgotten slipper.

*

Gill readied the VR box as Nonhle stood to act her story.

Stories should be *performed*, not just spoken.

"How the honey-guide bird punished the greedy man," Nonhle announced, fluttering her hands to emulate bird-flight. "The honey-guide has always been the friendliest of birds, fetching men from their fields and leading them into the forest to show them where to find honey…"

Gill fed in buzzing sounds recorded from the now extinct hive that had been near Camp's Bay.

Nonhle's hands froze in midair, her face horrified.

Gill cut the connection.

Nonhle desperately flapped her hands, as if they could coax words from her mouth. But there were no words.

Gill said nothing; standing up, to hug the old woman. Nonhle did not return the hug.

"Gone," she whispered. "All gone."

A tingling prickled inside her stomach. She was wrong. Not everything had gone.

He was back, flicking his tail.

*

Without a story, she could not sleep.

Empty, hollow, old memories of her own mother reading something to her, but those words were gone too, eviscerated and evaporated over time. Nothing left but the Monster of pain, returning in undulating waves, as if slithering around inside her, with scales of razor blades.

Nonhle cried, despite being tired of crying, knowing it would help little.

No stories. What is the point?

Gill.

She sighed; her pillow was wet and salty, sharp to her nose. A distraction, at least, from the clawing Monster within.

What shall I do with you? Why won't you leave me?

There was no answer.

Gill.

Yes, Gill had made a new story for herself, when she'd challenged her father. A harder story in many ways, but a new one.

So what—if she can't remember the old, what was to stop her making new stories too? Somehow, the Pain Monster was part of her—and if it was part of her, she could place it within a story.

A completely new story.

How do you transform a Monster that feels as if it's slicing your body apart?

How do you transform a Snake?

No good friend would ever hurt you like that.

Family?

Maybe, but still not quite right.

Ever-present, unshakeable.

The Pain stepped outside of her, for the barest of moments.

Watching her, flickering between empathy and dispassion.

Then it was back inside her, a painful, strange angel.

She did not believe in angels. An ancestor, maybe, searching for something too?

"What are you?" Nonhle asked, before finally falling asleep to silence.

*

Her door creaked. A giant snake was slithering in, a Cape Cobra, brown-hooded, wet fanged, rearing.

Nonhle screamed.

Smash. She winced at the flash of pain across her face.

It was Gill, bent beside her in alarm, broken shards of a tea-mug beside her on the floor.

"What the hell, grandma?"

"S-s-sorry child, a bad dream. You frightened me."

"Nonhle." Gill sat next to her on the bed and she could sense a tingle in her voice. "Our account has gone crazy; we'll be hitting fifty million by the end of today—your gamble has paid off."

Nonhle laughed, sitting up to wipe hot drops of tea off her face. The Man with No Name had thought he'd won, when she had asked for a royalty cut in addition—and then had allowed herself to be pared down to zero-point zero one percent of all Mountain Top earnings on her stories. But Nonhle knew the value of her stories—and the terrible expenditure gap fissuring a divide far harder than that giant red wall, between the Top few and the Bottom many.

A very small fraction of so very much can still be a lot.

The No Name Man's parting look had carried a veiled accusation that she had overvalued her stories—but they were not just hers, they were from her family, her clan—and a deep history.

Thank you, mother, wherever you may be.

"Pack your bags, Gill," said Nonhle. "We are heading up the Mountain after all."

And, as she spoke, a new story was forming inside her, as if words were knitting together from internal puncture wounds and her scarred innards, the Snake gnawing frantically at her throat and tongue, trying to silence her.

The old woman smiled. *Words will not be stopped.*

(iv)The Day Nonhle Wished to Stay

The helicopter ride up the Mountain was terrifying.

Neither Nonhle nor Gill had ever flown before, carbon taxes curbing only the richest. Nonhle was stunned at how far the Mountain threaded its rump to the distant horizon, far beyond the table top plateau. She clutched the new BawoMa close in front of her, despite them being strapped together. It had cost her quite a bit, but she always knew she had to take the avatar with her somehow—eventually settling for a Wi-Fi chip within a gravity-resistant, walking staff.

The 'chopper'—as the surly white pilot referred to it—circled in towards the flat peak, buffeted increasingly side to side in the busy breeze as it moved in towards an open flat space of rock marked with a bull's-eye target, adjacent to a small building.

The domes of The One Hundred and the spire Of the Fist sprawled towards their left as they approached the landing mark—it was only then that Nonhle noticed a small crowd cordoned off from the site.

The chopper landed with a jolt, but BawoMa cushioned Nonhle by lifting her slightly, hovering above the point of impact.

As they stepped out of the helicopter the pilot said: "Welcome to your story fans, Mamma."

He smiled.

Nonhle smiled back—very little stayed as it initially seemed. The air itself was changing all the time.

But, as she moved, she had to suppress a gasp of pain.

Some things don't change.

The crowd—forty or fifty people—tried to move towards them; but were held back by electric-cordons. They shouted and cheered as the pair walked past and into the small terminal hut.

A bored official chewing gum of uncertain properties was waiting behind a desk, leaning against it as if she had forgotten how to stand. "Welcome to Table Mountain, one of the Twelve and a Half Wonders of the World. We need you to read and thumbprint residential rules before you go."

A screen behind the official began to roll a numbered list of regulations: 1. No crossing The Wall without formal permission from The Five; 2. No fomenting of troublesome behaviour; 3…

Nonhle wondered if there would be ten rules, but there ended up being thirty-five.

"Frown into the camera," instructed the official to both in turn.

"For your ID chips."

"Hello dad," waved Gill, as if knowing it was a live security feed too.

There was no response, from either the camera, or the official.

"You have a meeting with The Five at seven tonight," she said eventually, "and *don't* be late."

Gill and Nonhle thumbed assent at the end of proceedings—by the time they had completed the screen-work, the crowd had dissipated, the helicopter long gone, as the clock tilted towards five p.m.

The sun was hanging low over the swelling Atlantic Ocean.

"What now?" asked Gill.

"Now we foment some trouble," grinned Nonhle.

"Rule Two," said Gill.

"Indeed, and that's just the beginning."

"But how? We're just two newbies and The Five will be watching us like hawks."

The sea breeze shifted, as the sun sank, carrying chirps and alien chattering on the wind.

They looked at each other and Gill turned, running off ahead along a less used path, obscured partly by mountain *fynbos*. Nonhle followed painfully, as quickly as she could.

Gill was waiting for her, pressed against one of two large wire enclosures in front of them: one was roofed over, with a tweeting shrieking mass of wild birds of all shapes and sizes. The other that Gill was leaning against faced across the rear of the escarpment, peering into the deep valley spine of the Mountain marching south. This cage was open to the sky and housed several medium dog-sized grey animals, rooting amongst tumbled rocks and vegetation.

"It's true; they're catching the animals. What for? And what *are* they?" Gill asked, stock-still.

"*Dassies*," Nonhle whispered, "rock rabbits... Gorgeous. Did we pack my wire-cutters?"

There were about seven or eight, congregating around a pile of rocks with a small hole at the base. Some distance from the group, close by the wire fence, a particularly large one was sunning itself on a flat sandstone ridge.

"City food!" said a drone, hanging silently in the air behind them and Nonhle jumped. "Now move; you have no business here."

But it was too late.

The *dassies* were fast disappearing down their hole, squeaking in alarm. The fat one roused itself and starting scrabbling to get through the wire, as if it had spotted another hole nearer by.

There was no way through the wire, though, and the squeaks grew louder, more terrified.

"What is it?"

Nonhle looked up, screening her red eyes from the sun's glare with her spread left palm.

"Eagle," she said. "Black eagle."

"More than that," said staff Bawoma. "Everything is always more than that."

The eagle stooped from out of the sky, a bursting flurry of feathers and beak and poised talons, latching onto wriggling grey fur.

Then they were gone.

Blood on stone, waiting for rain.

"Move!" barked the drone.

They walked, shaken, threading their way through vegetation and low bush towards the raised 'finger' of the Tower of the Fist.

The drone vanished on ahead of them, as if finally satisfied with their compliance.

"They're watching us like eagles, not hawks," said Nonhle, "but, in the end, we will be the hunters. Got to find our own safe bolt-hole too, though."

"What will you tell The Five, *gogo*?"

Nonhle stopped then, some way short of the residential area, under the screen of an alien thorn tree. A large green head stood on a grey concrete plinth, marked *CJ Rhodes*.

"They've resurrected part of Cecil John, I see," smiled Nonhle.

"Who's he?"

"Who's he indeed? I need to first find out what the living, the Five, want to hear," Nobhle said, looking at Gill. "Every audience is different, every story unique." *Subtle tales of slow revolution, of breaking walls and a just spreading of food, wealth and water.*

Much, then, still to live for. Almost one million people on the other side of The Wall.

One million reasons to live.

The Fist must open its fingers—or else they will be forced open.

Finger by finger... story by story.

First, though, she must capture her audience.

Nonhle smiled, remembering the crowd that had awaited them—open to her—and open to new stories too, milling, as if they were caged too, and in waiting.

"I am coming to meet The Five too," said Gill.

Nonhle grasped her elbow. "But your father is Thumb," she said. "Why face him now, given how bad things were between you when he left?"

"To show him I am grown and no longer under him, I am my own woman," Gill said, "and I'm sorry, *gogo*, both for what he has said and who he is."

Nonhle shook her head, wincing at the increased bite of familiar pain within. "We're not responsible for our families, *ntombi*."

Gill smiled tearfully; *perhaps at being called daughter?*

Is this really the first time I have told her this?

Daughter.

Nonhle crossed her arms against the internal scratching of Dumisani the *ichelesi*, the Honey Badger—she would need to feed him more compassionate, sweet thoughts soon, to ease the pain. Still, he was kinder than the Snake had been—fierce too, but this may be useful, should battle come—as it always did.

"As for *you*, Dumisani, you must learn some manners, if you continue to use my belly," Nonhle snapped, clutching her stomach.

Gill laughed, knowing at whom the words were aimed. "What about buying the cure for CRAPs?"

Nonhle hesitated, feeling the lure of cure, the call of painlessness. *But there is so much to do first…*

"All in good time," she said. "I know some pain will always remain, whatever I do, while that wall still stands. First things first, we see the Five and then find a way to blow up the wall, story after story."

"We have Jesus on our side too," Gill laughed. "They won't stand a chance."

"Let's go then," said Nonhle. "There's always work to be done —- those waters just keep on rising."

"Now *that's* my girl," said BawoMa.

Mama?

Nonhle swung her staff with one hand, holding the pain in her belly with the other.

"Let's go," she said, again.

They left the head of Rhodes, under the thorn tree.

Now, to face the Fist.

No, you never *do* get used to pain.

But still, you can cup it with love.

Already, Nonhle could feel that the Badger inside her was softening and changing into her mother.

Beautiful Meat

The Old One of the Flow, Mwari, stood despairingly on the shore of the Dead Ocean. Leaning for support on Bama, his Power-Staff, he wished: *If I were an eagle, I'd fly this water…*

But I am only human, trapped in human meat.

Nothing moved; nothing lived. The ocean lay before them, the dry earth behind. He scanned the water; an endless grey emptiness leaking into stacked clouds on the horizon.

Here I am, in search of new life, new beginnings. Instead, I find the Flow has stopped, dead.

What will Thwasa say?

Mwari waited, with growing dread, for his young apprentice. *Am I indeed who I say I am? A finder of flow and life? Or am I just an old fool, chasing a dream?*

Images of children with fly-faces and rat-ribs entered his head. That last town, the most despairing for food… I must find the Land I sense. A land of fruit and honey, somewhere beyond…?

Mwari turned.

The last vestiges of vegetation straggled above, on steep red dunes, recoiling from the dead ocean. The heat hung heavy, a wet blanket burning the air, but yielding no rain.

The *shusshhing* of sand on the slope was the first sign of arriving life. The young man with white hair and angry face appeared over the crest of the dune, slithering and sliding down on leathery feet, thin body hunched at a defensive angle.

He swore as he arrived on level beach and saw the empty sea.

Mwari sighed; the tall youngster was decidedly the worse for wear, after their thousand-mile journey—his paler skin stretched tight and long darkened by the ever-angry sun.

Thwasa's green eyes swung down to catch their gaze, cursing again. "What is this, Master? A mirage—or for real? And can we fucking drink it?"

He shook his head; when would Thwasa learn not to waste his words? *What use is empty cussing, spitting your precious water against the sky?*

Thwasa tapped the reed bag strapped across his back. "We're almost out of water and fucking food. We're not going to make it back to that last settlement, and they have precious little themselves anyway. It's three days away—and that's on good legs."

Mwari sighed again, wondering when thirst would eventually pin the young man's mouth shut. Still, he had a point.

He turned and walked stiffly down the slope to where the Ocean waited.

Or so he hoped.

But the water did not wait, nor did it lap, or move. It was flat, empty, and lifeless.

Mwari bent down with difficulty and scooped a cold splash into his mouth.

He turned to look at the paler burnt man, staying squat on his haunches, in the cool water.

"Well?" Thwasa asked impatiently.

Mwari spat.

There is nowhere to go—and nothing to drink. This is indeed the very end of the world. Clearly an age, and an age beyond, since rain last fell here.

"What now?" asked Thwasa.

Terse for a change—was the young man's tongue starting to stick to his palate too? Thwasa was an apprentice who'd matched him step for step over a thousand miles or more, so deserved every respect, however annoying he'd been along the way.

"I'm sorry, I haven't a clue," Mwari said, heart heavy, head and stomach light.

A faint offshore breeze fanned the Ocean of the Dead and, without thinking, Mwari turned to face it.

Always face the wind, Mandisa had constantly told him.

But there had not even been a breeze the morning she died.

Where too now, Blind One in the clouds?

Mwari had found Thwasa soon after the start of his journey, searching for new food and life. Thwasa was sullenly sweeping the floors of a madrassa. Food and a little water the young man had fetched him, even though Mwari was clearly a magician of The Flow, not a *Christlamic* supplicant.

Still, not too many clung to certainties any more, religious or otherwise.

The young man had then loitered in the doorway, while Mwari had told the learned of his quest to find new seeds and new life in order to resurrect the dying Earth. The elite of Islamic Christ had confirmed only the mystical mountain of *Hoerikwaggo* might still harbour anything of use—due south, towards the very end of the world, perched on an

158

island in the Ocean of the Dead.

The young man had wanted to come and, as paler men were few—some even supposedly endowed with magical talents and spiritual nous—Mwari had thought the gods might have earmarked him as a companion for the journey.

Now, though, many moons later, Mwari wondered whether the devils had duped him instead…

Thwasa stepped in front, making direct eye contact, face pimpled with hunger-fever. "What about magic? Can't you fly us to the other side?"

Mwari shrugged. "What other side? And as I've told you repeatedly, magic carries a cost—and we have nothing left, nothing with which to pay."

The sun was starting its slow descent, bright orange blaze barely denting or bouncing off the leaden Ocean. Mwari stepped around Thwasa, walking forwards to stand knee deep in water, savouring some wetness, however undrinkable.

"This Ocean," he said, "is the very end of the world."

"What about the promised island? Let *me* try," said Thwasa, moving alongside and holding his hand out. "Give me the Power-Staff."

Mwari turned to look at the young man's grasping right hand. "Do you see any island? And are you sure you're up to this?"

"Where's your faith, Old One?" he snapped. "What else have we got?"

Indeed. Mwari hesitated then. *Was this the time, finally, to start handing over? The young man has shown some promise en route, leaching water from clay, and finding hidden mangoes to eat.*

Mwari had once been young too, when blind Mandisa had finally handed over the Staff known as Bama to them.

"In my younger days," she'd told him, "Bama spoke. Take care of the spirit inside, and they will help you hear."

"Hear what?" he'd asked, but it was as if Mandisa had not heard them.

"You are different," she only said. "Magic thrives on difference."

Mwari did not need reminding he was different.

"Stop daydreaming, Old One!" Thwasa grasped at the Staff.

Mwari felt their right-hand bunch into a fist and resist.

The young man looked astonished—and then angry.

Remembering their Calling, the Old One let go.

Water flows best through open hands—and fists have little use beyond fights.

We need to drink, then eat, not fight.

Let it go…

The young man had indeed used Bama before, sparingly, but always under strict supervision.

I have no ideas left, nothing to suggest.

The young man stepped ashore and glared at the Staff—held wide between his two open palms—stretched in front of him. It was five feet of solid Cape oak, with several leather straps for grip, and a metal cap at the top, harnessing a small array of black squares.

An ancient Staff, from the time of the Metal Wizards.

Thwasa straddled his legs apart on the parched beach soil, bare leathery feet shuffling for a firm position. His loincloth flickered in the light sea breeze fanning off the water.

At least he remembers that. Always face the wind. Be prepared for what is coming.

Thwasa snarled at the Staff held out in front of him, as if focusing his frail strength into the thick wooden shaft cradled between his spread palms.

Then, without chant or invocation, he swung the Power-Staff heavily to the earth in his left hand, simultaneously roaring his desperation into the blue sky.

A call to the Gods from a dying man.

Mwari smiled sadly, moving forward to join the man, trailing drops of cool water from his heels. The dry land burnt his briefly softened soles.

The Gods, like the last of the animals, he'd learned on this long journey, were scarce indeed.

Mwari stopped.

Thwasa was grinning and looking behind him, out to sea.

The ground was trembling under their feet.

Slowly, the Old One turned, as turgid, listless water rushed out. Emerging from the sea, dotted in an erratic pathway to the horizon, were red stone pillars, stepping stone height and spaced evenly above the water.

"After you, Master," Thwasa grinned, waving the heavy Staff with some difficulty.

Mwari took the Staff—it was warm and sweaty. The hard, silver cap on the top of the Staff was glowing red, too hot to touch.

This was indeed an ancient Staff, full of temperamental magic from those long-gone Metal Wizards of old.

What kind of magic is this?

Thwasa's loincloth had been brushed aside from underneath.

Ahhh, man *magic then.*

Mwari turned away, quickly, and jumped onto the first stone near the shore, using Bama to balance, as if crossing a rope bridge. Slowly, methodically, given the stones were slippery, he stepped out towards the horizon—and, as he walked towards the clouds in the distance,

Mwari prayed silently for rain.

Step, shuffle, step, step, shuffle, step…

Mwari moved from stone to stone—head down, intent on not slipping. Until his right foot hovered over empty sea.

Teetering, he reared back onto the last stone.

A body thumped against him and he was choking cold water, bubbles flailing and rising. Mwari held on to the Staff, kicking his legs, eyes burning. Coughing, he felt a weight pull him upwards, onto craggy raised stone. He lay and gasped, holding scratched and bruised ribs from the rock's edge.

Thwasa was holding the other end of Bama and had pulled and stepped backwards onto the further stone behind, in order to make room for him.

"We've no bloody paddle, let alone a boat," said Thwasa, staring over still empty sea to a darkening horizon.

The stones had stopped.

Mwari sat coughing, looking towards the murky red-grey sky where the hidden sun was sinking—darkening the water, mist slowly rolling in. *Back to the beach, in this gathering dark… is a death walk.*

"We're fucked," Thwasa said from behind, "Unless…"

Thud… and rumble.

A small wave hit Mwari's back. Alarmed, he spun around on their haunches.

Thwasa was standing with legs akimbo, holding onto the Power-Staff in his right hand, his stepping stone split squarely in two.

"Uh—perhaps I didn't hit it hard enough?" he said, bringing both hands to bear on the Staff above his head.

"No!" Mwari said, holding his hand out.

Thwasa hesitated, Staff hovering.

Mwari looked him in the eyes.

The young man bent forward and handed the Staff over.

"So," he said, "what are *you* going to do instead, Master?"

"Pray," he said, dropping the Staff across his lap.

"But I thought you said the Gods were dead?"

"I know, but I just pray I'm wrong." Eyes closed, Mwari mouthed words from an ancient prayer to the Sea God, until his tongue stuck painfully to his dry palate.

He opened his eyes.

Thwasa was sitting, watching the water, in what looked like a vain search for fish.

Mwari turned to look over his right shoulder.

The sea went on forever and the mist had reared into the sky—large, but still distant clouds, too far, far away.

Mwari cried, tears rolling and spilling into the dead, salty sea.

What else to do? But what a waste of water—and not even the lightest of breezes to face into, either.

*

"Water," croaked Thwasa.

Mwari gave him the too-light gourd.

Thwasa tilted it back and emptied the last few drops.

Mwari took it back, reaching over into the water and scooping up a draught through the open lid. Placing it upright between his knees, he held Bama over the gourd.

Mwari whispered a blessing: 'To Mandisa and the parents who were ashamed of me. To the gods who have left the Earth.'

He took a sip.

It was fresh.

Mwari turned and gave the rest to the young man.

"You're a genius magician, Master," he croaked, as he took a swig.

Mwari shook his head, feeling weak and dizzy. It was a last and fading flourish, not to be sustained. Prolong the young man's life and he, at least, might just find a way to move on and live. *In search of new life, all I can do is delay death. And not for long, either.*

Mwari handed Thwasa a soggy, salty apple.

"So… which are you *really*," asked Thwasa, nibbling into the damp and floury fruit, "master—or mistress? Master, surely, given you have no tits?"

Mwari pulled his legs onto the stone, grimacing at the pain in their ribs. Memory flashes of children pulling down their trousers and laughing circled in painfully again.

The Blind One had always taught him to wrap up the nether regions well, and to be discreet in toileting; some might stone them, as if accursed of the One God.

Sometimes, difference needs to be covered.

"Come." Thwasa swallowed the core. "No secrets between the dying. I know you've seen my dick. Now show me yours."

"Either-or thinking kills magic," Mwari said, licking cracked lips, "Keep your possibilities endlessly refracted, like those rusted kaleidoscopes, from the Metal Masters of old."

"Yadda, yadda, ya—now it's *you* who talk too much. Show me your cock."

Mwari hesitated, ashamed, holding up a hand to keep the laughing children at bay. Mandisa had sent them all running one day and had taken over mentoring Mwari, reassuring him *everything* was natural, and *everything* was beautiful.

Even… him.

Thwasa was preparing to take his own loincloth off instead, with a challenging stare.

"Stop," said Mwari, standing with difficulty and working off the clasp holding his pelvic wrapping. Slowly, he pulled the cloth away, aware his legs were shaking.

Thwasa recoiled in shock.

He's a young man—he knows no better—but why do I still feel shame?

"Well?" Mwari asked, edgily.

"I. Have. No. Fucking. Idea."

"Good," Mwari said, but not feeling good. "There's magic in that. I am both master and mistress—and neither."

Behind him, the breeze was whipping up into stronger gusts.

"So… which one do you piss out of?" Thwasa asked. "The half-cock, or the hole?"

Mwari hesitated, fixing his loincloth back and turning to face the stiffening wind. "In the end, it's all just a piece of meat." *There is more difference in the shape and contour of the human face—why does my small organ difference have to always be so shocking to others?*

Darkness was coming in on the wind, the clouds now directly above them, and a chill shock of rain swept onto head and shoulders, pouring down his almost naked body.

Mwari tilted his head back and opened their mouth.

Mangilasayo!

This time, he did not regret their tears, although he was not fully sure what stung them free. Bama blinked in his right hand. *Is there someone else here, hanging in the damp air above me?* "Mandisa?"

Only the rumble of nearby thunder answered.

*

Hunger snaked inside, so the Old One stood on one leg, alternating, balancing, and keeping his circulation going in the gloom.

The young man was a deeper shadow in the dark, sitting hunched around his knees, and talking through his favourite meals as a young boy in the madrassa; *braaied* rat in *buchu* sauce seemed to be the all-time favourite, a repeating motif.

The rain had clearly lubricated his tongue.

Mwari resisted an urge to strike the younger man with Bama. The Staff had gone cold and damp; darkness always stilled its magic, and he knew hunger always fueled their own anger.

Both had dropped their cloths; what purpose could it serve out here, so far away from any habitation and in a still insistent heat? There was nothing left to hide, in any case.

"It *is* just a piece of meat," Thwasa had grudgingly admitted, looking down at his limp cock.

Both gourds were full of water, at least. The clouds had felt personal, somehow, and Bama's cap had glowed momentarily, as if in strange recognition of something—or someone.

Thwasa stopped talking.

Has he fallen asleep at last?

And then the question came, from out of the dark, like an arrow.

"You know what you always tell me about facing into the wind?"

"Yes…?" *This question is veiled and loaded, but how else to respond, without knowing what plucks the bow string?*

"That's easy for you to say, but not always *do*, given how you must piss, surely?"

Ah—masked animosity; finally unmasked—Mwari raised their Staff, ready to strike the talking, disrespectful shadow.

"No!" said Bama.

Thwasa recoiled, but Mwari stayed their strike. *Has Bama just spoken?*

No further sound, but Mwari felt shame fill his lungs. *There is too little life left to hurt anything or anyone. Fists hold back flow. Relax your grip. Hunger makes us* all *angry.*

"Tell me, Thwasa—why *do you* talk so much?" Mwari asked, instead.

Silence. *Is he ignoring me?*

Then, one by one, words came—slower words, less easy and less slippery off the tongue.

"Mostly… to keep the night away."

"What do you mean?" Mwari stood squarely, resting against Bama. *We will head back, defeated, in the morning—and we need to listen to each other too, properly, if we are to survive the return journey. Even though we have failed, and we carry nothing.*

"I don't remember anyone being with me at night," Thwasa's words dripped slowly, reluctantly. "I was two when I was left at the madrassa gates. There, they made sure I was fed, but I've *always* slept alone. I learned to speak back to the night, to keep the monsters away."

We share ashamed and abandoning parents. Are the young man's words just a constant assertion of existence?

"And then I spoke back to the day too. But, despite my words, I—I stayed alone—and lonely."

Peering hard in the gloom, Mwari could see Thwasa's back, slouched away, as if hiding from what he'd said. He could sense the young man's own shame, and his isolation too. *I had Mandisa, at least, who'd raised me as their own before making me apprentice to the Flow.*

Unsure of what to say, Mwari coaxed up their favourite bedtime song, remembered from Mandisa, guaranteed many solar seasons ago to always help him sleep: "*Tula Thul Tula sana…*"

And the years fell away as they sang, with Mandisa, the Blind One, hovering like a shadow on his shoulder. But—was that a man standing behind her—thin and sallow skinned, shining faintly in the darkness? Surely not The Ancient and first one of the Flow, //Kabbo of the San, the Early People?

If so, he was singing too and, as they all sang, the sea began sparkling, green lights flashing on and off around them.

Mwari stopped.

Mandisa and //Kabbo were gone, but dark shapes weaved alongside and around them in the water, flitting amongst the sea of stars.

"Fish," shouted Thwasa. "Food."

Mwari threw back his head to laugh, but stopped, noticing something very odd about the swimming patterns. *The—fish?—are swimming away from us, further up, but in a… straight line? Nature hates straight lines, preferring sprays and curves. Axiom Three of the Flow. It's as if an… an underwater barrier is keeping them in check, funneling their flight through the green and floating stars?*

Ahhhh… was this a wall—now broken and fully submerged here?

"Are you ready to get wet, Thwasa?" Mwari asked.

"What do you mean, Master?"

"Just call me Mwari," he said. "I think these steps are actually part of a broken and submerged wall. The fish are swimming along it; we must have just hit a larger broken gap. I reckon we can make our way along the underwater section. It's probably not too deep and it's got to head *somewhere*. Walls connect—or hide."

Mwari could not remember when he had last spoken so much.

"So—we go on?"

"We. Go. On." Mwari jumped in, holding Bama firmly to his chest, kicking hard to stay afloat. *It's fucking cold.* He followed the fish, making contact eventually with a slippery, underwater edifice, scraping his shins painfully.

"Bingo!" Mwari gasped.

"What?" shouted Thwassa, splashing along behind.

"A magic oath, from long ago," said Mwari, momentarily resting on a slippery, underwater wall fragment. "We follow the fish." *The Gods may be scarce, but the ancestors, at least, are alive.*

They followed the fish.

*

Mwari woke on the shore, where they'd finally dragged themselves off the wall, in the deep of night. Unable to see clearly and exhausted, they'd pulled themselves away from the sea, until reaching safer bush cover at the top of the slope.

Old journey habits, finding spaces where the occasional foraging dog-rat or starving vulture would not see them.

Here, though, what awaits us?

Mwari sat, with a groan, bruised right ribs from the earlier clash with sea-brick still aching.

Thwasa was sitting in front of him, grinning through his beard, as he ate from a pile of mangoes and plums.

"This is a fucking paradise," he said.

Mwari looked at him.

"Sorry—*paradise...* I'm also sorry for, uh, being an *isidenge* out there."

"Well," said Mwari, grabbing a mango with his right, and a plum with his left hand, "acknowledgement is the start of change. I've no doubt I was a bit of an idiot too."

"Terse as tin, irritating as hell," Thwasa wiped juice off his beard, before grabbing another mango. "My favourite fruit."

"Let's not start on food again," said Mwari. "Have you scouted?"

"Just over the rise, the fruit trees stopped me."

Mwari smiled and used Bama to lever himself up, minimizing strain on his ribs: "Of course they did."

Thwasa led them upwards, through a dense screen of waist high shrub—ripe and resilient, a good sign, as if this place were well blessed by rain.

The slope was overhung by fruit trees, dripping with mangoes, plums and figs.

"Leave the figs for now," grunted Mwari, pushing though the dense trees. "Our stomachs have had shock enough, with so much sudden food."

Thwasa was panting too hard to reply and Mwari smiled, no longer feeling quite so old.

The slope gave way to a wide shelf of stone and plants and Mwari whistled.

"What—is—it?" Thwasa joined them on the plateau, stopping suddenly.

A corroded metal hut hung crookedly near the hard slope edge, with a broken cable swinging from its empty doorway. Further beyond, a chaotic corridor of trees and tumbled brick houses led to a tall tower in the distance.

"Metal magicians," said Thwasa.

In the distance, through the trees, they could see the sparkle of the sea. The living Ocean of the Dead.

"This is an island," said Mwari. "It can't be *Hoerikwaggo*. That's a mountain."

"There's certainly plenty of fruit here—but what are you looking for in particular?"

"Seeds, life generators, life enhancers…" said Mwari, moving forwards with reverence, through the trees and ramshackle buildings. A flap of wings, and a burst of birds erupted from a building.

"Not hungry pigeons," said Thwasa. "What are they?"

Mwari smiled. "Fat red-winged starlings; I recognise them from pictures in books at the Jozi Shrine. We are indeed in paradise here. Eggs count too, although they're hard to carry safely."

Thwasa peered under a bank of broken stones, by an old and twisted thorn tree. "There's a metal head here, lying on the ground."

The head was mostly green, a man with a broken nose and white bird shit spattered across his face, name still on the battered plinth that the head had seemingly fallen from.

"He's seen better days," said Mwari. "Someone called 'Rhodes.' We can't eat that."

They froze at the bloodcurdling shriek.

Disorientated, they looked around, Mwari holding Bama defensively in front of them.

The shriek came again, from a heavily foliaged tree in front of them. They crept forward cautiously.

A large black bird hunched on a branch, curved beak used to shredding, its eyes blinking.

"What the hell is it?" whispered Thwasa.

"Black eagle," chuckled Mwari. "Got to be a good food chain here."

"We're not on it, are we?" Thwasa refused to move further, so Mwari sidled up closer.

The bird started to dance slowly on the branch, ragged claws clenching and unclenching in turn, head cocking first to the right, then to the left.

Bama was warm in his hands, the metal cap starting to glow as the sun's rays took charge of the new day.

Images flash. Mating in midair, tumbling downwards, and breaking apart—flying sated, but banished by partner, burning trees below but seeds within. Take—but go.

"What's wrong, Mwari?" Thwasa stood beside him, supporting him under the arm, holding Bama in one hand.

Mwari shook his head, dazed. "I think the eagle has just—spoken to me?"

Thwasa laughed, "What did the bird say, then?"

"I—I think it told me we're allowed just one bang here before we must go, never to return."

"Ha!" Thwasa grinned, but Mwari was not listening or watching, intently focused on a smaller brown bird, dancing further along the path.

"Jackpot," Mwari said. "Another old magic word—this is a honey-guide."

He set off after the bird. "You hear that humming sound, Thwasa? That's the call of heaven."

But Thwasa had remained behind, holding Bama, and Mwari caught his shout, muffled through the trees: "I think this fucking bird has spoken to me too!"

"What's that?" Mwari was pushing through bushes in excitement, chasing the brown bird, as the buzzing grew ever louder.

Thwasa's voice floated, urgently loud and insistent. "Bird says cover up—or else heaven's going to sting like shit!"

*

Standing on the summit of the island, looking down across the sea, with bags packed full of eggs, seeds, honeycomb and bees, Mwari hoped they had the queen bee herself inside too.

If not, the entire swollen left side of my face will not have been worth it.

Honey, though, was surely the food of the gods.

Ready to head home, but where is the way back?

The stepping stones, dots in the distance in the morning, were gone. Thwasa swore.

"Tide?" Mwari asked hopefully. *Who knows where else—or how much—it has rained?*

A large bird alighted nearby, on the broken building with its swinging cable.

"Oh, hello *Nongqawuse*," Mwari said to the eagle.

"The bird's got a name now?"

"It's more than a bird. It's the living spirit of a prophetess who aimed to drive white invaders out of her country, a long time ago."

Thwasa laughed then, a belly-based guffaw, which gladdened Mwari's heart: "Seriously?"

"Yup, she's even told me that a lot of life is drifting here from a giant green land, even further across the seas than this."

Thwasa laughed again, but this time in obvious disbelief.

"We're all more than we appear," said Mwari shortly, stopping to listen to the eagle again. He sighed and licked a finger to check the wind direction. "Not easy; we're going to be heading straight into the wind."

"What are you talking about?"

Mwari inspected the Staff, "How are your arm muscles, Thwasa?"

"Like yours; not bad. We've exercised them enough. Why?"

"*Nongqawuse* wants to come with us, so we're going to fly."

"Seriously?"

"Yup, but we're going to have to hang on like sticky shit for a while. I've seen pictures in old books of women riding brooms—but they must have had superb stomach muscles and an incredible sense of balance. Look, hold here..."

But Thwasa refused.

Mwari looked at him over the Staff, "What's wrong?"

"Why can't we just stay here? We've got all we can eat or wish to drink here. We're going back to a fucking desert."

"But we need to make it better—and what about the others? I promised them aid."

"Yes," said Thwasa loudly, a vein jumping in his neck, "what about them? We both got abandoned. we both got treated like shit."

The wind off the sea was cold and the eagle shat on the roof.

Mwari offered Thwasa a part of the Staff, strapping a leather thong around his own wrist. "I *have* to help the others. Besides, I don't want to end up having to marry you."

Thwasa snorted a repressed laugh, but kept his arms lowered.

"Goodbye, my... friend. Thank you for coming with me on such a long and hard journey." Mwari turned into the wind, holding Bama aloft.

"Wait, I, I—don't want to be alone again."

Mwari turned.

Thwasa had lifted his arms in submission. "Alone, I am nothing."

Mwari smiled, fastening him on to the other end of the Staff. They raised Bama above their heads. "Grip hard and on my mark. On five; one, two..."

Bama pulled hard and their grips tightened, Mwari teetered onto his toes, as the Staff lurched upwards.

"Five." A mutual grunt of pain and effort as the Staff pulled them both off their feet and swung them down and over the sea, skimming above the waves.

Thwasa yowled with excitement: "*Yahhhh...!*"

Mwari focused on containing the pain in his face and ribs while steering towards the unseen shore, across the sea.

Nongqawuse swooped ahead, leading the way.

Mwari held a focus on the eagle, the breeze buffeting them as they swung underneath the Staff, their shoulders wrenched and aching, right ribs burning.

Thwasa seemed oblivious. "Look," he said, "a fish fin in the water below."

"Don't. Let. Go." Mwari grunted. *Not a fish. Sign of a long food chain in the water too, at least. That's the Ocean King, a Great White. The sea lives.*

The shore was coming, a ragged coastline of white, yellow and sporadic green. Mwari felt the cost of their flying effort, blood lacing his bitten lips.

Keep going, the far shore is almost here. Keep going, damn you, all pain will pass.

Keep going.

"Who's that?" shouted Thwasa.

Mandisa and //Kabbo were waiting on the shore.

Keep going... this young man, he must live.

Mwari died, as he had lived, face ever turned into the wind.

Thwasa it was who landed them, in soft sand—gently done, but with Mwari hanging and dropping limply onto wet sand, like a wretchedly broken doll.

Thwasa sobbed, then howled.

Above them, *Nongqawuse* circled.

Three Souls flash away, and so life flows, person gone. Call cousin vultures? Now, dead body is just a piece of beautiful meat.

Bonus Material

Commentary on stories

Of Hearts and Monkeys

In 2009, after being diagnosed with two unrelated—but both essentially chronic and incurable illnesses—I went for frequent walks on Silvermine, a mountainous region along the spine at the back of Table Mountain in Cape Town. It was there I first heard the whisperings of Noluthando Ngobo Bhele, on the stiff South Easter summer breeze.

So, one day I got back to my parents' home and started to write MamBhele's whisperings down, feverishly, and forgetting my own pain. I gave the story to *Noluyando Roxwana* who confirmed MamBhele's words resonated with herself as another umXhosa woman. So, how does one survive the Zombie Apocalypse or Umbulalasizwe? By listening hard and respecting each other's space—and working together. And, in hearing the stories of others, our own pain can be shared and forgotten. At least for story-time.

The Girl Who Called the World

This continuation of MamBhele's journey was inspired by a call from Crossed Genres, who were compiling an anthology around 'QUILTBAG' families—at that time relatively hidden or absent from SFF, despite SFF being ostensibly about new and diverse ways of being. And so *The Girl Who Called the World* found its way into *Fierce Families*—the story was an effortless write, despite being several years later than *Of Hearts and Monkeys*—it felt like revisiting an old friend. With a few suggested minor tweaks, *Noluyando Roxwana* agreed.

Thandiwe's Tokoloshe

This was the first time I was actively approached to contribute towards an anthology—in this case Fox Spirit's *African Monsters*—and it made me feel I had *arrived* as a writer. (It took me a long while to realise you are constantly 'arriving'—and, if you're lucky, each new time is a little further along the Not Paved with Gold Street of Writing.)

Which 'African Monster' though? Easy enough if you're a white South African, where growing up, the pre-eminent local monster was the *tokoloshe*—a small, evil, sprite like creature, full of spite. Fox Spirit Books asked me too, why the *tokoloshe*?

Have a look at Penny Miller's (1979) wonderful *Myths and Legends of Southern Africa* or, if you're more academically inclined, try Nhlanhla Mkhize's (1996) "Mind, gender, and culture: A critical evaluation of the phenomenon of Tokoloshe "sightings" among prepubescent girls in Kwazulu-Natal"

But, as for me, if you want the truth, the little monster called me to watch him…

The Tokoloshe smelt someone coming, even as the late afternoon air hummed with hot sun and clouds and a rainbow arch crumbled into a million dying pieces above his head.

Still, the river flowed strongly, swirling logs and leaves and dead fleshy things past him.

He stepped up onto the river bank to sniff the air, and he could smell the coming human was a she.

He grinned then, licking his sharp teeth, flicking fur out of his eyes and twisting his only garment, a leather strung hip pouch, into ready position. His witch would be pleased. The thick riverside bushes bustled with movement.

Ooh, a young smell. She whom he served would be very pleased.

He slung his penis over his left shoulder and fumbled in his pouch for his stone, but there was no time. The bushes burst apart and a skinny, dishevelled girl was staring down at him.

She looked tired and her trousers were torn, with both her legs bleeding.

I know, fuck those thorn bushes, he thought, but the girl's eyes opened wide in shock and she shrunk against the bushes.

He licked his teeth again, slowly, waiting for her to turn and run.

But she stood firm, returning his gaze.

He grabbed his penis, flailing it like a warning whip.

Still, she did not run.

Brave or stupid?

Either way, she was dead meat.

He leaped forward to grab her…

500 Photons

Writers often like the challenge of writing to specific and exact word constraints. You need to be extra careful to make sure each word counts. Add in the story conceit of a further constraint as to whether your words would *ever* be heard, as the intended recipient becomes ever more distant.

A meditation on my own increasing sense of mortality, as the time and space for words dry up. Make *your* own words count. Now.

God in the Box

This story was a first for me in several ways. My first 'big' sale, to the premier *SF* magazine in the UK, my first story where I wrote in 1st person POV as a woman, my first story to be translated. (The translation was fun—*Dieu sur ordonnance*, published in the *Utopiae 2003* anthology—and I was even flown out to Nantes in France and met Michael Moorcock, Terry Pratchett, Brian Aldiss, a very young Lavie Tidhar...)

All triggered by a numinous dream in which God appeared—as an asteroid crashing to Earth. Now how the hell—or heaven—can I make a story out of that? By finding the characters orbiting in tension around that asteroid...

Bridges

Bridges was entered for the *Aeon International Award* in 2009 and ended up as Runner-Up, with Ian Watson saying of it: This story, featuring a future South Africa in which apartheid never ended, is "politically acute and powerful, with its heart in the right place... and is in many ways a 'textbook story', because it's so well done."

Having grown up reading many of Ian Watson's wonderful books in the 1970's, e.g. *The Embedding*, *The Jonah Kit*, *The Martian Inca*, etc., I was thrilled to bits to get these comments on the story. But this was only the beginning of Bridges, which eventually morphed into my debut novel *Azanian Bridges*, under the supervisory encouragement of Farah Mendlesohn during my MA in Creative Writing (Science Fiction and Fantasy) at Middlesex University.

What started me building Bridges was the question What if Apartheid Had Survived? But, as the years have subsequently rolled by, I think in many ways it *has* unfortunately survived, in ugly but still recognisable, transmogrified forms...

Azania

Another first—the first anthology of SF by Africans for Africans—and any interested others—beating *Lagos 2060* by a few months. Azania was once touted as a possible name for a post-apartheid South Africa.

I was wondering about setting a story in space, and how to subvert the neo-colonial enterprise of much space-conquering fiction. Ah—what better way to do this, I thought, than to send astronauts from previously colonised countries to colonise a new world. But how do we stop ourselves repeating the mistakes of the past? Nothing like a touch of illness, to remind you of how small and fragile you are. I gave a distant tele-lecture to a US College course on 'World SF' about Azania. I was asked what this mysterious illness meant. All immigration comes at a cost, I said.

Lunar Voices (On the Solar Wind)
This story won the *Accessible Future* prize run by Redstone Science Fiction for stories positively integrating disability and adaptations in the future. I had completed my PhD on Cognitive Development in Deaf Children at University College London and had learned some rudimentary British Sign Language (BSL). In addition, I was partially deaf myself with discomfiting and intractable Meniere's Disease, and I was wondering how I might story such a beautiful language as BSL within a futuristic setting? Why in Space of course—in this story here, on the Moon—where no one can hear you scream.

(Busi Siyathola was my helpful umZulu reader, to ensure Phulani's account was culturally sound.)

African Shadows
This is my oldest story in the anthology, initially published in *Scheherazade*, a Brighton based SFF magazine. I visited the editor Liz Counihan to see the original artwork made for my story and loved it—an astronaut desperately alone in the vastness of space. It was the first time anyone had made art in response to my own art—pond circle ripples, creating new ways of seeing and being.

As for the story itself, it was triggered by an axiom I quickly learned, while working within an amaZulu psychiatric hospital: reality and knowledge can be very relative.

Mindreader
In my job as a clinical psychologist, I ended up specialising in work with children, particularly children with neurodevelopmental difficulties such as Autism. *Mindreader* was written in the aftermath of 9/11, with echoes of aggressive Bush rhetoric. I laced those two ideas across an 'emotional bridge,' heralding love, rather than guns. (I guess bridges are somewhat of a pervasive theme for me.)

Mindreader was positively reviewed by Lois Tilton (who reviewed for *Locus* at one point), although Lois said she did not think I had much knowledge in psychological research. I wrote to Lois, saying I was Research Director on a D.Clin.Psy. Programme. She replied: 'Oh. Sorry.'

I'll take that, thanks Lois!

The Paragon of Knowledge

This story was published in *The Future Fire*, a socio-political SF magazine in the UK. The story was prompted by considerations of disability and the naïve notion of an 'everyone will be tan' post-racial future. With regards to disability, I was thinking about whose stories are marginalised or appropriated—or, as in from the Department for Work and Pensions (DWP), here in the UK, *discounted*. Allied to this was the rise of social media and concerns about AI—who, or what, is gorging on our data—and our lives?

Case Notes of a Witchdoctor

It was published on Lavie Tidhar's wonderful but now defunct *World Science Fiction Blog*. I made a decision for my future working life, in 1981, after finishing a psychology degree at the University of Cape Town (UCT), that I would only work in then legally designated 'black' areas in apartheid South Africa. This was because I needed to familiarise myself with what was happening to the vast majority of my co-citizens in the country, but those who had no vote and were subject to state violence at the time. So I worked initially as a community worker, then as a psychologist with a socio-political organisation aimed at helping victims of state violence both recover and mobilise.

There were very few white people in the townships at the time and this white fear of township spaces seems to have lasted until current times, despite massive political transformations since 1994. So this is a story about the need to bleed our public spaces and versions of 'reality' together, akin to the *Hearing Voices Network* around experiencing and normalising 'psychosis' within the UK. (An old and enduring influence for me is RD Laing's *The Divided Self* and *The Politics of Experience and the Bird of Paradise*.)

As for the derogatory and still used colonial term for local African traditional healers such as *isangomas*, i.e. the 'witchdoctor'—to whom does this apply, within my story?

Dream-Hunter

A first story in Africa's premier SFF online magazine *Omenana!* And a story that gets reprinted in *The Best of British Science Fiction 2016*. A story where I was thinking about home, roots and multiple identities—as well as how do we stop 'domestic' violence? (There is certainly nothing domesticated about this vicious and often hidden or minimised form of violence.) With dreaming new and better ways of 'being a man'—and realising gender is multiple and rainbow too.

Thirstlands

Thirstlands was originally published in the NewCon Press anthology *Subterfuge*. (NewCon went on to publish my debut novel *Azanian Bridges* too.) *Thirstlands* is currently in the Solar-Punk anthology *Sunvault* (2017), looking at moving beyond grim dystopias and into new ways of living with (and restricting) global warming. The wellspring for *Thirstlands*—and the novel *Water Must Fall*, which has subsequently emerged—was global warming, the desiccation and disruption of resources and nature, and the need for us to co-operate and share, if we are going to survive.

The Guardian of the Grain

I lived and worked in Aotearoa, New Zealand, for a couple of years, primarily with Maori and Pacific Island youth with mental health difficulties. I was taken under the wing of a Maori psychiatric nurse, keen for me to be educated and aware of the political issues in the country. Coming from South Africa, however, I was not too surprised. It took me a good few years before I felt I could do justice to Anne, and even only then, by putting her on the Moon.

To the renaissance and survival of *Te Reo Maori*, once outlawed in New Zealand schools.

A Million Reasons Why

A story for the many, on the wrong side of walls and borders. And to everyone who manages—and finds meaning—in constant pain. Suicidal behaviour is a taboo for many, but I also wanted to demythologise the idea that it is the prerogative or domain of any specific group of people. Working clinically with suicide, I have found the most powerful intervention is reconnecting the person to someone of value, who provides a reason to continue. And yes, here I write what I know. Time to talk indeed.

And time for humans to unite and dissolve borders and barriers, so that we can find ways to struggle together with—and survive—the Climate Threat already upon us. But that's another story…

Beautiful Meat

A story for celebrating, not just 'tolerating', difference. And for celebrating the reverence for life, needed to sustain life.

Years ago, I spent some four nights and days on my own, in a hiking hut on the Drakensberg/uKhahlamba Mountains. A Booted Eagle shot overhead as I was looking down into a steep valley. Then another one followed, hard on its tail. I watched through my binoculars as the eagles locked together and started to spiral downwards, falling towards huge and sharp boulders at the bottom of the valley. Almost at the last moment, they split apart and I realised they had been mating, not fighting.

"A good evolutionary argument for premature ejaculation," said a friend, when I told him the story.

And I realised I had initially seen violence where new life was being created.

All of life is beautiful meat.

Writing Ourselves and Others

It took me a good few years before I plucked up the courage to write the 'Other', i.e. to me, someone who was not white and male. I firstly wrote as a 'white woman' in *God in the Box* (2003), set in an increasingly familiar London. Phew—that was picked up, published—*and* I wasn't scorned as a 'sexist imposter'! The leap to crossing the 'colour' divide took a bit longer for me though—part of my fear was that, given South Africa's history, it would be seen as a form of colonization of experience. Then, one day, I sat down and thought long and hard about it.

Slowly, a series of thoughts dawned. In *not* writing about characters of colour, I was in essence deleting them from my stories, replicating an apartheid mindset. Furthermore, I was holding on to an implicit internalized belief that perhaps the 'gap' between us was so large, I would get it completely and catastrophically 'wrong'. Again, apartheid had taught us that the 'racial' gap was an unbridgeable chasm—which in essence meant we needed to be kept apart. I realized, with some degree of horror, that in excluding characters of 'colour' in my writing, I had thus been—at least partly—colluding with an apartheid mindset.

So in 2004 I wrote about 'Kerem' in *The stone chameleon* (Young Africa imprint; Maskew Miller Longman), a so-called 'coloured' character in a futuristic Cape Town. The book 'passed' the test read of several selected township readers. Phew again—but this time, I knew it was *right* to write about the 'Other'—as long as it was with respect. Further, as long as I checked the voices I was using with someone from *within* that culture—and if the characters felt 'right' for that particular story.

I eventually came across Nisi Shawl and Cynthia Ward's (2005) book on *Writing the Other*, which has also proved a useful tool. The book itself uses an acronym—'ROAARS'—which covers what the authors see as central potential areas of difference to be considered in your characters, along axes of intersectional identity, i.e. Race, (sexual) Orientation, Age, Ability, Religion and 'Sex' (gender): <http://booklifenow.com/2010/03/nisi-shawl-and-cynthia-ward-on-roaars-and-the-unmarked-state/>.

Lauren Beukes wrote a great guest blog on 'Writing the Other' for The World SF Blog: http://worldsf.wordpress.com/2011/04/27/guest-blog-lauren-beukes-on-writing-the-other/

I'm not going to repeat it—you can read it for yourself, as Lavie

Tidhar has left the site up—but one of the points that particularly resonated with me was her idea that anyone you write about is 'Other'. That is, at some level, we are all 'Other' to each other—and one way to bridge that 'gap' of difference, is to ask.

So, although I stand partly outside now, I am still proud to be (South) African—and to continue to write stories about where I come from and visit annually, trying ever harder to get them to reflect the richness of the people there/here. When I anxiously handed my story *Of Hearts and Monkeys* to an umXhosa reader, Zandile Mahlasela, I had an irrational fear it would be full of inaccuracies, because I was no longer resident in South Africa and 'out of touch'. I was extremely relieved when Zandile eventually replied that it was fine, suggesting some tweaks.

I will *always* need a cultural advisor or editor, because SF to me, should be a world fiction, representing everyone. I am thrilled to have an umZulu clinical psychologist (Busi Siyathola), reading *Azanian Bridges* and now my novel, *Water Must Fall*—both books at least partly set in Kwa-Zulu Natal.

And, on the dangers of Internet translations, and cultural-linguistic context. I consulted a Zimbabwean of Shona heritage about my short story *Azania* in *AfroSF*. 'All fine,' he said, 'But why on Earth have you got your main character saying in chiShona: "Oh, excrement!"'

'I was trying to making her swear,' I said lamely, to his laughter.

He gave me a much better word. *Duzvi*!

Or as the French say, *merde*!

If in doubt, ask.

Finally, there has also been some interesting genetic-cultural research which suggests that in certain places, variation *within* cultures is much wider than variations *across* cultures—i.e. we may be more different to someone we perceive as similar to ourselves, than someone we see as completely different. Also, perhaps not surprising given Africa as the 'cradle' of humankind, variation within Africa is wider than variations in the rest of the world combined; Africa is indeed the original and the richest, most subtle 'stew' of people.

In the end, 'race' itself is a dangerous fiction, as we all carry parts of each others' ancestors within us. We need to be aware we are 'other' too—and decentring our own perspective, is partly what living and writing is about. Self and other will always be in relationship and, as Deeyah Khan's (2017) brave documentary *White Right: Meeting the Enemy* shows, when we really get to know someone else, we mostly realise that, in the end, we are all just human beings trying to build our lives with others, whilst simultaneously fighting the grave. (Although that knowledge alone may not be enough to shift perspectives, as there are also issues of resource access and structural inequality, stemming from long colonial legacies.)

But, if anyone wants some advice (or a workshop) on "How to Write Being a White Male", I'm your man!

The Sticks and Stones of Becoming 'Disabled'

'Sticks and stones may break my bones,
… But names will never harm me.'

Rhymes and resonances:
This traditional English children's rhyme, used down the ages as a retort to disempower playground name-calling, was apparently first coined by William Kinglake (1809-1891), in his book *Eothen* (1844), although he actually referred to 'golden sticks and stones.' *Eothen* was a recording of Kinglake's trip through Syria, Palestine and Egypt, so it may well be a corrupted translation of an Arabic or Middle-Eastern saying of the time.

One of the earliest records of this phrase—as reported above—is in T*he Christian Herald/Recorder*, dated 1862—the magazine was founded in Philadelphia in 1848, and 'is the oldest existing periodical published by African-Americans.' The phrase appears to be a (perhaps co-opted) Christian call to 'turn the other cheek' and attempts to disempower the aggressor, by hiding (but surely also internalizing) any pain caused. It is also of no little significance this phrase occurs during the American Civil War, with slavery as a central source of conflict—and where one can only imagine the brutality of the words being tossed at this time and place, let alone other sources of accompanying and aggressive violations.

As both story writers and readers, we are familiar with the power of words. Words can transport us to new places, new emotions, and new perceptions. But, so too, can they also constrict, imprison—and yes, even hurt us. Words do sting—and they can surely damage and harm too. Words carry power—amplified by associations and historical resonances—it is no accident, with regards to racial epithets, that the 'N' word in America (and the corresponding 'K' word in South Africa) are now publicly proscribed, although they retain reduced but still ongoing current usage, within enclaves, and for various purposes… *But what, you may ask, has all of this to do with 'disability'?*

The denigration and oppression of 'disability':
Well, the 'disability' label itself is an evolving umbrella word, also having historically transmogrified from various negatively connoted terms, e.g. 'cripple', 'spastic', 'handicapped', 'retarded' etc. I trained as

a clinical psychologist in South Africa—during the *Apartheid* State of Emergency in the nineteen eighties—and initially worked in forensic 'learning disabilities.' At one point I presented—as mitigatory evidence to a court judge—a psychometric (intellectual) assessment of a young black man being charged with violent theft.

The (old white) judge got irritated with my careful qualifiers about the racial-cultural caveats needed on psychological tests. "Just tell me," he snapped, "Is this man an idiot, an imbecile—or a moron?" (Terminology sanctioned by the *International Classification of Diseases* until as recently as 1977; ICD-IX. And terminology also associated with involuntary sterilization and the eugenics movement, attempting to 'erase' disability/difference—and carried enthusiastically forward by the Nazis during World War 2, Germany.)

Some would argue 'disability' is itself also becoming a loaded term, with a history of prior discarded negative terms and associations—the word may perhaps imply a lack of ability in certain areas of functioning, a concept in keeping with the 'medical model', i.e. entailing 'deficits' situated as internal and individual. The *Disability Rights Movement* 'social' model of disability, however, involves a conceptual shift towards considering 'disability' as a social concern and responsibility, caused not necessarily by an internal 'deficit', but by lack of recognition, access and support for all of its differently abled citizens (Vanderhooft, 2013).

So, as per the Union of the Physically Impaired Against Segregation's (UPIAS) 1976 statement:

"In our view, it is society which disables physically impaired people. Disability is something which is imposed on top of our impairments by the way we are unnecessarily isolated and excluded from full participation in society. Disabled people are therefore an oppressed group"
(Dawood, 2017, p.22).

Representation Matters:
Oppressed and marginalized groups need their 'voices' to be heard by society, if meaningful change is going to occur. Recognition will be boosted by representation—so, as always, representation does matter! There has been hitherto relatively little good representation of 'disability' in SF. (By 'good', I don't mean tidied up, 'PC' representations, but explorations of fully human characters struggling within societal contexts that are challenging; and may require addressing and change.) *Flowers for Algernon* by Daniel Keyes (1966) is an early example. A recent successful 'Disability in SF' anthology, focusing on the socio-political nexus, has been Kathryn Allan and Djibril al-Ayad's (2015) *Accessing the Future: A Disability-Themed Anthology of Speculative Fiction.*

A website repository by the Finnish writer Maija Haavisto heralds '*crip-fic*', a term she has ironically re-coined, in an attempt to subvert 'heroic and inspirational' societal narratives of disability, which tend to patronize and 'other' experiential accounts of people with disabilities: <http://www.fiikus.net/?cripfic> Nicola Griffith (2017) suggests the 'FRIES' test for discerning the use of 'disabled' characters in fiction. "*Does a work have more than one disabled character? Do the disabled characters have their own narrative purpose, other than the education and profit of a nondisabled character? Is the character's disability not eradicated either by curing or killing?*" (And Nicola moves on to providing a rolling list of fiction that seems to pass the 'FRIES' test: see below.)

The Sticks and Stones of 'Disability':

As for me, I have chronic and ongoing encounters with three incurable illnesses from over ten years ago (Meniere's Disease, TMD and CP/CPPS—none terminal), that eventually necessitated an incorporation of 'disability' into my own self-identification. Partial deafness, constant jaw and pelvic pain, and urinary problems. It took me some years before I both accepted a 'disabled' label—and was willing to share it with others—such is the tenacious stigma and social shame around such terms (Dawood and Williams, 2018; Wood, Qureshi and Mughal, 2017). See, too, Nicola Griffith's (2016) Blog on 'Coming Out as a Cripple.'

At first, I thought all of this would mean the end of my writing, given it is on top of a day job. But my passion to write remains kindled, although I have learned to slow down and regulate my activity, to conserve my energies—and so I write less, through pain, but with a little more care…Still, at least I write.

But the difficulties *do* require acknowledgement and adjustment and (for me) reduced productivity and focus. There are costs to illness and disability—sticks and stones are both felt within and may still persist in various places without—witness difference as 'deformity' or coming from 'evil'.

So, How Then, to Carry on Creating?

For anyone interested, there is a fascinating book by Arthur Frank (2013) called *The Wounded Storyteller*, which addresses how people try and create narrative meaning from the chaos of illness. Another source of help for me has been the ACT model, (i.e. Acceptance and Commitment Therapy). 'Mindfulness' and Acceptance (rather than denial or avoidance of) illness and pain has been heralded as important factors in learning to cope with many conditions (Kabat-Zinn, 1990; Khoury et. al., 2013)

I have struggled somewhat with this notion—how can you completely 'accept' something which is inherently unpleasant? The recent book by Ray Owens (2014) was a great help—entitled *Living with the Enemy*, it adopts a pragmatic approach that acceptance also acknowledges a tension in the relationship, given it is hard to completely 'befriend' illness and pain. But also of importance for me is that the book moves away from a dominant discourse around 'battles' and 'conquering' illness with 'bravery'. (Presumably then, those who 'fail' to force their illness away and regain health are not 'brave' enough?) These contain (Western) individualistic notions that put the person as the main instrument of their life, actively shaping and changing their fate by 'defeating' the Dragon of Illness.

I am not brave. Illness has largely 'defeated' me, as some might say, but I continue to write, both as part of acceptance and resistance. And I have realised my strength actually lies in the relationships that envelop me—it is my family that sustains and enriches me. I am lucky indeed! And, given my illness and pain is largely invisible to others, I have learned to let them know, as and when appropriate—and thus work modifications have kept me working too. It's a cool modification too—a standing desk, given sitting exacerbates my pelvic pain (Wallace & Dawood, 2018).

And that's the other part of the ACT Model—the essential partner to Acceptance—Commitment. Commitment means engaging with life, despite illness and pain, sometimes even because of it. It involves becoming aware of the values that make your life worth living—and pursuing them. Writing is part of who I am and what I have learned to recommit to—and there are many other, better writers out there who continue to write, despite significant impediments and 'disability'— For those interested, I have listed just a few below.

But Why Do We Write?

I believe, in the end, we write not only to testify or destroy—but to create and build, together. I write because the personal is political. When I presented to a network of National Health Service pelvic pain providers on how services needed to change, in order to meet the needs of people with Chronic Pelvic Pain Syndrome, I met some of my 'sisters' in CPPS—e.g. endometriosis is a common—but not the only—cause of CPPS, amongst women. They introduced me to literature showing that their pain is minimized even more by the medical profession—that is, women are frequently seen as 'hysterical' and exaggerating of pain and are often dismissed by health professionals when they seek support.

Disability is intersectional. As a white, privileged hetero and cis-gendered male, I have additional implicit systemic/structural supports to help me cope and manage—it is no accident 'austerity' within the UK is seen by many as a war on the poor, women and the 'disabled': Guardian, November 2017: <https://www.theguardian.com/society/2017/nov/17/women-and-disabled-austerity-report-tax-benefits-reforms>.

As Alice Wong (2018) argues in the *Disability Visibility Project*, 'disabled' stories of resistance and hope are desperately needed, in these dark times: <https://disabilityvisibilityproject.com/author/alwong199/>

***

To read about some SF/F writers experiences with disability and illness:

Nicola Griffith (2014). My Health. <http://asknicola.blogspot.co.uk/2014/08/my-health.html>

Nicola Griffith (2016) Coming Out as a Cripple. <https://nicolagriffith.com/2016/04/25/coming-out-as-a-cripple/>

Nicola Griffith (2017). The FRIES test for disabled characters in fiction. <https://nicolagriffith.com/2017/11/04/the-fries-test-for-disabled-characters-in-fiction/>

Helgadottir, M. (2017) Problem Daughters: Interview with Nicolette Barischoff. <https://margrethelgadottir.wordpress.com/2017/01/08/problem-daughters-interview-with-nicolette-barischoff/>

Nalo Hopkinson: (2013) The Geek's Guide to the Galaxy. *Lightspeed,* 37. <http://www.lightspeedmagazine.com/nonfiction/interview-nalo-hopkinson/>

Kameron Hurley: (2010) *Where Have All the Brutal Women Gone?* <https://www.kameronhurley.com/when-power-fades/>

Jay Lake (2014) *Last Plane to Heaven: The Final Collection* <http://www.jlake.com/2014/08/27/last-plane-to-heaven-the-final-collection/>

Rose Lemberg (2018). Writing While Autistic. <https://www.patreon.com/roselemberg/posts?tag=writing%20while%20autistic>

Nnedi Okorafor (2017). How Nnedi Got Her Curved Spine. *The Manchester Review,* 18. <http://www.themanchesterreview.co.uk/?p=7897>

Ada Palmer (2017) Campbell Award and Invisible Disability. <https://www.exurbe.com/?p=4269>

Nisi Shawl: 'I am Strong: I'm Invisible'. <https://blog.seattleacupuncture.com/i-am-strong-im-invisible-by-nisi-shawl>

Fran Wilde (2018): 'We Will See You Now'. *Uncanny Magazine, 20.* <https://uncannymagazine.com/article/will-see-now/>.

***

Bibliography

Bury, M. (2001) Illness narratives: Fact or fiction? *Sociology of Health & Illness, 23*(3), 263-285.

Dawood, R. (2017). Understanding the socio-political dimensions of disability within clinical psychology, *Clinical Psychology Forum, 299,* 21-24.

Frank, A. (2013). *The Wounded Storyteller.* University of Chicago Press. (Second Edition.)

Kabat-Zinn, J. (1990) *Full Catastrophe Living: Using the Wisdom of Your Body and Mind to Face Stress, Pain, and Illness.* Bantam Dell.

Khoury, B., Lecomte, T., Fortin, G., Masse, M., & Therien, P., Bouchard, V., Chapleau M., Paquin K. & Hofmann, S. (2013) Mindfulness-based therapy: A comprehensive meta-analysis. *Clinical Psychology Review 33,* 763—771.

Lambert, M. (2017). Austerity has trampled over disabled people's rights. But the UK won't admit it. *The Guardian, 4th September.* <https://www.theguardian.com/commentisfree/2017/sep/04/austerity-disabled-people-rights-uk-un-government>

Owen, R. (2014). *Living with the Enemy: Coping with the stress of chronic illness using CBT, mindfulness and acceptance.* Routledge.

Parks, T. (2011) *Teach Us to Sit Still: A Sceptic's Search for Health and Healing.* Vintage Books.

Shawl, N. (2013) Invisible Inks: On Black SF Authors and Disability. In *WisCon Chronicles 7, "Shattering Ableist Narratives".* Ed. JoSelle Vanderhooft; Aqueduct Press.

Vanderhooft, J. (2013, Ed.) WisCon Chronicles 7, "Shattering Ableist Narratives". Aqueduct Press.

Wallace, G. & Dawood, R. (2018) Out of sight but on our minds: Invisible stigmatised identities and disclosure, *Clinical Psychology Forum, 301*: 33-37.

Wong, A. (Ed, 2018). *Resistance and Hope: Essays by Disabled People.* Disability Visibility Project: <https://disabilityvisibilityproject.com/resist/>

Wood, N., Qureshi, A., & Mughal, F. (2017). Positioning, telling, and performing a male illness: Chronic prostatitis/chronic pelvic pain syndrome. *British Journal of Health Psychology, 22*(4):904-919.

Writing Speculative Fiction for Personal and Socio-Political Change

Nicholas Wood (& Anneke Sools.)

Introduction

This article was initially accepted as a chapter for a new book, to be published by Palgrave in 2019, entitled *New ideas for new times: A handbook of innovative community and clinical psychologies.* However, I had been in discussions with Prof. Anneke Sools from Twente University, having seen her research into the construction of alternative futures through stories. With permission from the editors, we rewrote this chapter to include details of her approach too. This is my original chapter, which is sufficiently different from the rewrite with Anneke, to be considered separate. I will focus on writing Science or Speculative Fiction, as an act for both personal and political change, framed for psychologists and 'lay' people and illustrated via sections from my novel Azanian Bridges. As many of the ideas below were intertwined from our discussions, I will refer to 'we,' to include Anneke, as I am indebted to her ideas on story.

The discipline of psychology has an ambivalent relationship with fictional narrative, to say the least. Freud's dealing with 'phantasma' precedes later critical accounts of fantasy in clinical practice as unreal, escape, being unable to face the facts. I would argue that in this way, an understandable yet problematic opposition between fact and fiction is constructed. Drawing on the inclusive view proposed by Brockmeier (2013) and Herman (2011), we depart from the idea that "narrative [is] a psychologically fundamental practice of meaning construction, a practice which cuts across the putative divide between fiction and nonfiction" (Brockmeier, 2013, p.7).

In other words, the mind does not 'mind' whether a story is 'real' (i.e. happened in reality) or imagined (i.e. not —yet- happened); it has capacity to perceive imagined story characters and situations as real (Schiff, McKim & Patron, 2017). In this ability lies the potential to create new experience (Sools, Triliva & Filippas, 2017). Truly new experiences depend on difference from the past; for as long as known, past experiences are repeated, newness cannot take effect.

From this view, psychology could benefit from a change in perspective from looking at what is (and at how current experience and behaviour came into being) to what *could* and *should* be. This requires changing focus from the question of factual truth of an imagined future (whether personal or collective), toward its psychological relevance, i.e. how meaning is constructed through stories (which can be more and less 'fictionalized') by both author and reader.

I will initially outline my motivation for reading and writing science fiction, particularly growing up in Southern Africa. We aim to consider how writing, reading, and sharing stories can scaffold ideas about changing the self and the future—not just for individuals, but potentially larger groups and even whole communities. Together, we propose ways forward for promoting the creation of stories that embrace the struggles of now, but also open-up potential ways of building healthier and communal models for alternative—and hopefully better—futures.

1. Why Write Science Fictional Differences?
I have written (and drawn) stories and comics ever since I can remember, growing up in Zambia and then South Africa. Eventually, I gave up the comics, because my illustrations never matured into my teen years. But I have kept up the writing, through thick and thin, through health and now, enduring illness (Wood, 2015).

So, *why* do I write? And, even more specifically, why am I writing *this*?

The short answer is, because I want to both make sense of the world—and to try and write a better world into being. And this book—proposing 'new ideas for new times: a handbook of innovative community and clinical psychologies'—seems to me to be about stretching the boundaries of the psychological profession, to engender positive and progressive change.

For I am a writer and a psychologist, and the two identities have, to date, sat rather warily alongside each other. My writing nom de plume is an—admittedly very *thinly* disguised 'Nick Wood'—as opposed to my more 'respectable' professional full name Nicholas Wood. So why does my professional identity feel more 'respectable' than my fictional writing?

Probably because I write genre fiction—and not just any genre, but *science fiction* (SF)—a form of fiction that has long been sneered at in more 'literary' circles. Growing up as a privileged white young male during apartheid in South Africa, however, reading science fiction offered an escape from a pending militarised future to reinforce the iniquitous status quo. Most importantly, though, science fiction is premised on a crucial question that needs constant asking, as it moves beyond the constraints of 'accepted reality': '*What if things were different?*' So, I knew—and from an early age—that there were alternatives to the grand narrative of apartheid—which was why the censors were such a powerful force within State officialdom at the time.

SF faces forward, proposing alternative models of the future—
different ways of living, organising and being within the world. Such
models are, of course, a threat to any entrenched and/or oppressive
status quo—and it was no accident a number of SF novels were
banned for periods in South Africa— such as Heinlein's 'Stranger in
a Strange Land,' Mary Shelley's 'Frankenstein' and Anthony Burgess'
'A Clockwork Orange'—alongside more overtly political novels
challenging apartheid (McDonald, 2009).

Implicit within one of the central questions of SF is the realisation
that things *can* be different from the prevailing system—and seeking
this difference can be a worthwhile, if difficult, goal. This was the
aim of the political Struggle during apartheid, or as Nelson Mandela
eloquently put it, at the end of his 1964 Rivonia 'Treason' Trial:

> I have cherished the ideal of a democratic and free society
> in which all persons live together in harmony and with equal
> opportunities. It is an ideal which I hope to live for and to
> achieve. But if needs be, it is an ideal for which I am prepared to
> die (Nelson Mandela Foundation, 2007).

2. On Reading and Empathy

The field called the psychology of fiction (Oatley, 2011) investigates
empirically how readers experience fiction and non-fiction through
identification with characters and situations, and through immersion
in story-worlds. The central claim of this field is that reading fiction
"permits us to become imaginary travellers and experience people
from other times and places and consequently leads to a greater
understanding and sympathy with people unlike ourselves and beliefs
unlike our own, even perhaps changing our sense of who we are in the
process" (McKim, 2012). Reading fiction can from this point of view
be considered an ethical practice that enhances empathy (Nussbaum)
through identification. But how does this work?

Gaining empathy from reading is a mixed process of partial and
wholehearted identification and distancing at various points within a
story. Moreover, it is a process that is different for each reader and
situated in time (as I change as reader, my identification may also
change). Importantly, by writing down your identification process, it
can deepen in a way similar to the processing of emotions through
expressive writing (Niederhoffer & Pennebaker, 2009).

3. The Seeds of Story

The other reason why my writing pseudonym 'Nick' feels less
'respectable' than my professional epithet 'Dr. Nicholas Wood', is
perhaps also down to what capitalist society values. Within western

capitalism, conventional salaried work is viewed as a more 'legitimate' or 'useful' activity than a 'recreational' activity such as writing—particularly 'make believe nonsense', as someone once categorised science fiction to me! Other examples of differential societal values, both implicit and explicit, involve the remuneration of 'work' (however ethically compromised) and 'economic productivity/GDP' over the care of children or the fetching of water for survival (usually by girls and/or women).

So, with work, after graduating, I spent two years as a community worker within the black townships surrounding Cape Town before starting professional training in clinical psychology at the start of 1985. Half-way through my first year of training, a partial 'State of Emergency' was declared by the white regime, granting police special powers to detain, impose curfews and control the media and funerals. Armoured troops were called in to occupy the townships. I avoided conscription by moving frequently and staying ahead of the Military Police—aided and abetted by stonewalling parents and a senior black clinical psychology supervisor. After qualifying, I chose to work only within legally designated 'black' hospitals.

When I was training as a clinical psychologist, South African psychology at the time was a predominantly white and western affair, and the emphasis was on individual models of therapy; learning the Diagnostic and Statistical Manual of Mental Disorders—at that time, the 3rd of what now feels like an endless iteration; and the emphasis was on writing case reports and research in 'objective scientific' fashion. It was with some relief I joined a nascent organisation called the Organisation for Appropriate Social Services in South Africa (OASSSA), as they recognised psychology in South Africa was, in fact, a tool to enforce an individualised status quo, and that there could be no mental health without social justice (Hayes, 2000). What I had also learned from my earlier time as a community worker, was that engagement within larger, collective communities—rather than individuals in sanitised clinic rooms—held the best key, to maximise chances for lasting and positive change. Clinical psychology (CP) needs a community focus, if it is going to challenge the socio-political context of mental ill health (Cain, 2018). And it also needs stories and books. Books of all sorts. *So where do the seeds of a story come from?*

From 'real' life: I met 'Sibusiso' when I was a young intern psychologist (trainee) and he was brought to me, for 'therapy'. That was the start of a case report that quickly spiralled beyond the individual, to end up focusing on 'there is no normality in an abnormal society.' I immersed myself in Sibusiso's case and place and asked those around him, who knew him best. And I read, on politics and amaZulu culture amongst other things. All writers start as readers; sometimes in the broadest sense of the word, for example, watching and interpreting the events around us, learning to story our lives.

And, when it came time to fictionalise his story, in the SF novel *Azanian Bridges* (2016), I reread 'Sibusiso's' now yellowed case report. Fiction is transforming what *has* been, into what *might* be.

Sibusiso was silent and seriously depressed.

How, then, to start hearing his story?

4. A Bridge to Azania
The bridge starts with just one young man.

> Silence…
>
> Silence shrinks an already small room and I stare at the young man who will not talk, wondering how I reach out across the space between us, how to make his words flow. He stares across to the picture on the wall behind me: his eyes are hooded; his body is slumped. The room is a tight box of peeling institutional yellow, mould-flicking corners of the ceiling, the narrow walls groaning with a history of mad voices . . . or so I've been told. The young man's head is cocked: as if he's listening. Perhaps the voices in the wall have overwhelmed him. Me, I've never heard them, sitting as I am on the right side of this small square desk, panic button comfortably within range on the wall next to me.
>
> "What do you hear, Sibusiso?" I ask, normalising his experiences, just in case.
>
> He flicks a glance to my mouth, as if unsure that's where the voice has indeed come from, but his eyes scan back behind me.
>
> How indeed to build a link between us?
>
> (Wood, 2016, p. 31).

I immersed myself in 'Sibusiso's case and place and asked those around him, who knew him best. And I read, on politics and amaZulu culture amongst other things. All writers start as readers.

And, when it came time to fictionalise his story, I reread his now yellowed case report.

5. The Story Seeds are Sharing What you Know—but Learning Too
The young man named called 'Sibusiso' is a nom de plume, of course, given he is loosely based on that case report I wrote up as part of professional Clinical Psychology training. As Bladon (2018) states, it is an ethical necessity to ensure confidentiality when fictionalising clinical material. The other main character, Martin, was a clinical psychologist. Now *that*, I know. (For an overview of clinical psychologists in fiction, read Goodwin, 2017).

The building blocks of fiction are life experiences and our experiences with others and the world around us—writers mix and match the best they can to disguise characters, but no character is ever a naked creation. And I had wanted to give voice to 'Sibusiso'—someone I met and came to know over weeks and, eventually, six months of talking and even playing together in 'therapy', someone who had been badly damaged by a violent political system, for daring to try and make a difference.

My initial brief (from a white supervisor) had been to 'fix him with some Cognitive Behavioural Therapy' (CBT)—but I needed to hear 'Sibusiso's' understanding of his severe low mood first. "I dropped a pencil," he told me gloomily, "A girl picked it up and gave it back. But I could tell from her look that she had bewitched the pencil—and me."

Amafufanyana. One word capturing the central theme in the small but illuminating story 'Sibusiso' told me—but only in our third sessions, after trust had been built to a degree. *Amafufanyana*—the isiZulu term for bewitchment or possession. I decided I needed to learn from 'Sibusiso' first, rather than try to teach a model of therapy that may feel very alien. A bridge across a river—the Umgeni River in the book—required a solid storied base be established on both sides first.

I could tell he was torn—his cultural heart believed he was 'bewitched' but his 'modern head'—his words, not mine—was both sceptical *and* afraid of my judgement. Knowing I had so much power to contest or validate his stories, I opted for validation of both 'organs'. He had clearly been broken by the assertion of his own voice and why should 'heart' and 'head' be a choice, when they are so often in messy conflict anyhow?

I suggested a traditional healer might be helpful. He was both relieved—and worried. It turns out he wanted to see us *both*. So, by month three, 'Sibusiso' was well set with a *sangoma* (traditional healer) and increasingly conversant with CBT. Given what was happening within his life and the country, though, individualistic models would *always* eventually be found wanting. It was around this time, that he told me about his political activism.

"What about you?" he asked me, "Have you done your military service?"

The bridge of story always needs at least two sides, in building and holding a creative centre.

6. What is the Water on the Ground? The Impetus for Developing an Idea.
The spark for writing *Azanian Bridges* came when I was living and working in London at the time—the original anonymised case report now yellowed by the passing of a quarter of a century. Then the so-called 'Tottenham Riots' happened, and I was reminded of the 'Soweto

Riots' (Uprising) of 1976 in South Africa—'riots' echoing across decades and places as deliberate media discourse; used to take away the agency and humanity of the participants, all searching for a way to express their own oppressed and marginalised stories.

Why Azania? This was a term for the new South Africa envisioned beyond liberation—the Dream Country that awaited. (And was eventually discarded, in a less radical naming break with the past, in post-apartheid South Africa.) By 2011, with minimal structural shifts in wealth distribution and ongoing violence, the 'rainbow dream' of the 'New South Africa' was fading fast.

And then, 'Sibusiso's' voice came back into my head. *'What about me?'* he asked, *'What would I be doing right now?'* (There was no way of knowing, of course. His case report was anonymised, the past effectively untraceable.) But, over the twenty-five years living and working subsequently in South Africa; Aotearoa New Zealand and England, I had become aware of the subtle toxic pervasiveness of racism and institutionalised white patriarchy. Not an easy topic to broach with white people in particular—or to facilitate an open discussion around (DiAngelo, 2018; Eddo-Lodge, 2017; Sue, 2015; Wood & Patel, 2017).

What would Sibusiso say to this? Right here, right now, in the twenty first century, in a parallel universe where apartheid remains, and we can sit and relax with the characters, safe in the knowledge that this is *just* a book—and set in another reality too.

But, in the reality of *Azanian Bridges*, Nelson Mandela fulfils his Rivonia Treason Trial Declaration and *does* die, alone, in solitary confinement for his ideals, on Robben Island—*and* there is a white-right coup. Not a million miles away from some countries right now.

Write what you know—and acknowledge we are all flawed in some way. The key is becoming aware of this—and wanting to be better, or to make things around us better. Flaws revealed in fiction—or 'alternative facts'—can be illuminating for readers, and are very human, encouraging identification. They are also less threatening to confront. The hard conversations are to be held by the characters.

We eavesdrop—and we learn.

Vicariously.

Plenty has been written about how fictional worlds can build and hone our empathy (Dam & Siang, 2017)—but, just to make sure, I plonked an empathy device squarely into the book, as a central McGuffin . A plot engine, driving change—because story is about change—both of our circumstances and how we see ourselves and others.

7. The Challenge of Change

Sibusiso eyes the machine straddling the table between us with obvious doubt.

"It looks like a box the Security Police would use."

I look at him with surprised shock; forthright views indeed for an endogenously depressed patient, especially a black one. But the night nurses did report he'd been more talkative this morning, more assertive.

"It's okay Sibusiso, I've tried it on myself—it doesn't hurt, it only amplifies your brain waves and makes me understand your experiences a whole lot better; it works better than any language could."

"What's wrong with my English, black man that I am?" Sibusiso slumps in the chair again, his eyes veiling over.

I knew I would have to engage him quickly, before he regressed further into a depressed stupour.

"Stand up, let's move around a bit," I call; behavioural activation always helps alleviate mood-based psychomotor retardation.

"*Ja baas,* have you been in the army, *korporaal?*" He stands, but sullen, angry and hostile.

This is not going well. I hesitate, unsure of whether his question is seriously meant or a bit of loaded sarcasm. But he continues to stand and stare at me directly, as if in defiance of cultural respect for his elders, waiting...

I smile to break the tension: "We're here to treat you, not me—your family were worried and brought you here because you'd stopped eating."

Sibusiso shook his head: "No, it doesn't work like that. You expect me to share things, hurtful things, dangerous things, but yet you say nothing about yourself, nothing about who you really are, away from your work? And the white army patrol our streets, shooting and whipping us."

Is this where his head injury comes from?

Silence...

I sense there is no way forward, without a big step of trust, a leap of faith.

"No, Sibusiso, I've never been to the army. I'm a secret draft dodger, a good few years back now. I've moved addresses many times and they've given up chasing me—at least, I hope they have, with all their energies in the... black townships, as you say." The word 'black' sticks to my tongue like glue, but Sibusiso has given me enough cues he wants me to verbalise colour, although I still worry it polarises us…

He watches me and relaxes just a little. Then he chuckles, looking around the dingy yellow room: "Well, if you speak the truth, I can probably be sure this room is not bugged."

Is this one reason why his words have been so guarded, so hard to come by? It seems behavioural answers lie not just in a man's mental state, but in their surroundings too. It's a wide gulf between us indeed, even in this cramped and stale room, where we're standing so close, we can smell each other.

Sibusiso is sweating, although the sun's mid-morning heat has yet to build strongly. He stretches his arms in response to mine and looks down on me from across the table; he's tall, thin and powerful. I feel the weight of early middle-age years and the spread of my stomach: "Shall we sit again?"

He takes the back of his chair and moves it, appraising me coolly from a standing height as my own chair squeaks, swivels and spins unexpectedly beneath me.

"I'll do this on one condition," he says.

I stabilise and root myself by planting my shoes firmly against the concrete floor, grasping the table in front of me.

"What's that?" I look up to capture his glowering gaze.

"You must go first, doctor," he says.

Ag, I'd not expected this.

I can see by his stare this is not negotiable. I hesitate, racking my brain for a therapeutic response that would open him up again, a psychological jujitsu phrase that would put me back in control, with therapy moving forward as planned.

"Okay," I say. That's not it! (But what else can I say; who else will agree to do this?)

I take a deep breath and clip the primary cap onto my scalp. He watches me closely; his eyes measuring mine more than they did yesterday.

I hold the second cap up to him and he flinches away. "You can't read me if you're not connected," I say.

He lifts a warning finger: "Promise me you do it the way I want."

I nod and fumble with clipping the electrodes in place, glad he's had his head tightly shaved since coming onto the ward. I am sweating too, even though it is not as hot as yesterday, a drop of sweat falls on the table between us, my collared shirt sticks to my back.

We face each other over the Box, which is plugged in, green dials flashing.

"Ready?" I say, breathing deeply and dreading I am breaking

ethical codes across the board. There is still time to stop, to unplug the machine, and unclip our caps, to return to words...

But Sibusiso just smiles and nods.

I flip the switch on to 'export' and wait. For me, I feel nothing. All I can do is think calming thoughts about surf rolling across Durban North beach, which should hopefully hide my more intimate thoughts. At the same time, I concentrate on sending him positive thoughts that should hopefully pulse along these wires with a mood of optimism and change.

His eyes are closed and his face twists with amusement, concern, a bit of disgust, sadness...joy? I struggle to read the fast flash of feelings as they wash over his face like the sea—his mouth open, as if gasping for breath, but no sound emerges.

Silence . . .

I catch flashes of fire in my head, smoke stings my eyes and I fall as something hits me on the head. Glazed, I look up to see a white policeman swinging his *sjambok*.

Dogs are barking nearby, big dogs. Wetness drips down my face and my clothes are damp. I look around the shack-ridden dirtied landscape. There are hundreds of us, but hemmed in, milling, the Peace March broken as gas infiltrates our lungs and purple spray marks us as enemies of the State.

I cough and switch the machine off. Shit man, a bit of resurgent identity feedback, despite the one-way setting? I'm scared too of what Sibusiso may find, afraid of the effects of mixing brain waves, merging identities, even though our huge differences are mapped onto our skins.

Sibusiso opens his eyes and looks at me, smiling peculiarly in what looks for a moment like self-recognition.

"Well?" I ask.

"You're mostly okay doctor—a little more racist than you think, but a little less racist than I ...worried."

8. Whose Story is This?

I rewrote the ending many times before I decided on the 'right' one. One of the pivotal decisions was around whose voice needed to linger most in the reader's mind. We know of the primacy and recency effect and I decided, in the end, that both belonged to Sibusiso. The start and end of the story is his.

How can one write about a life of someone who has lived an 'existential chasm' away from one's own story and lived experience?

With due care, respect and seeking feedback from cultural 'insiders' to try and ensure there is some verisimilitude in the telling (Shawl and Ward, 2005). And you are bolstered by the realisation that, at the heart of all stories, everyone is human. What unites us is far bigger than what may divide us: Witherspoon et al., 2007).

And, if Sibusiso was around, we may well have tried co-writing this book. It certainly felt ethically dubious that a privileged white writer should be the sole financial beneficiary from a novel about apartheid. So, I asked for advice from other South African writers, and I eventually agreed, with my publisher and the relevant organisation, to split the authorial royalties with a body dedicated to encouraging and fostering 'black' writing in South Africa, *Long story SHORT* (Masilela, 2015). Who knows, perhaps Sibusiso is a member?

And then I let *Azanian Bridges* loose on the world.

9. Which Stories Get Heard?

It was a hard slog to get published. South African publishers did not want it—'too close to home' as it were, from the feedback. (If any are interested, there are more details in the online interview of me by Geoff Ryman, 2017.) But being 'close to home' was one of the main points of writing *Azanian Bridges*! There is a need to focus on the realities of 'now', if we are to shape a new future (Hall, 2015).

Geoff Ryman (2013) himself spearheaded the 'Mundane' movement in Science Fiction—which maintains SF, i.e. Science or Speculative Fiction, should focus on the Earth-centred, more malleable near-future scenarios, rather than pursue fights of fantasy into a distant, space-faring and less certain future. That is, it should focus on imminent realities and crises, as a form of activist 'thought experiment,' to address the critical—and *proximal*—issues of the age. Streeby (2018) collates SF 'climate fiction' or 'cli-fi', as an exemplar of this, going on to detail writing workshops being run by black feminist activist adrienne marie brown [she uses small letters for her names], focusing on building an indigenous and intersectional reclaiming of the climate futures, i.e. via giving voice to the dispossessed and the voiceless (Hall, 2015; Medak-Saltzman, 2017)..

As for *Azanian Bridges*, I eventually found a UK publisher and it has sold reasonably well, been positively reviewed in *The Guardian* and *The Financial Times* amongst other places, as well as being short-listed for four major SF Awards in the USA, Britain and Africa. *The Guardian* calls it: '*an intelligent examination of prejudice in all its forms and a convincing portrayal of characters under extreme stress.*'

Not bad for a debut novel, I think.

But has it changed anything or anyone?

A book is a stone thrown into the rivers of the world.

I've seen some ripples from the 'Bridge and have received some very interesting feedback—for all stories end up being transformed by conversations they provoke, new readings—and the even newer stories they may help foster.

10. Feedback from the Bridge

Some writers suggest that instead of focusing on reviews of past work—which may infuriate rather than please you—it is best to just get started on the next book. One of my flaws is a tinge of narcissism—I love to see my name in print. But I'm also genuinely curious as to what others think of my work. How else can you improve on your art—and your mission?

Out of the good number of reviews I've seen on *Azanian Bridges*, one of the most interesting is by a reviewer on Amazon called Ken Arenson (2018). He liked it, on the whole, referring to it as 'a gripping read'—phew! But he outlines one of his two criticisms thus:

> Also, the book's McGuffin does not acknowledge the debt owed to our present-day fMRI and/or EEG-based machines using AI that are on the road to reproducing dream visuals. (For example, see Miyawaki et al, 2008, Visual Image Reconstruction from Human Brain Activity using a Combination of Multiscale Local Image Decoders; Horikawa et al. 2013, Neural Decoding of Visual Imagery During Sleep; Horikawa 2015; Horikawa 2017).

Nice, I thought, a work of science fiction being critiqued for not quoting its sources. So the real and 'academic' world intertwine again with a work of fiction—worlds collide and leak, universes mesh, reality is an unruly beast, at best.

And that was one of my intended points in writing *Azanian Bridges*—apartheid may have gone, but its source and legacy still leaks corrosively all over our current world. We need to be vigilant and active in challenging this, in our constant fight for Martin Luther King's 'Dream', half a murdered century old now. Stephen Lawrence's murder, closer to British homes is—even though a quarter of a century ago—still bleeding. How *do* we heal this? (Patel & Keval, 2018).

11. What Makes a Story?

I heard an anecdote from a colleague that Professor Stephen Frosh from Birkbeck University referred to a story as a series of events with 'a beginning, a muddle, and an end.' That certainly feels true for me, as a description of the writing process! Most stories involve change over time, whether that be a plot/story and/or character 'arc' (Booker, 2004). Arcs are part of a curve and is a metaphorical allusion indicating that interesting stories don't go in straight lines—we don't always just get what we want—the curving conflict in the middle, heightens both tension and engagement.

What, then, gets a story going?

Prof. Anneke Sools from Twente University in the Netherlands says it's a combination of 'desire' and 'imagination'.

Desire:

Sools, Triliva and Filippas (2017) argue that in their focus groups with unemployed Greek Young Adults, the root of stories is desire—a desire for things to be different. This may appear superficially in keeping with the (Hollywood) notion that you start off with someone wanting something ('motivation')—and the story is about their muddled struggle to obtain that thing—with eventual success and/or failure (endings: Booker, 2004).

However, desire is something much more profound than basic motivation—and is often unconscious. Abensour (1999) argues there is a need to learn how to desire, and how to desire *differently*. Desires have been hijacked by a media saturated with neo-liberal consumption ideals—you can become fulfilled, by what you buy. Desire has been trivialised and run dry for most, in times of austerity (Cain, 2018). The point is not to assign 'true' or 'just' goals to desire but rather to 'educate desire', to stimulate it, to awaken it. Not to assign it a goal to desire but to 'open a path for it'. Abensour (1999) continues: "Desire must be taught to desire, to desire better, to desire more, and above all *to desire otherwise.*"

But what drives a story after desire creates it?

Imagination:

The power of the story comes from imagination, however. If we can't imagine things differently—which seems to be the imprisoning intent of the neo-liberal phrase 'there is no alternative'—then we are trapped to repeat and survive the present; something which the austerity agenda appears intent on engendering (Psychologists for Social Change). For imagination requires the freedom to play and think—scarce resources indeed, when survival can be the sole and enervating focus of just meeting basic human needs.

Desiring differently thus depends on the imagination. In the case of the Greek adults in Anneke (et. al.'s) study (2017), I would say there was a deprivation of imagination resulting in truncated desire—i.e. imagination is crucial to 'desire differently'.

Resourcing Stories:

But, first and foremost, stories need time and imaginative spaces to grow and breathe—how do we create and sustain this for all our communities, where public libraries, as the repository of stories, are under attack? A safe space to think and share with each other, finding ways to excite our desire—and spark our imaginations. Then, better stories will come.

12. Building Science Fictional Stories

I have run writing workshops in township high schools with seventeen-year olds in South Africa, near Cape Town, focusing on the speculative question: what would you like South Africa to be, in thirty years' time, when you are fully fledged adults? This creates the tension between the real 'now' and a close but imaginary future—these 'thin' stories are projections of our desires and values and as Sools et al (2017) argue, need to be close enough to feel obtainable, yet distant enough to 'stretch' and be different from the given constraints of now. Their methodology was letters written from 'future selves' describing what it was' like' in the Grecian future, with changes both desired and targeted.

So, stories rooted in desire rest on values—what is important for us—what do we want to build and sustain, and what else do we want to challenge, that perhaps prevents us obtaining our visualised dreams? What is our 'bridge' from a hard present to a desired future? And what is feasible or believable—for investment in a story requires the story to feel both consistent, credible—and achievable.

In the township schools, the 'bricks' to build stories for participants were pencils and papers, as the school computers had been stolen. But, most importantly, the shards of stories were around us, in each other. We spoke long and hard and playfully at times about what was important to them—and me.

And then we wrote. Most of the students wrote short personal pieces not directly reflecting this theme, but were still poignant pieces reflecting relationships, ethnic identity and environmental concerns. Two students wrote present-day stories; the third, Noluyando Roxwana (17), wrote a story with a 'leap' to a monochromatic 'racial' future, exploring what loss of diversity might mean. (I managed to persuade the publisher of the South African SF magazine 'Probe' to publish this story and to send Noluyando a copy.)

What was the 'engine' for her time leap?

A dream.

No, this was not a hoary use of a dream in a story where all is restored on waking. The dreamer woke a changed person towards the end of the story. (I was also aware that dreaming amongst traditional amaXhosa can be a sacred vehicle for change, where contact can be made with ancestors, and, in this story, the future can be shown.)

What a wonderful time machine. Stories come from our ancestors too and we aim them towards new and desired visions of a better world for us all. And stories just happen to be true, too.

If you're in doubt, just ask Sibusiso.

13. Just Doing It: Ten Steps for Turning Story Seeds into Trees

Everyone lives surrounded by stories—our sense of who we are, is itself a storied experience (Brockmeier and Carbaugh, 2001). We all carry within us the capacity to create stories. When running a story writing workshop, these may be helpful steps to bear in mind (Bolton, Field and Thompson, 2006.).

i.   Meet in a safe space and lay ground rules of respect (and confidentiality if needed) for all the stories to be created and heard.

ii.   Emphasise we create stories out of events all the time, so *all* are story-tellers.

iii.   If necessary, remove critical (self) censors about what is a 'good' and a 'bad' story—stories have intrinsic value, both in being made, and being told.

iv.   Choose (or imagine) a main character (or 'protagonist) and then,

v.   What do they want to be *different*, from how things are now? (Values and Desire).

vi.   Plot a sequence of events to show them either achieving this (overcoming obstacles: 'happy' ending) or failing ('tragedy.') If failing, what *might* they have done differently to experience success? Or what else needs to be different?

vii.   Share stories and listen respectfully.

viii.   Create a group/community of stories, centring around a theme or identity, seeking positive changes, via storying them into existence.

ix.   Witness and celebrate new possibilities—self-publishing, internet stories etc.

x.   Keep writing—stories of hope, resistance and change.

To stories of new and fairer futures for all.

Bibliography

Abensour, M. (1999) "William Morris: The Politics of Romance," trans. Max Blechman (Ed.), in *Revolutionary Romanticism: A Drunken Boat Anthology*. San Francisco: City Lights Books, 1999)

Arenson, K. (2018). Fiction with an authentic ring of an imagined future South Africa, if still under the boot of Apartheid. *Amazon.com* Retrieved 26th April, 2018: <https://www.amazon.com/gp/customer-reviews/R1A6QNT609TJNW/ref=cm_cr_dp_d_rvw_ttl?ie=UTF8&ASIN=B01B1E9P7M>

Baldwin, C. (2015). Narrative ethics for narrative care, *Journal of Aging Studies, 34*, 183-189.

Bladon, H. (2018). Should psychiatrists write fiction? *British Journal of Psychiatry, 42* (2), 77-80.

Bloch, E. (1986). *The Principle of Hope*. London: Basil Blackwell.

Bolton, G., Field, V., & Thompson, K. (2006) *Writing Works: A Resource Handbook for Therapeutic Writing Workshops and Activities*. London: Jessica Kingsley Publishers.

Brockmeier, J. (2013). Fact and fiction: Exploring the narrative mind. In: M. Hatavara, L.-C. Hyden & M. Hyvarinen (Eds.). *The Travelling Metaphor of Narrative*. Amsterdam & Philadelphia: John Benjamins.

Brockmeier, J. & Carbaugh, D. (2001). *Narrative and Identity*. John Benjamins Publishing Company.

Bruner, J. (1991). The Narrative Construction of Reality. *Critical Inquiry, 18* (1), 1-21.

Butler, J. (2004). *Precarious life: The power of mourning and violence*. New York: Verso.

Cain, R. (2018). How Neo-liberalism is damaging your mental health. *The Conversation*. Retrieved 10th December 2018. <http://theconversation.com/how-neoliberalism-is-damaging-your-mental-health-90565>

Dam, R. & Siang, T. (2017). The Power of Stories in Building Empathy. *Interaction Design Foundation*. Retrieved: 26th April 2018. <https://www.interaction-design.org/literature/article/the-power-of-stories-in-building-empathy>

DiAngelo, R. (2018). *White Fragility: Why It's So Hard for White People to Talk About Racism*. Beacon Press.

Eddo-Lodge, R. (2017). *Why I'm No Longer Talking to White People about Race*. Bloomsbury.

Georgakopoulou, A. (2006). The other side of the story: towards a narrative analysis of narratives-in-interaction. *Discourse Studies, 8* (2), 235—257.

Gergen, K.J. (2015). From Mirroring to World-Making: Research as Future Forming. *Journal for the Theory of Social Behaviour, 45* (3), 287—310.

Goffman, E. (1959). *The presentation of self in everyday life*. Garden City, N.Y.: Doubleday.

Gwyther, G. & Possamai-Inesedy, A. (2009) Special Issue: New methods in social justice research for the 21st century, *International Journal of Social Research Methodology*, 12:2, 97-98.

Hall, S.D. (2015). Learning to Imagine the Future: The Value of Affirmative Speculation in Climate Change Education. *Resilience: A Journal of the Environmental Humanities, 2* (2), DOI: 10.5250/resilience.2.2.004.

Hayes, G. (2000). The Struggle for Mental Health in South Africa: Psychologists, Apartheid and the Story of Durban OASSSA. *Journal of Community and Applied Social Psychology, 10*, 327-342.

Hofmann, W. & Nordgren, L.F. (2016). *The Psychology of Desire*. New York, London: The Guilford Press.

Josselson, R. (2004). The hermeneutics of faith and the hermeneutics of suspicion. *Narrative Inquiry, Vol 14* (1), 1-28.

Linton, S. & Walcott, R. (2018). *The Colour of Madness: Exploring BAME mental health in the UK*. Skiddaw Books.

Masilela, J. (2015). The Long and short project: Getting South Africans to read. *Mail & Guardian*. Retrieved 25th Apr 2018: <https://mg.co.za/article/2015-03-26-long-and-short-of-it>

McAdam, E. & Lang, P. (2009) *Appreciative Work in Schools*. Chichester: Kingsham Press.

McDonald, P. (2008). *The Literature Police: Apartheid Censorship and its*

Cultural Consequences. Oxford: Oxford University Press.

Medak-Saltzman, D. (2017). Coming to You from the Indigenous Future: Native Women, Speculative Film Shorts, and the Art of the Possible. *Studies in American Indian Literatures, 29* (1), 139-171. University of Nebraska Press. Retrieved December 13, 2018, from Project MUSE database.

Melges, F.T. (1982). *Time and Inner Future. A Temporal Approach to Psychiatric Disorders.* New York: John Wiley and Sons.

Mishler, EG (1999) *Storylines. Craft artists' narratives of identity.* Cambridge MA, London: Harvard University Press.

Nadir, C. (2010) Utopian Studies, Environmental Literature, and the Legacy of an Idea: Educating Desire in Miguel Abensour and Ursula K. Le Guin. *Utopian Studies, 21*(1), 24-56.

Nelson Mandela Foundation (2007). *Rivonia 'Treason Trial' Speech.* Accessed 30th Apr 2018 <http://db.nelsonmandela.org/speeches/pub_view. asp?pg=item&ItemID=NMS010&txtstr=prepared%20to%20die>

Nunn, K. P. (1996). Personal hopefulness: A conceptual review of the relevance of the perceived future to psychiatry. *British Journal of Medical Psychology. 69* (3), 227-245

Ochs, E., & Capps, L. (2001). *Living narrative: Creating lives in everyday storytelling.* Cambridge, MA: Harvard University Press.

Patel, N. & Keval, H. (2018). Fifty ways to lose your … racism. *Journal of Critical Psychology, Counselling and Psychotherapy, 18* (2), 61-79.

Ryman, G. (2013). The Mundane Manifesto: *SF Genics*, Retrieved 10th December 2018. <https://sfgenics.wordpress.com/2013/07/04/geoff-ryman-et-al-the-mundane-manifesto/>

Ryman, G. (2017). Nick Wood: 100 African Writers of SFF. *Strange Horizons*, March. Retrieved 10th December 2018. <http://strangehorizons.com/non-fiction/100african/nick-wood/>

Salvatore S. (2016). Cultural Psychology of Desire. In: Valsiner J., Marsico G., Chaudhary N., Sato T., Dazzani V. (eds) *Psychology as the Science of Human Being. Annals of Theoretical Psychology, Vol 13*. Springer, Cham.

Schiff, B., McKim, A.E. & Patron, S. (2017). *Life and Narrative: The Risks and*

Responsibilities of Storying Experience. OUP, USA.

Schuhmann, C.M. & van der Geugten, W. (2017). Believable Visions of the Good: An Exploration of the Role of Pastoral Counselors in Promoting Resilience. *Pastoral Psychology, 66*, 523.

Shawl, N. & Ward, C. (2005). *Writing the Other: A Practical Approach.* Aqueduct Press.

Smit, B., McGannon, K.R. & Williams, T.L. (2015). Ethnographic creative nonfiction. In: M.Gyozo & L.Purdy (Eds,) *Ethnographies in sports and exercise research.* London: Routledge.

Sools, A., Triliva, T., & Filippas, T. (2017). The Role of Desired Future Selves in the Creation of New Experience. *Style, 51*(3), 318-336.

Sools, A. (2012). "To see a world in a grain of sand": Towards Future-Oriented *What-If* Analysis in Narrative Research. *Narrative Works, 2*(1). Retrieved 10th December 2018. <https://journals.lib.unb.ca/index.php/NW/article/view/19500/21152>

Sools, A. & Mooren, J.H.M. (2012). Towards narrative futuring in psychology. Becoming resilient by imagining the future. *Graduate Journal of Social Science, 9*, 203-226.

Sools, A. M., Mooren, J. H. M., & Tromp, T. (2013). Positieve gezondheid versterken via narratieve toekomstverbeelding. In E. T. Bohlmeijer, L. Bolier, G. Westerhof, & J. A. Walburg (Eds.), *Handboek positieve psychologie. Theorie, onderzoek, toepassingen.* Amsterdam: BOOM.

Sools, A., Tromp, T. & Mooren, J.H.M. (2015). Mapping letters from the future: Exploring narrative processes of imagining the future. *Journal of Health Psychology, 20*, 350-364.

Sools, A., Triliva, S.& Filippas, T. (2017). The Role of Desired Future Selves in the Creation of New Experience: The Case of Greek Unemployed Young Adults. *Style, 51* (3), 318-336.

Sools, A. Triliva, S., Fragkiadaki, E., Tzanakis, M. & Gkinopoulos, T. (2018). The Greek Referendum Vote of 2015 as a Paradoxical Communicative Practice: A Narrative, Future-Making Approach. *Political Psychology, Vol. 39* (5), 1141-1156.

Squire, C. (2012). Narratives and the gift of the future. *Narrative Works.*

Streeby, S. (2018) *Imagining the Future of Climate Change*. University of California Press.

Sue, D.W. (2015). *Race Talk and the Conspiracy of Silence*. Wiley.

Witherspoon, D.J., Wooding, S., Rogers, A.R., Marchani, E.E., Watkins, W.S., Batzer, M.A. & Jorde, L.B. (2007). Genetic Similarities Within and Between Human Populations. *Genetics, 176* (1), 351-359.

Wong, A. (Ed, 2018). *Resistance and Hope: Essays by Disabled People*. Disability Visibility Project: <https://disabilityvisibilityproject.com/resist/>

Wood, N. (2015). How to talk to someone with an "untreatable" lifelong condition. *British Medical Journal, 351* doi: <https://doi.org/10.1136/bmj.h5037>

Wood, N. (2016) *Azanian Bridges*: NewCon Press, England.

Wood, N. & Patel, N. (2017). On addressing 'Whiteness' during clinical psychology training. *South African Journal of Psychology, 47*(3), 280-291.

Lightning Source UK Ltd.
Milton Keynes UK
UKHW010639280422
402201UK00002B/327